PRAISE *for* ALICE LICHTENSTEIN'S *The Crime Of Being*

The Crime of Being reads with the intensity of a first-class mystery, but Alice Lichtenstein's intricate shifts from one character to another, and her deft interweaving of sub-plots with all the shades of good and evil belong to the finest literary tradition. I haven't been able to do much of anything but read Alice's remarkable book since it arrived.

—ROBB FORMAN DEW, National Book Award-winner, author of Dale Loves Sophie to Death

---

Alice Lichtenstein's novel—as gripping as it is timely—excavates the complex roots of hatred and need for hard-won, radical empathy. A deeply human, fully-imagined story for our divided times.

—ELIZABETH GRAVER, author of *The End of the Point*

Alice Lichtenstein's loving inquiry, exhilarating range, and expansive devotion to her people inspire us to reckon with the inescapable truth: Each of us and all together must endure and live beyond the crime of *be-ing*.

—MELANIE RAE THON, author of *The Voice of the River*

Brilliantly written, filled with edge-of-your-seat suspense and wisdom, Lichtenstein's tale of a hate crime's polarization of "the perfect village" is both timely and timeless, a moving and necessary book.

—ELIZABETH EVANS, author of *As Good as Dead*

During the brilliant and explosive opening pages of Alice Lichtenstein's *The Crime of Being*, bullets fly. Thanks to one teenager's violent and racist act, the minds and hearts of people in a small, Upstate New York community are forever fractured and divided. Al... Lichtenstein delves deep into the viewp...

characters, presenting the disparate voices of victim and perpetrator, and those who surround them. It's a feat of extraordinary writing, all mounting toward a terrifically tense final confrontation. A tour de force of unsparing insight and empathy.

—Adrienne McDonnell, author of *The Doctor and the Diva*

The Crime of Being is a fast-paced, urgent story of how we live now. Alice Lichtenstein tells some hard truths with poise, wisdom, and compassion.

—Hilma Wolitzer, author of *The Doctor's Daughter*

A brilliant, riveting, and emotionally charged story about the crime of black life...vivid insight into the interior life of an African American teenager, who is the victim of a hate crime in his predominately white community. *The Crime of Being* reveals the emotional and psychic toll of anti-black racism, what it means to breathe while black in a white world.

—Jallicia Jolly, Institute for the Humanities,
University of Michigan

The Crime of Being is real and relevant. Alice Lichtenstein magnifies the most dangerous fractals of hate with wisdom and grace—with love. Her prose is fluid and full, a linguistic framework of compassion and generosity, and the story it tells compels us to be more than bystanders in this only life we have.

—April Ford, Pushcart Prize recipient, author of
The Poor Children and *Death Is a Side-Effect*

The Crime *of* Being

Also by Alice Lichtenstein

The Genius of the World

Lost

11/13/2019
For Vicki,
With love + admiration
for your work—and you!
Alice

The CRIME of BEING

Alice Lichtenstein

ISBN: 978-0-9984906-9-4

Cover and interior design by Stewart A. Williams.

This book was typeset in Electra.

"Tell us what moves at the margin. What it is to have no home in this place. To be set adrift from the one you knew. What it is to live at the edge of towns that cannot bear your company."

—Toni Morrison

"To insist on being who we are is a political act."

—Carl Phillips

For Iris and Sarah, my teachers, my astonishing daughters

and for

Safay, Emily Ann, Sheryl, and Sasha, whose strength and courage light the way

CONTENTS

PART I

INCIDENT

Good Friday

ONE

THEY HAVE THE DAY OFF FROM SCHOOL, so they are hanging out in Town Park, he and Woody and Sam and Ryan, all his buds from track, when the Chevy rolls through the gate. The gate isn't really a gate, it's two stone pillars, topped with nasty-looking eagles, wings spread, beaks open like they're about to grab something. The park is small with perfect grass, almost as perfect as the grass at the golf course where his dad works. It's the park where Gunther and his friends and most of the kids from the high school like to hang because it's perfect for cruising: an asphalt drive loops the center of the park and exits through the same gate. Whenever someone drives through, everyone stops what they're doing (even if it's nothing) to check out who it is.

When the Chevy pulls in, everybody looks, not just because the color of the pickup is so red, lipstick red, cherry red, and so shiny, the sun glinting off patches still slick from the Self-Wash, but because everybody knows whose truck it is (Sean, Sr.'s) and who's driving it (Shawnee Padrushky) and their curiosity is roused because everybody knows that

Padrushky, though seventeen, doesn't have a license (he's failed parallel parking twice), that he can't be driving legally without a licensed adult, and that Sean, Sr. anyhow has forbidden his son to drive unless he pulls all A's this semester and so far he's failing Chem.

That's how it is in this town. Everybody knows everybody's business. What car you drive and what grades you get are the least of it.

Gunther and his friends get to their feet, begin to saunter toward the truck that's bucked a curb in a squealing stop across the grass from them. They plan some joshing to the effect that no wonder Padrushky don't have a license, he still got to learn to park.

When they rise, they feel it's almost a right, a responsibility, to greet the man, to needle him, but also to convey a measure of admiration for his cunning, his guts—swipe your dad's truck, wax it, drive it without a license in *daylight*. They are swaggering a bit, grinning, but a little nervous, too. In the end, they plan to bestow their collective thumbs up. But who is this new version of Padrushky, usually a quiet kid, a loner dude who is isn't exactly known for breaking the rules?

Sam and Ryan lead the way. Gunther and his best friend Woody back a few steps. Ryan reaches the driver's door first; Sam closes in on the other side of the truck. Then Padrushky's rolling down the window to Ryan's, "Hey," pitched somewhere between friendly and not. Gunther and Woody, coming up slow, trailing their fingers along the side of the newly waxed truck as though it were satin.

Then Padrushky ducking, grabbing something from off the seat. Ryan leaping backward like he's been slapped; Sam, stumbling, his arms flying up. He shouts—"Dude's got a gun!"

How does Gunther know to run? One look at Padrushky raising the .22 as he opens the driver's door, his eyeball swimming into the crosshairs of the scope that's aimed right at him, and Gunther knows it's not show and tell. He knows he's gonna die if he doesn't get moving. His brain is running the race of its life as he flies across the park, through the gates, across Main, left to Tilden. He's running for the safest cover he can think of, the police station, six blocks away, running until his feet go numb, running on nothing, his stomach kinked, his breathing hard. Right on his heels, Padrushky's screaming, *I'm gonna kill you nigger.* Cars squealing, people shouting. He gets a sense the world has pulled up, but he's still moving.

Pounding up the steps of the police station, he reaches the entryway, yanks hard on the brass door handles. The doors don't budge. He yanks again, screaming *Help!* Through the heavy glass doors, he can see cops talking to cops, secretaries sitting at screens. *Help* he screams again. He doesn't see the white buzzer to the right of the double doors. He doesn't see the intercom, perched like an old transistor above it. Seconds he has, less, and now he has nowhere to hide, nothing to do but roll up in a ball, make himself small as he can in the corner.

He can hear Padrushky's sneakers slapping the pavement, his choking breaths, his garbled slurs, *You're a dead man,* and he believes him, his mind roiling with fear and yet scrambling for a plan. He raises his head, forces himself to look up at the kid who's pointing the rifle right at him so close he can taste the smell of metal in the roof of his mouth, can hear the click of the trigger as the barrel lifts, catching the light.

Gunther kicks out hard at Padrushky's shin. He pitches his water bottle with no time to aim. The blast of the gun spikes his head, splits it; his left arm is on fire. *That's it,* he thinks. *I'm dead.*

Padrushky aims the rifle again, but this time the doors are opening, the policemen are screaming. They point their guns at Padrushky who hesitates, then runs, fleeing back the way he came.

"Hold it," the policemen shout, and Padrushky drops to his knees on the sidewalk.

"I want to die," he says. "Let me die."

"Drop the gun."

Gunther sees it all. He sees Padrushky prop the .22 on the sidewalk, rest his throat on the tip of the barrel.

"No," the officers shout and he shouts, too. *No.*

The rifle fires. Padrushky's down, writhing and moaning and holding his jaw.

Police sirens explode out of nowhere. The sound bleeds into the ringing in Gunther's ears and drowns out all others. In minutes, men are lifting Gunther, strapping him into a narrow cot that they slide swiftly into the back of the ambulance. Then the men take their seats in the front. Others are waiting for him inside, blue uniforms and blurred faces. His arm is on fire, his head screaming. "Get my mom," he bleats. "My mom and dad."

Crouched near his shoulder is a woman with a long blonde braid that sweeps his cheek as she presses her pale fingers to the side of his throat. "Don't worry, hon," she says. "We're getting them. They'll be here soon as possible." He closes his eyes, hot tears flood his lids, sliding across his cheekbones, finding the corners of his mouth, the wells of his ears. His body starts shaking.

"Easy there," someone says. "It's okay." And someone else shoots something into his good arm, *this will help,* and almost instantly a sleepy high begins to suck the fear right out of his body. He's so grateful to be inside the ambulance, to be wrapped tight in this blanket, to be strapped tight to this bed, people telling him over and over they're going to keep him safe. Pagers are beeping, and radios are speaking like robots, and the ambulance is accelerating faster and faster; the G forces press down on his body, his hips and his stomach and the tops of his thighs. Gunther closes his eyes. His eyeballs feel heavy in their sockets, so heavy they might drop out the back of his skull. He sighs. This might be his own personal space ship, shuttling him off to the moon.

TWO

All morning Maggie Cannon has been dodging the jittery sensation that she should call home—a hyper, caffeine-fueled anxiety that makes no obvious sense, since she and Gunther have already gone over what she expects him to do around the house before he hooks up with his friends and heads for the park. On waking, she'd completely forgotten that the kids were off from school, and that Gunther would be home today, alone, until she came down for breakfast and found her son, earbud in place, happily shoving cereal into his mouth. "Good Friday," he informed her as though he had pulled off a personal coup, and she'd felt compelled—why?—perhaps because she was jealous of his freedom on such a glorious day, the first decent weather they'd had in months, to remind him in a stern voice that he had such and such responsibilities before he took off. "Ok, Mom. Chill. You don't have to be such a—" and then his voice trailed off, and she checked the clock and decided it wasn't worth pursuing.

So why the jitters? She trusts her son not to be stupid. Gunther and his friends run track. One dirty test and you're off the team. They're self-policing for that reason. Straight arrow—at least for now. On a day like this, most likely they'll be bare-chested, tossing a Frisbee in Town Park, showing off for the girls.

"All rise." It's the bailiff, Sergeant Ryan, in his somber bass.

Maggie stands. She doesn't know why but she loves this ritual. All rise and the deliberation room door opens—the judge emerges. Today it's Judge Adkins, a small mountain of a man in his black robes, trailing two lawyers, the Legal Aid rookie who looks all of twelve years old in his too-large suit, his off-kilter tie, and Marcia Hemperer, the prosecutor, tall and svelte in her taupe linen sheath.

Judge Adkins steps up to the platform, and the lawyers fan to opposite sides of the front row of benches to confer with their clients.

Judge Adkins takes his seat at the wooden desk. A moment later, the audience sits; Maggie, too, shifting her attention from the laptop on her desk to her steno machine. Inhaling, she rests her fingertips lightly on the row of slippery keys. They remind her of her first piano, a toy that made a sound like a poorly plucked guitar, but which she loved at the age of five more than life itself.

Then Deputy Ryan announces Hunter versus Gruen, and Maggie is typing with hummingbird speed, recording the lawyers, the witnesses, the plaintiff, the defendant. Their words flow around her and through her, a nearly unceasing mantra of sounds and syllables that she translates into key strokes, chords of words. She finds it hard to describe to people when they ask (and they do) exactly why she enjoys her job so much without sounding to herself like a Zen cliché or a stoner. She might be called the court amanuensis, or copyist or scrivener, but to Maggie, the art of stenography is almost mystical. It requires a state of mind in which there is no experience of the self, no membrane, no judgment. When she's recording, she is transparent, she is fluid, but she is also electric, a hot wire crackling with transmission.

Marcia Hemperer is cross-examining a witness, a middle-aged woman with a no-nonsense manner wearing a blue rayon blouse, when abruptly she stops speaking. Maggie brakes her typing, poised to start again after Marcia has consulted her notes or her client or whatever it is that has snagged her attention mid-sentence. Maggie looks up. The witness and the rest of the courtroom are riveted. Deputy Ryan, striding at a near run, is heading down the aisle toward Judge Adkins, waving his outstretched arm at him like desperate child. The hairs rise on Maggie's arms, and her fingers stroke the air like butterfly antennae, recording the details of the scene in her mind. Over the years of being a stenographer, she's developed the habit of typing an invisible copy, a backup, of what she's seeing and hearing. She's never seen a trial disrupted like this. Ever.

Bailiff Ryan is up on the platform, whispering in Judge Adkins' ear, and Adkins is shaking his head lightly, a shake of disbelief. His fingers squeeze the head of the microphone as though it were a lemon. Maggie cannot record these details for the record, but they are being recorded by her brain for her own record.

Then the bailiff steps back, and Judge Adkins is leaning across his desk; he is pointing to *her*, summoning *her*, as though she were a lawyer, to approach the bench. Both lawyers turn to her, looking baffled; the jury, too. Maggie feels her ribs lock against her breathing; her cheeks fire up in a rush of shame. She felt this way in fifth grade when Mrs. Churt summoned her to the front of the room for cheating on her math test—an accusation so deeply untrue that she couldn't find words to defend herself—and made her apologize to the class. She's been found out. But what is her crime?

At the bench, Maggie blinks, confused. Judge Adkins leans further toward her, his hand still covering the microphone. She can see a few bumps of sweat on the top of his lip; his breath is heavy with mint.

"You need to go with the bailiff," he says. His voice is tense, but kind, kinder than Maggie can remember hearing it. "Good luck."

Good luck? Now shame is turning to dread like quickly shifting weather. The room is blurring in her peripheral vision, and Bailiff Ryan is putting his arm around her shoulders as though she were a distraught parent or spouse, escorting her down the side corridor toward the rear door of the courtroom. She's not going to escape.

In their wake, Maggie hears Judge Adkins slam his gavel, adjourning the court. "What's going on? What is this, George?" she whispers, ventriloquist-style, barely moving her lips.

She's known the man for years and though no one would call them friends, she's always been careful to ask after the wife and kids, the state of his health. He might give her a clue. But Bailiff Ryan's face remains stone as he grips her arm and hustles her out the door and across the landing to the room opposite.

At high noon, the conference room is bathed in a pinkish light from the stained glass panels across the tops of the tall windows, crown jewels of the old courthouse. A police officer in uniform, a youngish man, not someone Maggie knows, is standing with his feet splayed, his hands crossed lightly against his groin.

"Mrs. Cannon?" His voice quivers a little, not police-like at all.

"Oh God," Maggie says. "What's happened?"

THREE

THE POLICE ARE PUSHING the thicket of onlookers back, back, back across the street to the far sidewalk. The air is filled with the shrieking of sirens as the ambulances slide in, unload their gurneys. Woody pushes to the front of the crowd, trains his cellphone on the scene. Others, too, are recording, snapping photos. The crowd is electric, jazzed. Kids from the park boast about what they saw and what they heard. But he and Ryan and Sam were right there. From the start. They saw it all.

Then the EMTs in florescent green bibs, aliens on the streets of Lake Village, run up the path to the Police Station, grab Gunther, strap him to their rolling bed. Another team shovels up Padrushky, crumpled on the sidewalk. Blink. Blink. And you've missed it.

Woody lowers his phone. He is shaking so hard he can barely type: *My friend Gunther Cannon got shot in daylight, Main Street, Lake Village, NY, doing nothing. I don't know if he's alive.* With a whoosh his tweet goes out into the world, its cluster bomb of information exploding as he and Sam and Ryan turn foot and head for the hospital.

FOUR

THE NURSE AND THE EMERGENCY ROOM doctor are dressed in green, their heads covered in tight white caps. With the gurney still moving, someone's sticking a thermometer in Gunther's ear, a cuff to his upper arm. Someone else pries open his eyelids, sticks bright light into his eyes. Everyone has a clipboard, acts like they've never seen a kid shot in the arm before. They haven't, a nurse tells him, reading his mind. He is their very first.

Then a curtain is pulling back, and he's rolling into the little theater. Beeps and smells of rubbing alcohol and Band-Aids and some gunk he once put on his face to smother a pimple. He's cold all of a sudden, shivering; his toes are ice, and his ears are still ringing like he's front row at a rock concert.

"How are you doing there, son?" A voice booms, a man's, one of the white-capped people. White and green.

"My mom and dad," he says, because all he can think, his whole purpose now is to make sure his parents know what's happened to him, to make sure they can find him.

"Nurse?"

"They're on their way, Doctor."

"So they'll be here, soon. You in a bit of pain?"

A bit? In his mind's eye, he sees the Human Torch bursting into flame from head to toe.

"On a scale of one to ten—"

"A lot," he says.

"More pheno," the doctor orders.

The nurse stops writing on her clipboard and checks the tube stuck in his upper arm.

"The good news," the doctor continues, "you're going to live."

"Doctor Walker," the nurse protests.

"Joke. I mean you're lucky. The bullet broke the ulna but seems to have missed the artery. You'll be up and socking balls in no time."

I got shot.

"What we don't know is what kind of break you have, so you'll be getting an X-ray, *toute de suite.* After that we'll hook you up to some fluids that will take that pain away for a longer amount of time. Sound good?"

"Yeah." Put out the flames. The smoking defeated Torch.

"Roll 'em," the doctor calls over his shoulder as he and the nurse push aside the curtains. Orderlies grab his bed and wheel him out of the room and into the hall.

Suddenly, there is screaming. Someone's being stabbed with a screwdriver or hacked with a chainsaw. "Out of my way!" shouts a nurse. Gunther lifts his head for a glimpse of the gurney with its screaming passenger as it rushes by. A tuft of blonde hair slicked with blood sprouts from the top of a head bandage like a weed in pavement. Padrushky. He's sure of it. Suddenly, he's freezing again, his teeth chattering like crazy, his body shaking. Padrushky rolling down the hall right past him, screaming his head off. Gunther tries to stop his teeth, but he can't. The screen in his forehead lights up: the gun pointing, aiming. Once again, he's sure he's going to die.

FIVE

BRUCE CANNON IS ON HIS HANDS and knees on the rough, down around the 7th hole, plucking up maple wings (something one of his employees should be doing, frankly, but he can't wait for habitually late Harry) when his cell phone rings. He's always a little pissed to be interrupted when he's in the flow, but he's used to his employees asking questions they think are emergencies, when most of the time, they're not. *The golf cart stalled on the Ridge Road*, "Check the gas"; *the lime hasn't come yet*, "Call the supplier." Sinking back on his calves, he pulls his cell out of its holster without looking at the call screen. Across the fairway, the Club's Border Collie is barking at geese attempting to settle on the putting green. He plugs an ear, crouches away from the sound. "Yes?" he says, allowing a little grit in his voice.

"Bruce, it's me." Maggie, sounding tense.

"What's going on?"

"Gun's been shot. He's not dead. I'm in a police car on the way to Foxwood. You need to get there."

"Gun's been *shot*?" Instantly, adrenaline floods his brain, breaching his desire to stay calm. "He's alive? You're sure?"

"I don't know much, but the police—"

"What do they say? What happened?"

"Something in the park. Someone shot at him. They don't really know anything yet." Her voice is rising, cracking. "All I can say is *get here*."

The cart's top speed is thirty, and Bruce hits it easily as he careens onto the asphalt lane and heads for the Clubhouse. *My boy's been shot. My boy's been shot.* A hard rubber ball of fear caroms in his chest. *My boy*—He brakes and swerves to miss a cart parked on the lane, then floors it. Most of the Friday afternoon golfers are inside the clubhouse, eating lunch; they'd rather not play in the noon sun. But a few diehards look up from their game, waving gaily as he flies by.

◈

The police car crosses the intersection against the light, then speeds down Main Street past the little cafes and shops with their striped awnings; the curbside cement planters spilling bright pink petunias; the lampposts fluttering crisp blue flags emblazoned with the Chamber's new slogan: American's Most Perfect Village, then hangs a hard right up Grover.

"Whoa—" Maggie gasps, grabbing for the handle above her door with one hand, and bracing against the dashboard with the other.

"Sorry, Ma'am."

"No, no, I'm with you. The faster the better."

Lights flashing, siren blaring, they scream through the wealthy section of town with its tilting slate sidewalks and stately homes set back behind wrought iron fences and immaculate stone walls. Most of these houses are occupied by doctors and the away people, who return each summer to Lake Village, their skin deeply tanned by Florida winter sun.

Working in the courts, Maggie doesn't interact much with summer people, but Bruce does. He's known some of them since he was a boy, growing up in Lake Village, helping out at his father's hardware, then caddying at the Club. Bruce was that fair-haired, pink-cheeked local kid, who always showed promise, who occasionally made a good pal of one of the scion's sons or consummated a summer crush in the gazebo past the ninth hole with one of the lithe daughters.

The CB on the dashboard crackles, a staticky metallic voice flares and dies. "Did you get that?" Maggie asks.

The policeman shakes his head. "Too many on the frequency."

Ahead, the hospital comes into view, a red brick behemoth that shrinks the neighboring houses to doll-size. A security guard stands in the middle of the street, across from the main entrance, stopping traffic, waving them on past the onlookers, the police cars. And just then, the radio releases its one clear piece of information: *Shooting suspect now in custody, identified as seventeen-year-old white male, Lake Village resident, Sean Padrushky, Jr.*

"They've got him," Maggie says, squeezing her fist. "Good." Then the name hits her. Sean Padrushky, Jr. Her gut tightens. Sean Padrushky. *Shawnee* Padrushky.

In her mind's eye, she sees the little boy, pale as paper, who wanted to take piano lessons, even though *they don't got a piano,* his mother told her over the telephone. She, intrigued, agreed to teach him anyway. There were always pianos being given away. They'd find one.

Oh god. Shawnee Padrushky, six years old, unsmiling, nearly mute, hunched beside her at the piano in the living room, his slender fingers resting on the keys. After one lesson, he'd memorized the scales in the book; after two, he could play a minuet by ear. He was her piano student, if only for a few months. But so long ago. Before she worked at the Court. Why the hell did Shawnee go after her son?

SIX

He opens his eyes, hoping to see nothing, hoping, but only dimly, to have a mystery solved: Heaven or Hell? He expects the latter, aches for it. He wants to join Satan and his wily crew. He wants to join a band of brothers with the courage to create chaos. The ceiling is a dim shade of eggshell; the light muted. The man in the chair beside the gurney is uniformed, sweating heavily. The follicles of dark hair slick at the back of his neck. There is another man in the room. Another police officer, his shoulder holster exposed.

"Mr. Padrushky? May I call you Sean?"

When he moves his jaw, the pain answers; chiseling through the bone, spiking his skull. Call me whatever you want, just don't call me mister. Ha-ha, a line his father says, thinking he's badass.

"So I guess you been through a lot."

Manly voice, so steady, like a priest's, like Father Rand's. Ha-ha.

"Are you hurting bad? They give you something?"

On a scale of one to ten, his pain is one thousand, but that's not the point, the point is he fucked up; he's supposed to be dead.

"So, this will sound funny with your jaw like that, but you have the right to remain silent. Anything you say can be used against you in a court of law. You have the right to have an attorney here during any questioning. If you cannot afford a lawyer, one will be provided to you at government expense. Do you understand?"

He opens his mouth. "Miranda. I get it." To his ears, his voice sounds like a frog with a sore throat and the words come out in slo-mo, sagging like a stretched wad of gum.

The man nods. "Okay, you can talk then. I wasn't sure." He clears his throat. "So, knowing your rights, are you willing to answer my questions without an attorney present?"

He hears the defeat in the man's voice. The man's got to ask it, but the man doesn't expect nothing. The man doesn't know the Plan. Haha. "Yeah."

SEVEN

THE CHIEF SURGEON'S OFFICE is not like any doctor's office Joanne Padrushky has ever been to, no calendars or charts or tab-eared copies of out-of-date magazines, the labels with the doctor's home address carefully removed. Instead, it's got built-in shelves stuffed with books, a leather couch and a matching armchair. The surgeon, a middle-aged man with the long face of an actor she's seen on TV, sits behind his desk, a long plank of cherry, resting on what look to Joanne like giant anvils. The surgeon reaches across his desk to shake her hand, then gestures her to take a seat. "Mr. Padrushky's on his way?"

"I haven't been able to reach him. He's surveying up North."

"Then we'd better start. I understand that the police want to arraign your son, but I told them I need to get him into surgery as soon as possible."

Joanne nods, her gut tightening. She slips her hand into her jeans pocket, closes her fingers around the slippery coolness of her rosary. *Emergency surgery.* No one has told her nothing. One minute she's cleaning the whelping box out in the yard; the next, a police officer is at her door, telling her to get to the hospital, her son's been shot.

"But here's the good news. Your son was lucky. Extremely so. The path of the bullet went up past his left jaw, missed the optical nerve and the brain stem to shoot out the other side above his ear." While he is talking, the surgeon is pressing up under his own jaw, then tapping a spot behind his ear. "Ordinarily a bullet of that caliber, angled in that way, at that range—"

"Angels," Joanne says.

The surgeon looks at her, surprised. "That sounds about right."

"My son was saved."

"Indeed."

Outside the surgeon's office, the police chief is waiting for her; a Detective So-and-So with him as well. They are polite, both of them. They keep their voices low, saying how sorry they are about all of this, that it's a tragedy, as though they were the guilty ones. They want to talk to her in private, they say.

The room behind the nurses' station is crowded with boxes of supplies and smells like bleach. The police chief, dead ringer for the Colonel with his too-scrubbed face and white goatee, backs his butt against the metal shelving; the detective in a suit and tie, sits on a cardboard box. When the Chief asks if she wants them to bring in a chair, she shakes her head hard and locks her arms across her chest. "What in hell's going on and when do I see my son?"

The Chief cuts a look at the detective who shrugs lightly, "Tell her."

"Your son's under arrest, Mrs. Padrushky, for attempted murder."

"No, you got the wrong kid. It's a mistake. It's not Shawnee. It can't be."

"Your son waived Miranda, Ma'am. He confessed."

And now, Joanne does want to sit. She sinks slowly to the floor, her back pressed against the closed door. The detective is eye-to-eye with her now like he planned it.

"What did he say?"

The detective coughs lightly, wipes the back of his wrist across his upper lip, catching his nostrils. "He told us he took his father's brand-new truck, his father's .22 caliber rifle and set out to rid the world of—the 'n' word. He told us he planned to find Gunther Cannon, *take him out*, then shoot himself. Luckily, he failed. On both counts."

"No. No. No." A gun? A plan? Her head whips back and forth like a loose sail. "No. Not my son. No."

The Chief puts his hand on her shoulder. "I understand, Mrs. Padrushky. It's a shock. A big one. It isn't easy. And your husband isn't here. But just so you know, off the record even, you need a lawyer. A good one. Right away."

In the alcove that houses the vending machines, Joanne calls the only lawyer she knows, her brother, Lyle. He lives in Albany, and she can't even remember what kind of lawyer he is. The secretary answers, and when Joanne starts to say it's an emergency, her voice stalls, and the woman puts her right through.

Then her brother is on the line, her big brother, who she only sees once a year on Easter. It's his wife's family, he says, they take up a lot of time, but she knows the truth: he can't stand Joanne's husband, Sean, Sr. The feeling is mutual.

"What's up?" Her brother's voice is plush, tight around the edges.

"Shawnee," she says and to her dismay the sobs break in harsh squawks, in the horrible strangled sounds that a chicken makes before its neck is fully snapped. She's not a crier; never has been. It's something she learned a long time ago, in their father's house.

"Whoa, what's going on?"

She tells him what she's been told.

"He waived Miranda? He's a moron. He's nuts."

Joanne sucks back what she'd like to say. "What do I do?"

"Where is he now?"

"Prepping for surgery."

"Where's your husband?"

"Up North. Out of range."

A string of curses rush by her ear, sounds pulled from the mud and hurled at her. Like she needs that.

"I'll cancel the afternoon. I'll get there. Your son's insane. No, I mean it. Insane. It's all we've got. Sissy?"

"Yes."

"Tell Shawnee to shut the fuck up from now on."

The bed in Shawnee's hospital room is made up tight, awaiting his return from the OR. It could take hours, the nurse tells Joanne. She should go home, catch some sleep. The nurse is heavy-set with a complexion that looks as if it's been boiled. She'll be lucky if she sleeps in a hundred years, she tells the nurse. She's not planning on going nowhere, she says.

She seats herself by the window, thankful that the curtains are drawn. Even as she got to the hospital, the citizens of Lake Village were jamming the lobby, the television reporters circling the building in blank white vans. Her son is the focus of everyone's attention, it seems; her son, and Gunther Cannon, the only black kid in Lake Village High School.

She presses the speed dial, and the phone rings and rings until the voicemail comes on: "You have reached Sean Padrushky, Sr., surveyor at-large. You got something to say? Leave a message." She can't. It's Good Friday. A beautiful spring day. In her mind's eye, she sees her husband, ankle-deep in mud, looking out over a swamp somewhere in the North Country. Once she asked him why he travelled so far for work, and he laughed. *'Cause up North I can be as crazy as I want.*

Joanne clears her throat, starts to push out a greeting when Sean picks up.

"What's going on?"

His tone is gruff. In the background, she hears the sound of convenience store music. Or maybe he's at the bar. "Shawnee's in the hospital. He shot someone and his self."

"What the fuck?"

"Listen. All's I know is he took your truck, your .22, went after a kid—" She holds her phone away as the blast of obscenities screams past her ear. She hasn't even told him that the kid was black. "He tried to kill himself, Sean. The bullet went up behind his jaw and out below his ear, missed his optical nerve, missed his brain. God showed mercy."

"Shit. Who'd he shoot?"

"Another kid. I don't know much. I guess he's okay. He's alive."

Through the phone, Joanne hears one sharp wheeze, then another, another and another. "You got your inhaler?"

"I don't need a fucking inhaler. Did you talk to Shawnee?"

"I couldn't. By the time I got here, he was out cold."

"He's going to talk to me. He's going to explain himself. What was he thinking, stealing my gun, my truck?"

Joanne snorts at that; she can't help herself. *Thinking?* "How long will you be?"

"Forty-five minutes. I'll be hitting the gas."

She turns to the curtain, strokes its hem. In her mind's eye, she can see her husband driving like a crazy man, pushing eighty on the two-lane from Richfield County. "Don't get yourself killed on the way. I need you in one piece."

◆

When the police came for her, the car with its siren and lights set the dogs off in a hurricane of barking that upset Sophie, the bitch, trying to catch a few after pushing out ten pups in the middle of the night. Joanne dropped the hose, got to her feet.

"Shut up!" she called to the dogs, knowing full well they wouldn't quiet down until they wanted to. The driver's door was opening, and an officer was getting out. A trooper in his deer-soft hat and trooper shades. The high sun glinted off the roof of the car, nearly blinding her. Her mouth tightened. Did Sean Sr. do something stupid again? Only a week ago, he'd gotten pulled over for a tail light and missed getting a Breathalyzer by the skin of his teeth.

"Mrs. Padrushky?"

She nodded. Over the years, she'd had her dealings with the police. She wasn't intimidated.

"Can I help you?"

"I hope so. Anyone else home? Your husband? Kids?"

It wasn't Sean then. "Me and the dogs. My son."

The officer nodded. "Right now, you'll want to come with me."

"What for? My bitch whelped last night, and I haven't had a wink of sleep." The officer widened his stance an inch or two, touched his holster. He's nervous, Joanne remembers thinking. People give off signs just like dogs.

"Your son's been involved in an incident."

"My son's in his room, sleeping."

Behind Joanne, a few of the dogs were still barking, pawing the chain link with their claws, still anxious about the stranger.

"Sean Padrushky, Jr. is your son, correct? Chief Rinehart sent me to tell you. Your son's in the hospital, Ma'am. But don't worry, he's alive. Now you can either come with me or take your own vehicle."

Joanne blinked. The man wasn't lying. "I'll take my own," she said.

The corridor outside Shawnee's hospital room is strangely quiet as though the staff has been deployed to other emergencies. Still, Joanne tucks her chin, narrows her vision and makes a beeline toward the bank of elevators. Her heart is beating like mad. Her armpits, pricking. She doesn't want to leave the hospital when Shawnee's in surgery, but she's got to trust in God that he'll do okay without her. She knows what happens next, she grew up with police raids—her father, her brothers. The hard knock on the front door. The polite or not-so-polite request to enter. The cops are going to go to the house to search Shawnee's room. She's got to get in there before they do.

EIGHT

HIS PARENTS ARE THERE, right outside the x-ray room when he comes out. They grab the sides of his gurney, lean way in.

"Gunther," his mother says.

"Gun," his father's voice right over the top of hers.

There they are, those tears he didn't ask for, doesn't want, trickling down the sides of his face. He tastes them in the corners of his mouth, feels them reach his chin. He's bawling now, big ballooning swells of sobs, his mother and maybe even his father, too, as they close in around him, their arms holding him and each other, their heads bowed over his.

"My baby," his mother is saying, "you're safe, thank god you're safe," and his father is shaking his head, his shoulders heaving. "I'm sorry, I'm sorry." Their words make him cry harder like he was afraid they would. "It's okay, son," his father breathes. "You're going to be safe. You're okay now. Tell us what happened."

"Shh," his mom says. "He's still in shock, can't you tell?"

He feels the tears heating up again, slow bubbles speeding up fast.

"He tried to kill me, Mom."

His mother clutches his arm as the gurney moves; she's glued herself to him; it's like she's a helium balloon that he's afraid will fly away. He's so tired, he could drop through the floor. His limbs are sacks of concrete. Except his left arm, the arm with the bullet that whomps with pain.

In the room, the orderly slides him from the gurney into the hospital bed as deftly as though he were a hot pizza straight from the oven. "Someone will be in to check on you soon."

His mom eyes his bed, wondering, he imagines, if she can fit in beside him. She tries to slide her arm around his shoulder. "I don't want to hurt you," she says, "but I want to hug you."

"Forget it," he tells her, but it is exactly what he wants. He wants her to hold him like he was a little kid again. He remembers how he liked to sit on her lap and stroke the soft skin under her jaw. She would laugh and pretend it tickled. It was so soft. When he touched that patch of skin, he thought of cream.

His mother kisses his cheek, then pulls a chair close to the bed. "I can't even imagine what you're feeling, Gun. We know you were chased—"

Hunted. "He had a gun, Mom; he was pointing it right at my face."

"It's unbelievable. But you're here, honey. We've got to focus on that. You're here."

His father rests his hand on his shoulder. "That's the only thing that matters, Gun. You're safe."

Gunther looks from his dad to his mom, two middle-aged people, not bad-looking for their age. His mom is proud of how fit she is. She's always bragging about how she can keep up with the twenty-something's in Zumba. His dad, a big guy, could have played college football if he hadn't wanted to do other stuff. He is their son; they are his mom and dad. Not their *black* son; not his *white* parents. That's what they want to believe. But what's happened, he can't explain to them. A storm blew in and dug a deep pit in the sand. He's at the bottom; his parents, looking down from the top. *They* are safe in this world; *he* isn't.

NINE

ON SHAWNEE'S DOOR HANGS A POSTER of a pirate's skull and crossbones. Underneath, he's written *Forboten* in black Sharpie on the blonde wood, an act that earned him a belt from his father. Joanne hasn't been in the room for months; not even a peek. Shawnee's good about laundry; she even hears the vacuum from time to time. Now Joanne grasps Shawnee's doorknob, bell-shaped, shiny. *She'd thought he was asleep.* It's locked. She swallows and butts the door with her shoulder. The plywood creaks under her blow but doesn't budge. Once as a girl, she read a fairytale about a pirate with a secret room, murdered girls inside. Her teeth want to chatter, but she won't let them. Shawnee locked the door from the inside.

She runs downstairs, out the front door, down the front steps and around to the back of the house. Looking up, she sees the black curtains billowing from Shawnee's open window. The hydrangeas below are crushed to one side. This is how he escaped. While she was in the basement with Sophie, he was risking his neck, jumping out the window, stealing his father's new truck, taking his rifle. He must have put the truck in neutral, pushed it out of the garage so quiet it didn't wake her or the dogs. A sob leaps from her throat, so sudden, it's almost a bark. Stop that, she scolds herself. There's work to do. She's got to grab a ladder and get into that room.

Coming back into the house, Joanne hears Sophie's faint cry coming from the master bedroom upstairs. What the hell's she doing in there? The whelping box is in the basement, but almost instantly she spots a trail of blood going up the stairs to the second floor and down the hall. Sophie's dragged her babies somewhere, looking for her, maybe, or for somewhere safe.

Sophie's a first-timer. Anything can happen. They get confused. She's seen it before. And in the hurry to leave the house, she might have left a door open somewhere; all the doors for that matter.

She checks her watch. Three o'clock. Her mind's spinning. There's no way she can handle the big ladder by herself. And any minute Sean Sr. will be getting to the hospital. She's got to get going, but she has to check on Sophie.

The dog is lying on their bed, the pups stuck to her teats. All but one, which Sophie holds between her forelegs, licking its crown, licking and licking. Joanne takes a deep breath. Focus. A mutant gene. A collapsed lung. These things happen. Yet she can't help thinking there have been times when she's been able to save a pup. When she's been there to suck out the mucus or give the shot. *When she's been there.* Sorrow cracks her breastbone. *He left through the window when she was asleep.* She hasn't been a good mother to her dogs or to her son.

"C'mon, Sophie," she says. "Come on, give her up. You done a good job, girl. Time to say good-bye."

Sophie rolls her eyes in Joanne's direction, but keeps on licking.

"Come on, girl." Joanne reaches for the dead pup.

Sophie growls.

"Enough," Joanne says, dropping her pitch. "Leave it." With one hand, she whisks the pup away from Sophie; its weight in her palm no heavier than a bar of soap. Sophie shifts, stands, shaking off the nursing pups.

"Stay," Joanne commands, wondering if Sophie will obey. "First things first," she says by rote, but nothing seems in order today. She goes into the kitchen, grabs a freezer bag from the drawer beside the sink, slips the pup inside and seals it. Next, she rolls out the bottom freezer and sticks the bag between the peas and the blueberries. You do this sometimes, you have to.

Back in the bedroom, Sophie has crapped on the rug. Joanne feels the anger shoot through her body. Usually her dogs are her best friends. Now it feels as though they have betrayed her. She has never ever hit one of her dogs; she won't now. Without a word, she rips a page from the magazine beside the bed, something Sean's reading, a hunting magazine, and scoops up the crap and the rest of the puppies. She grabs Sophie by the collar and hauls her back downstairs.

TEN

In the Recovery room, Gunther shivers beneath the thin sheet of the gurney, his eyes shut against the over-bright light. Only a minute ago, he was telling the anesthesiologist about track and then he was dreaming about track. It was a great dream. He was flying over the hurdles, chest forward, front leg stretched, his trailing leg so close to the bar, he could feel the hairs on his knee. *Perfect form!* Coach shouted as he crossed the finish line. Now, gazing at his left arm, he realizes that he isn't going to regionals, that he, the best hurdler on the Lake Village High Track team, the team's star, isn't going to race at all for the rest of the season.

The cast runs from the elbow down over the middle of his hand. It's royal blue and heavy as an x-ray bib. He is going to sit out the rest of the season. The backs of his eyeballs burn, and the tears start, only no one asks what he is crying about, because they're getting used to seeing him cry. Big things, little things. He's like the old fountain in Lake Village Park, a lion, that dribbles all the time out of a metal pipe in its mouth, little kids crack themselves up making jokes about that stupid dribble. He probably did once, too, but after a while no one cares.

It's still the afternoon, but it might as well be night, Gunther thinks. Someone has closed the blinds, so the room is in deep shadow. He does not want it to be night, because every time he closes his eyes, the movie flicks on, the worst part, when he's curled in the corner of the entryway outside the police station, and the gun is pointing right at him, and Padrushky pulls the trigger, and he thinks he is dead.

Within the hour, his parents told him, the detective's stopping by, and he's got to tell his story. All of it. Which sucks, because he's still so tired.

"Mom?"

His mother reaches for his hand. "Are you awake now? How do you feel?"

He shakes his head. Why did he ask for her? He wishes he could fall back into the good dream and fly again.

There's a knock on the door so loud that his mom and dad jerk their heads.

"Come in," his dad says, sounding gruff.

The man is short, balding, wearing the black, rectangular glasses of a movie director. He opens his suit jacket and flashes an ID. "Lance Peters, detective. Good time to visit?" He reaches for his dad's hand, his mom's, then touches his shoulder. "I see they've got you patched up already."

Gunther nods, shifting his arm a little to show that he would shake hands if he could.

"I'd like to get your side of the story now, Gunther. The sooner we get the details the better."

His side of the story. Is there another? "Okay."

The detective seats himself in the chair beside the bed and takes out his phone and a notepad. "Tell it from the start." He presses the record button on his phone. "I need to hear about your whole day, the start of your day, every little thing you can remember even if you think it's not important."

"The whole day. Okay. Do you want to know my breakfast?"

"Sure."

"Same as always. Wheaties, OJ." He remembers he promised his mom that he'd come back after hanging out in the park to clean up the winter crap in the yard. Then she handed him money for "a decent lunch" which meant a sub from Harry's or a slice from Dom's. "So after that, my buddy Ryan—"

"Ryan Fitch," his mother adds.

Peters nods and scribbles. "Go on."

"Ryan comes by, picks me up, my friend Woody—Woody Peterson—and my friend Sam Dover, and we head for Town Park."

"What are you planning to do there?"

"Nothing much. Chill."

"Were you planning to meet anyone?"

Gunther shakes his head. "No one special. You know, everyone hangs out at the Park. It's Good Friday. No school." He sees the moment he woke up to sunshine and birds and the text that Ryan was coming over to pick him up with Sam and Woody. How he wishes he could go back.

"Go on."

"Sam and Ryan and Woody and me were sitting on the grass at the top of the loop and that's when Padrushky drove up in his dad's pickup. Everyone knows the kid doesn't have a license; it's like what the fu—sorry—what the heck? We get up to check it out. You know. What's with the wheels, dude? Ryan's in front, and Sam, me and Woody are behind, and then Ryan's about to say hi or something when Padrushky reaches down for something. It's a gun. Sam jumps back and yells—"

"How did you know to run?" the detective asks. "He might have wanted to show you what he had. To brag or something?"

Gunther blinks. Is this man crazy or stupid?

"Son?"

Why is he everybody's son? "The way he looked at me. I can't explain it. Someone looks at you like that, you know you're going to die." He hears his mom gasp, his dad, too, but the detective scribbles some more.

"Was it personal? Was there bad blood? Did you cross Padrushky at some point? Or he, you? Were you after the same girl? Did you bully him?"

Gunther feels his lungs tighten; his ears heat up. Does he have to say this? He guesses he does. "I might have taken the kid's pencil one time, stuck it on my lip and goofed for the rest of the class. I do stuff like that; I can't help myself sometimes. I like to make people laugh. But I'm not a bully."

Detective Peters looks down at his clean white hands. "Was it your race?"

He was raised not to be paranoid, but the instant Padrushky aimed at him, he knew why Padrushky wanted him to die. "Yes, sir."

"You certain?"

His parents are looking at him with weird faces, horrified and sad at the same time. Is he betraying them? Is he telling a secret that he isn't supposed to tell? "The school's really small. We know each other, but we're not in the same group. I'm on the track team; he's more a loner type, I guess."

"A nerd?" The detective smiles at him like they are in some sort of joke together

"I don't know."

"But you feel he'd targeted you?"

"You heard what he was shouting?"

"Tell me."

He looks at the man. His face seems kind enough, though kind of blank. "I—" He clears his throat and opens his mouth, willing himself not to lose it. "'I'm going to kill you, Nigger.'"

His mom chokes like she's swallowed wrong. "Sorry," she says, turning away and coughing into her hand.

"That's pretty bad. He never said anything like this to you before in school?"

"We never really talked except, you know, a 'was-sup' when I sit down in Global. We got assigned seats next to each other."

"And the goofing off."

"Yeah, well. I mean that one time."

Detective Peters shakes his head lightly. "I wouldn't worry about that. It doesn't sound too serious. Gunther, is there anything else about Shawnee Padrushky that makes you think you were targeted? You alone and not your friends? Anything else about him that stands out in your mind?"

Gunther presses his lips, inhales, exhales. "There's one thing that happened in class. The teacher was passing out the homework, and when Padrushky stuck out his hand, I saw these black loops on the inside of his wrist. Double infinity." It was a tattoo he'd never seen before. It's embarrassing to remember that he thought it was cool.

"Double infinity?" the detective asks. "What's that mean?"

He didn't know, either. At lunchtime, he drew the tattoo on a napkin for Woody. *Nah, not infinity, dude, those are eights. Eighth letter of the alphabet, 'H'.* Then he got it.

"It stands for *Heil Hitler.*"

Detective Peters' pencil stops moving.

Padrushky's a Nazi? he asked Woody. *Guess so, dude,* Woody said. It didn't seem to bother Woody too much. But the thought of *Heil Hitler* on the kid's wrist had really bothered him. Gunther wasn't even sure if he was Jewish, but his mom was.

"One more thing." His mom's eyelids are fluttering the way they do when she's nervous.

The detective squints at her. "Mrs. Cannon?"

"This is probably nothing, I know, but I thought I should mention it. Shawnee—Sean Padrushky, Jr.—was my piano student years ago, before I stopped teaching. He was six, I think. Maybe a little older. His lessons only lasted a few months. He quit. I don't know why."

Gunther watches his mother blush. She's got dark brown hair, curly, to her shoulders, and deeply tanned skin that's naturally that way she once explained, because she's *Sephardic*, a kind of Jewish.

"So Padrushky knows the family? Knows your house?"

"It was a long time ago."

"Has there been any contact since then? Between you and Mr. Padrushky? His parents?"

His mother shakes her head. "It was silly to mention."

"It's not silly, Mrs. Cannon. Gunther, anything you remember about that time?"

"Not really. No." But he does remember. He remembers watching the little kid sitting on the piano bench right next to his mom. He remembers her holding his hand to show him where his fingers went on the keys. He remembers how excited his mom was that this little kid was so good at piano, and he remembers being jealous because, even back then, the last thing in the world he felt like doing was playing the piano, no matter how many jelly beans his mother promised him to practice.

"Okay, this is all valuable. The white supremacy affiliation; the lack of motive other than—" The detective clears his throat. "I'll put it this way—it's going to be quite a case."

ELEVEN

SOMETIMES JOANNE'S HUSBAND LOOKS handsome to her, sometimes he looks like a monster. Even from a distance she can tell he's out-of-control today, a cave man. He's standing at the nurses' station in his muddy work boots and pants, his shirt falling out of his belt, his arm raised and his voice hoarse and high, wrangling about something. He's like a maverick fire hose, spouting, spouting, spouting. She slows down, takes a deep breath. She needs this like Satan needs a match, but of course, she expected it.

At ten paces, he spots her, leaves off whatever the big discussion he was having, comes toward her. Then it's a quick nod, no hug, never a hug. His face flushes hard, and his hands come up to cover it. She puts her arms around him; one tight squeeze. He is her boy, too, after all.

Sean steps back. "Where in hell have you been?"

"Home."

Joanne watches his eyebrows shoot upwards. "You went *home*?"

"I got dogs to feed. Have you talked to a doctor?"

"Fuck if they'll tell me anything. I'm just the kid's father." Sean shoves his hand in his pocket, squeezing the pack of cigarettes that she knows is always in there. "Nobody's said anything. Lyle's in town, I guess you know. He's beating on the DA's door; no one has told him shit either. Lyle figures the DA's pinning stuff on Shawnee as fast as he can, but he's going to press for release on recognizance." Sean looks up at her, his black pupils shiny with rage. "What the fuck did that kid think, spilling his guts?"

Joanne blinks. "What stuff?"

"The detective talked to the victim—"

"Gunther Cannon."

"You know his name already?"

Joanne feels her forehead tense, a thundercloud of headache hovers just behind her eyeballs. "The piano teacher's boy. You know who he is." She watches her husband's eyes narrow, filtering the information. *Black*. "What's going to happen, Sean?"

Her husband snorts. "What's going to happen? We're going to fight whatever bullshit the DA comes up with. That's what."

Joanne reaches for Sean's arm. "Listen, before Lyle gets to the hospital. I got to tell you something. Not here. Somewhere—" She casts her gaze around. The waiting room across from the nurses' station is empty except for a TV ablaze in orange and blue, a banner of bad news trailing along the bottom of the screen. "Quick."

In the waiting room, they settle themselves in chairs tucked in a corner.

"I went home to check on things. His bedroom is locked." Crackles of electricity flit through her skull. The headache breaking open.

"Shawnee's?"

"His door is locked. I tried it. He got out the window. But I'm thinking—I'm thinking someone's got to get into his room. You know, get *inside*, before the cops, in case—" Her throat gums, and she coughs sharply, telling herself there's no time for tears. "We can't tell nobody. Not even Lyle."

Sean's eyes widen, his dark brows, arching. "You're smart, woman."

Joanne stands, red lights knife her brain tissue. She would like to grab her head and tear out the pain. "We've got an hour."

TWELVE

IN ALL THE YEARS MAGGIE HAS WORKED as a court reporter, recording people's stories, translating scenarios of grief, of violence, of addiction, and fraud, she has always been struck by the sheer human beingness of the perpetrators and their victims. They are bodies, emotions, needs. They are physical presences with body odor or thick black hair; blue eyes splintered with flecks of green, scrawny arms or heaving belly fat. They have names, voices, language—vowel sounds that stretch like rubber bands. Such variety. Sometimes she wishes she were a composer and could write the music that would capture the suffering on both sides of a crime.

But as much as she used to feel she was the link between their voices and their written stories, now she realizes there was a gap. She was recording statements, utterances, fragments, but she had not in the least, captured the utter vulnerability of being a victim.

"Bruce," Maggie says. "Look."

It's three o'clock. Gunther, medicated, is sleeping heavily.

Bruce goes to her at the window. Below, the street is filled with white vans, corralled by metal barricades. Lights rigged on poles burst with artificial brightness on what seems increasingly like an artificial day. "The circus begins."

Maggie steps away. Only a week ago, they were sitting in the high school bleachers, cheering Gunther as he sprinted hurdles, his chest high; only days ago, they were high-fiving the other track parents, as triumphant as their kids. "'Heil Hitler'? A neo-Nazi? Where are we? Is this happening?"

Bruce covers his cough with a fist. He is not a man who cries. It is a skill he prides himself on, Maggie thinks, like making a campfire or pitching a tent, something that took practice to accomplish and that his father must have taught him by example.

He coughs again, looks at his phone. "Everyone and his brother is trying to reach us."

"Do you hear me?" Maggie snaps. "What's wrong with you?"

Bruce lowers his phone, his nostrils tensing. "Do you hear yourself? Give me a break, Maggie. 'Is this happening?' Yes, it's happening, okay? It's happening, and I'm just as freaked out as you are."

His admission softens her. They're in it together. She turns her gaze to Gunther. "I feel so guilty."

"Come on. One crazy kid."

Maggie inhales deeply. "I hope so."

"Listen," Bruce's voice is strained, "we know what the kid said; we know about the tattoo, but I don't think it's going to help Gunther if we dwell on that stuff. He knows he's black. It's not news. It hasn't been for a long time, so let's just shut up about it."

"That's what you want? Me to 'shut up'?" She looks at Bruce. His eyes have gone hard, not one ounce of remorse.

"Frankly, you liked that kid. Even though he was weird, and Gunther didn't like him. You thought they should be friends."

"He was shy. They didn't have a piano—"

"It was a big deal when he quit lessons."

"What are you talking about?"

"You went around, all bummed, that you'd lost your prodigy—"

"I never called him that. Shawnee wasn't a prodigy." He was a serious little boy. He reminded her of herself at that age when striking even one note was thrilling.

"Gun took it that way. He drew a picture for you. Don't you remember?"

Maggie shakes her head.

"A big kid with yellow hair next to a little kid, crayoned brown? How can you not remember? The mother was holding the yellow kid's hand. Gun gave it to you, so you wouldn't feel so bad."

"No," Maggie says. "That's not what I remember." This is true. She doesn't remember Gunther's drawing. She remembers being worried that Gunther, about to start first grade, was still the only black child in the school.

Gunther groans, his body arcing, resisting something in his dream. Maggie and Bruce move swiftly to his side. His face is dark, ashy against the stark white pillow.

Maggie presses her palm to Gunther's forehead. "A little feverish," she says.

◈

It's been a long time since Maggie has been allowed to gaze at her son's face, a long time since he's allowed her to touch him. Friends tell her it's the same for them. Their fingertips shoot voltage and their breath reeks. Their sons won't go near them. *Separation* is the term they use, the necessary trial of good parenting. *Healthy*, they insist as though describing a diet of grains and leafy vegetables. Maggie would like to believe that her friends are right. But is it more than that? Is Gunther separating from them as *parents* or as *white* parents? That's the question she can't ask her friends. It's a thought she doesn't want to think, a thought she'd like to extract from her brain, no matter how painful. A thought that seems to have wrapped itself around the tissue and the fiber of who she is.

Gunther's eyes open, glassy, frightened. Maggie takes his wrist. "I'm here," she says quietly. And the words or her presence seem to reassure him as he sinks back to sleep.

Once he was a baby with huge dark eyes and tiny gathered lips. Lying on his back in the crib, his nostrils pulsed with his sleeping breath like underwater fronds. Now, at seventeen, Gunther's jaw is Batman sharp; his brows thick and arched. Her friends go out of their way to tell her that Gunther is handsome. They are speaking in code, she thinks. What they are really saying is that they hope that Gunther's good looks will guarantee him a successful future. That he will, in some sense, *pass*.

THIRTEEN

CHARLOTTE WALKMAN IS NOT SHY about pushing to the front of the crowd in Town Park. She wants to get a good look at Sean Sr.'s pickup, sitting astride the curb where Shawnee Padrushky abandoned it. If someone gives her an eye, she can give it back. The way she looks at it, this is her town, her people. She's a *local;* three generations in the graveyard if not more, and even if she didn't witness the incident, somehow this is her story to tell.

Charlotte knows the Padrushky's, went to school with them, attends the same church; she knows the Cannons, too. Bruce Cannon? She's been crushing on him since freshman year in high school. Maggie Cannon? They're work friends. Maggie stenos for City Court; she, for Family.

Charlotte uses her broad shoulders and her elbows to squeeze in next to Johnny Scheim, Lake Village's code enforcement officer and his wife, Betts. Neither one of them greets her with more than a glancing nod, their attention captured, like the others in the crowd, by the sight of the bright red Ford. Charlotte leans across the police tape as far she dares. Wow. It's the new truck, all right. The nerve of the kid. Suicidal. Charlotte knows exactly how much the truck cost and what kind of payments the Padrushky's must be good for. Her cousin-in-law, Mort, owns the dealership and details like that make their way into dinner conversation, let's say. The lucky thing, it's not banged up. The unlucky thing is that the man won't touch his truck for months, wrapped up tight like it is with yellow tape and guarded by state police.

The weather is not what it was this morning. The clear sky is now sheathed in gray. A light scrim of mist raises the smell of iron from the newly laid sod beneath their feet. To Charlotte, the truck looks dead drunk. Like it's been through something it will never recover from. *Shawnee Padrushky.* She says the name out loud, shaking her head. Talking to herself out loud is a habit she's gotten into being a single person. Sometimes she feels like a kid launching a kite, hoping that someone will take notice and join her. What she would say, if anyone asked, was that she's watched that boy grow up in church. The angel with the golden curls and the big blue eyes that stared and stared. Marked for a vocation, people said. God's grace, they said, given the father he got.

All around her, people are talking in hushed, amazed tones, and shaking their heads, frowning, united in disbelief at what occurred this morning right here in this place. Under the gray drizzle, it feels to Charlotte like a funeral. It's the death of *something*, she thinks, though, thank god, neither of the boys died.

Already the incident has been reported on the TV, the radio, the Internet. Everybody in town has heard the reported facts as well as the speculations. The tech savvy are privy to the hundreds of tweeted hypotheses, the loads of unsubstantiated rumors that the high school kids, some witnesses, have put out in cyberspace. Charlotte has read a bunch of them, the charges of bullying, Gunther on Shawnee; Shawnee on Gunther; the girl trouble assumptions; the festering jealousy. None of it explains why Shawnee Padrushky hunted down Gunther Cannon.

Twisting this way, that way, Charlotte maneuvers through the crowd and across the street. Ahead, the entire block from Main Street to the police station is closed off by State Police SUVs parked end-to-end like small, metallic elephants. Charlotte recognizes Billy Malone, her neighbor's son, new to the force, standing stiff as a statue beside his car.

Beyond them, yellow tape stretches lamp post to lamp post, preventing the swelling crowd from reaching the path to the police station's now-boarded-up entrance. As soon as Charlotte's lunch break came, she was down here. The rest of the town, too, it seems.

Charlotte, breathing hard, presses up to the police tape. People are snapping photos, pointing, texting. *Seeing is believing*. Just beyond the tape is a square of sidewalk marked in chalk, a square of sidewalk she must have trod a million times, she thinks. It's where Shawnee must have knelt only hours before, trying to blow his brains out.

"I can't believe it," she mutters aloud, the thought too large to keep to herself. Shawnee Padrushky, the altar boy, the acolyte; Father Rand's page turner at the organ; then, the organist himself. Such a nerdy kid. So devoted.

Charlotte spies Holly Grant, the Court's Chief of Protocol. Her back is turned, but Holly's unmistakable. A real carrot-top. Charlotte moves toward her. She needs to talk to someone solid. Someone who might take away this strange feeling that the world has shifted and cracked.

Just then, to her left, a spotlight bursts on, as distracting as an explosion. In its beam stands a news reporter, his microphone aimed at someone. "Oh crap." She doesn't care who hears her. It's Dewey Harter, of all people. Screwy Dewey in his racing-striped pants and ballooning windbreaker. Why the hell is *he* being interviewed? He's the high school football coach, not the mayor. But there he is. Dewey Harter, 1999 Division 1 draft pick out of Lake Village High, local hero, his blonde crew shining in the light, his lips, way too pink, gabbing into the mic like he's the winning quarterback at the Super Bowl.

Charlotte edges closer. No matter how much she hates Dewey and his pink lips, she wants to hear what the blowhard, has to say.

"So, Mr. Harter, you've lived in this town all of your life; you went to school here; you coach here, do you think there's a racial angle to this horrific incident?"

Charlotte watches Dewey shove his hands in his pockets and pull his lips wide. His tongue thrusts out, pulls in, a toad-like tic of his she well remembers.

"Our little town might lack diversity," Dewey Harter says. "That doesn't mean we're bigots."

FOURTEEN

WOODY AND RYAN AND SAM ARE SITTING under a willow they used to call their clubhouse, when they were a lot younger and met afternoons to play. Sometimes they were snipers hunting guerillas in Kabul, like Ryan's dad; sometimes they were magic-driven, trying to conjure snow days or fencing with light sabers made from sticks. That was before they all got into sports (except Woody) and video games and in the off-season, beer.

The willow's long branches dangle like beaded curtains shielding them from the river and the drizzle. Woody, his back against the trunk, is smoking a joint, and the others are looking at their cellphones, pinging like little pinball machines in their palms. An hour ago, they were at the police station, telling the detective exactly what they saw and heard in real time, right there, at the cab window, at the raising of the rifle, at the opening of the driver-side door. Since then their nerves have been calling for a doobie to take the edge off, but they don't dare smoke one with the Regional meet coming up.

"Here." Woody sails the lit end past them. "You can catch a little."

They sniff, lifting their noses like hounds, appreciating the scent.

"I can't believe this shit," Ryan says. "The dude was going to waste him."

Sam sits up, grabbing his knees. "Fucking psycho."

Woody takes another hit, feeling his chest expand, the smoke burning lightly in his lungs. "Padrushky's a Nazi," he says, matter-of-fact.

"Why do you say that?" Ryan reaches for the joint, then pulls his hand back.

"He's got the tattoo and everything."

"What tattoo?"

Woody props himself up. "Why am I the only one who knows this shit?"

"When did fucking Padrushky become a Nazi?" Sam asks.

Woody shrugs. "Heck if I know."

"I thought Nazis hate Jews," Ryan says.

Woody feels the high coming on, his head cushiony and his mouth smiling even though there's nothing funny. "Jews, blacks. They probably hate everybody except Nazis."

"I never think of Gunther as 'black'," Sam says. "It's weird. I guess he is."

"No, duh," Ryan says.

"You forget about it," Woody says.

"Which means you do think about it." Ryan, always the smart ass.

"I guess so," Sam says.

"Before you get to know him." Woody contemplates the joint's lit end, before taking another toke. "I was kind of scared of Gun. In the beginning. A long time ago."

"Wha-?" Ryan pings him with a pebble, and Sam turns to him, incredulous.

"I didn't think he was going to waste me or anything, just like, I didn't know him, didn't know how to talk to him. I never talked to a black kid before."

"Me, either, actually." Sam digs at the soft ground with a stick.

"Oh jesus," Ryan says.

Woody brushes the spot on his shin where the pebble landed. "You mean you never notice?"

"That Gun's black? Of course, I notice; I'm not blind. I just don't give a shit. He's my teammate."

"Do you think Padrushky was scared of Gun?"

"Fuck no." Ryan is scowling. "Like you said, Padrushky's a fucking Nazi. They should've hauled that kid away a long time ago."

"True that," Woody says, raising the joint to his lips.

"Hey," Sam says, "save some for Gun."

Woody shakes his head. "Track." Then he remembers. "Oh, right. I'll roll him a fat one," he says.

FIFTEEN

THE LINE TOWARD THE CASHIER moves forward, and Bruce slides the slice of peach pie from a rack strategically placed to tempt onto his tray. He already knows the pie will taste like sweet glue, hardly a taste at all, but he can feel his blood sugar sinking fast. He's grabbed a carton of whole milk, too, even though he shouldn't, and sets it on his tray. A little more than fifteen years ago his father died of a heart attack right behind the counter at his hardware store. That's when Bruce's doctor read him the riot act on his cholesterol.

At the register, the cashier rings Bruce up without even a "hello," for which he is grateful. To her, he's just another hospital visitor in a state of shock. He gathers up a plastic fork and a straw and heads for the patio. He's still mad at Maggie. *I feel guilty*, she said. Guilty for what? Raising Gunther in Lake Village? *Adopting* him?

Still, he's sorry he reacted the way he did. He prides himself on being the calm one. For that reason, he's considered a good boss: He doesn't take shit, but he also doesn't give any. And here he is giving

Maggie shit that neither of them needs. He guesses he'll text an apology as soon as he has a few bites of pie. He'll bring her a slice. No, not pie, chips. Chips are her weakness.

At the table, Bruce pulls his phone from the front pocket of his khakis. There are a million texts, it seems. A million calls. He scans the screen. It looks like the news channel out of Albany; right on top of it, Utica, Binghamton. He puts down the phone to take a bite of the pie. The phone on vibrate buzzes on the table like a flipped June bug. Friends, work, radio, TV, newspapers. His gut spurts a jet of fire. He forgot to take a pill. Hiatal hernia, the doctor told him at his last check-up.

Bruce closes his eyes. How the hell is he going to answer all of these? He digs his thumbnails into the sealed edge of the milk carton, working the carton flaps back and forth to loosen the spout.

"Need help?" It's a girl in a candy striper apron. He must look pretty pathetic, he thinks.

"Nah," he says, "I'm going to tear it." And he does, spattering the table and his hand with milk. Feeling foolish and hoping the girl's moved on, he dabs the table with a napkin, sticks the straw into the carton. The sweet milk coats his throat.

He presses 7 on the cellphone, the shortcut to his mother, then holds his breath, imagining what he will say and how he will say it. Stay calm, stay calm. His mother's phone rings and rings. She's probably forgotten it somewhere or can't hear the ring tone. After his father died, she sold the hardware store building and moved into an assisted living center overlooking the lake. One time he found her phone at the base of a palm tree in the main lobby; another, in her medicine chest. On the tenth ring, the recording comes on, his mother commanding in a flat voice to, "Leave a message. Please." The beep is like a starting block he can't push off from. What can he say? How can he muster a reasonable tone? He can't. His voice, when he finds it, is as bland as the milk he is drinking. "Bruce, here. Try me again."

SIXTEEN

The driveway is blocked by the troopers' cars, one parked straight; the other, sideways. An officer stands at the door, gun drawn like he expects to be ambushed. Sean Sr. pulls up on the shoulder of the lawn, braking so hard the old truck pitches forward and back. Then he's out of the driver's seat and up the lawn and in the grill of the officer, someone he doesn't recognize, though he's pissed beside most of these fuckers at one bar or another.

"What's going on here?" he shouts. "Who the fuck let you in my house?"

The officer's Adam's apple lifts and lowers. "Sir, we have a warrant to search the premises."

The dispute has set the dogs barking, scrambling at their chain link enclosures like they have something to add to the conversation. Joanne veers across the lawn to quiet them.

"Let me see the warrant."

The officer lifts his radio to his mouth and mumbles into it.

"Sergeant Talbot is coming."

"Let me into my house, you asshole."

The officer flinches. He does not know the protocol on this one.

Then the front door opens, and Sean Sr. gasps. He can't help it. His stomach rises hard and fast. His knees buckle. Three men in black, wearing battle helmets and body armor, crowd the doorway, their rifles slung over their shoulders like bagged geese. In their arms are boxes overflowing with notebooks and papers: Shawnee's laptop and what looks like folded flags sealed in plastic.

Sean Sr. backs down the stairs. The sky above him is too blue and the sun too bright. This is deep shit. Really deep. What has Shawnee done?

SEVENTEEN

AS YOU DWELL IN SILENCE, OBSERVE. That's how they met; he and SST, his mentor.

The computer screen is a glowing rectangle, a portal that he passes through into a world where he is seen. He types:

—All the kids around me want to be black. They love rap music and try to act black. They talk as though they do not know English and wear immodest clothing. They treat the one black kid in the school like he is white and look up to him like he's a BBMOC, even though he was raised by white and talks like white and probably doesn't know black any better than they do.

Within minutes, the Brothers are typing back to him:

—That's too bad, brother. Stay strong. Keep modeling what it is to be white and proud.

—Just be white and let your European spirit soar.

—White is Might, keep it tight.

On and on, they offer their fist-bumps of support, signed with beer stein emoji's, endlessly toasting him. It feels good.

Then, this:

—*Be gracious. Be silent. As you dwell in the Silence, observe.* SST.

He blinks, feeling his heart speed up. *As you dwell in the silence.* A paralyzing chill runs through his arms and legs. The pressure of emotion inside his skull. *SST.* He knows what the initials stand for. "*Sic semper tyrannis.*" *Thus always to tyrants.* John Wilkes Booth's cry after he shot Lincoln. His fingers tremble as he types his reply. *I am silent. I dwell in high corners, weaving my web, ready with my poison.*

SST's reply follows almost without pause. *If you are ever alone and need someone to talk to, PM me. P.S. my friends call me 'Sic', ha-ha.* After this, he and Sic message day and night and do not run out of things to say.

This is the memory Shawnee clings to as the pain shatters his jaw; as his shame in failing his mission flays his self-worth. Sic, are you laughing or jeering?

EIGHTEEN

PEOPLE ALWAYS ASK HOPPER, Why'd you want to become a DA? Their underlying question, he knows, is, What made you such a prick? They've got theories—you were bullied, your father was a cop, you're a sadist, you've got a self-righteous stick up your ass. That might all be true, he wants to tell them, but so what? He's not the one selling drugs; he's not the one beating his wife or robbing banks or conning senile old folks. He's the one who convicts criminals; brings the bums to justice, stands up for what is right. People hate him for it.

Now it is Saturday morning, and he is sitting in Chief Reinhart's office. On the desk between them is a pile of notebooks, the kind you pick up for a dollar, with the mottled covers and wide ruled lines.

"Take a look," Chief Rinehart says, handing him a pair of rubber gloves. "It's going to rock your world."

Hopper slips the gloves on easily and draws the top notebook close. He knows he's handling evidence; the thought practically makes him pant. He flips open the cover. There, in handwriting as neat as a schoolmarm's, the boy has written: *This book belongs to Sean Padrushky, Jr. Mess with it and you die.* Nice, Hopper thinks. Beneath that epigraph is the date written European style, day, month, year. The month in German. Beside it, a neatly penned logo, the right angles of a swastika embedded in a circle.

"Oh shit," Hopper says. "What do we have here?"

"A philosophy and a methodology."

Hopper looks at the Chief. "A plan?" This is a real case, the good stuff.

"It couldn't get more detailed. Plus, a suicide note. Turn to the back."

Hopper breathes out hard through his mouth. There are scrawlers, and there are typists. There was once even a note composed entirely of words cut from a newspaper held down with packing tape, a work of art that read like a telegram composed from all the miseries of the world.

Shawnee Padrushky's suicide note is tucked into a cardboard pocket taped inside the back cover, two neat lines in the center of the lined paper.

I thought there was more that I would want to say when I said good-bye, but it turns out there isn't. I thought he loved me. He didn't.

Hopper blinks. He reads the note again. He is not a psychologist, he thinks. He is not qualified to understand this. But in an instant, he finds himself growing angry, angry as hell. This note would put a fucking dagger through any parent's heart. No good-bye; no thank you; no appreciation at all.

He has two boys of his own. One son runs a restaurant on a tourist island off the coast of Georgia; another works in the tech business in California. They never wanted to go through upstate winters again, they said, which is why they both lived so far from home. Maybe this was the truth, maybe it wasn't. Hopper doesn't care. They are good sons. They keep in touch. He and his wife try not to interfere too much in their lives, but if the boys need something, he and his wife are there.

Hopper folds the note back along its creases, sticks it into its special sleeve. Removing his glasses, he rubs his temples. Then again, maybe the *he* isn't the boy's father? Would the Padrushky's want to pursue this mystery? Explore the angle, say, of Sean Jr. as jilted lover? Heartbreak accounting for temporary insanity? Unlikely. No sane family would subject their seventeen-year-old son to a public confession. Surely, they would realize this wasn't a reality show: This was real life. And frankly, he can't see a jury believing Padrushky's crime was motivated by love, not hate.

"Is this my copy?" Hopper taps a black, three-ring binder, inches thick.

The Chief nods. "I sent a duplicate to Lyle Carullo, the Padrushky's lawyer; the kid's uncle, out of Albany."

"Keep it in the family, I guess. I don't know him. If I was them, I'd be mortgaging my house, getting the best lawyer money could buy. We're looking here at pulling together a grand jury, for sure."

Chief Rinehart blows heavily through his mouth as though he had been holding his breath for a long time. "It's a biggie, all right. It's got hate crime written all over it, and we haven't even looked into the hard drive."

Hopper blinks. "You've got the hard drive?"

"Shit, like I said, we've got everything."

As soon as Hopper gets to his office in the annex to the courthouse, he shouts at his assistant to hold his calls, then shuts the door. Opportunity of a lifetime? Career case? Even skimming the journals, Hopper knows what he's got: the possible indictment of Sean Padrushky, Jr. for pre-meditated second-degree attempted murder as a hate crime, which in this state is a felony that knocks out youthful offender status and bumps you up a class. When you total the numbers, Padrushky is looking at a possible twenty-five years in federal prison, maximum security. No parole options. The seriousness of the charges is enough to make Hopper breathless.

NINETEEN

THIS APRIL MORNING, the atmosphere has a smeared quality, the heavy blankness of a hot August afternoon. Father Lambert, his phone to his ear, heads over to the air-conditioner, turns it on. Father Lambert has been on hold to Bishop John for a full five minutes, but suddenly, there is a stop to the choral music and a throat clearing. "Father Lambert?"

"Your Excellency."

Then Father Lambert is explaining the situation. A boy, a parishioner, but not just any parishioner, a teenaged boy, the only boy of his age to come forward on Maundy Thursday, *a boy whose feet he, Father Lambert, held as he washed his arches, dried his toes (but Father Lambert doesn't say this)*—a boy who used to play the organ at Mass every Sunday like a conquering angel, a boy whom *the Bishop himself* once noted seemed marked, just possibly, for a vocation—is now lying in his hospital bed, recovering from self-inflicted wounds. He has confessed to the attempted murder of a classmate, who, thank the Lord, has survived the attack. Even as he speaks, Father Lambert is listening intently to the breathing on the other end of the line, monitoring its purr.

"God is merciful," the Bishop says.

"You do remember the young man? Shawnee Padrushky?"

"I remember him, indeed. Father Rand's protégé."

Father Rand. Father Lambert presses the tip of his tongue against his front upper teeth, before letting it relax. The Church hierarchy, he thinks, is a three-dimensional chess board. Bishop John, gazing down from above, knows, of course, what's happening on every level. Father Rand's reassignment a year ago was his move. "With your permission, I would like to hold Mass this evening to support the Padrushky family. Our church family needs this as well." *Sabbatum Sanctum,* Easter Eve. The last day of Holy Week. Jesus's body lies in the tomb. No Mass for this day unless there is an extremely grave or solemn situation.

"You must. A Mass for *both* of the young men. Let us keep both victims in our prayers."

TWENTY

THIS SATURDAY MORNING, Joanne sets herself to shoveling shit. She has her scooper, and she has her rake. She has her plastic bags and her rubber gloves. Nine dogs. A lot of shit. And even though she's trained each one of them to do their business in the far corner of their run, still it isn't like the shit is piled neatly in one heap, one neat shovelful. No one can train a dog to do that.

Sean Sr., dressed today in clean jeans and his pearl-buttoned shirt, shoves the toe of his cowboy boot through a metal diamond in the chain link fence and rests his elbows on the top bar. "You're not coming? You'd rather stay with the dogs?"

She rakes the dark turds into her shovel, considers flinging them in his direction. "If you haven't noticed, I got a bitch who whelped for the first time; I got a pack of dogs to feed. Of course, I'm coming. After I do my chores." She ignores Sean Sr.'s gawping. Go ahead. Gawp. Run the mouth. Who the hell headed off to the bar, while she sat by their son's side all evening and through the night?

Yesterday in the darkened hospital room she sat, watching her son sleep and wishing that she could disintegrate into the shimmering particles of dust caught in the single beam of moonlight that had escaped a crack in the blinds. When she was a girl, she stumbled into places of light and dark, dust glittering in a sunbeam, dusk inside the barn, and she believed God was about to speak. She would freeze in place, every vein electric with anticipation, her heart open to His word, waiting, knowing that she was among the chosen. But no. Dusk eventually dimmed to dark, the sun beam drained of light. Crickets rasped, and the cows lowed. God was silent; she moved on.

Shawnee wasn't talking, not a word. When the nurse asked him if anything hurt, his jaw, his head, he said nothing. When the doctor asked him if he needed something to help him sleep, he stayed still as a rock. They gave him something anyway. The nurse, a plain girl, heavy set, wore a slim cross around her neck, and when she went to the supply room to get the bed pan, she leaned close to Joanne's ear and whispered that she was praying for her son.

"Me, too," she said. And she was, her rosary clicking as precisely as a second hand through her fingers. *Hail Mary, full of grace.* Through the peppery light, her son's pale skin shone white as shell; the bandages wrapping his skull waxed even brighter. In the cot beside his bed, she did not sleep, her mind like a restless tongue probing, probing. Who was her son? What had he become? She remembered the quiet baby, the good baby, the baby so easy you could forget he was there. She remembered the little boy who saved his tooth money to give to the Mission; the boy who sang like an angel and learned to play the organ from a priest. A boy marked for a vocation it was whispered. She had believed with the others that that might be true. And now he was being called a psycho, a crazy person. He'd tried to kill Gunther Cannon, the police were saying, just because Cannon was black.

That couldn't be the whole story. Maybe if her son would talk, they'd learn something. Maybe Gunther had done something to Shawnee that he wasn't saying? Maybe Shawnee was afraid of him? She knew only two things about Gunther Cannon: he was Maggie Cannon's, the piano teacher's, son, adopted, and he was black. But there was more to know. She was sure of this. There was more to know, and she was going to find out what it was.

TWENTY-ONE

THE WHOLE CANNON FAMILY looks up when the DA enters Gunther's hospital room, introduces himself. "Is this a good time?" he asks.

"Good as any," Bruce says, coming forward to shake Hopper's hand.

Hopper is a tall man in a well-tailored suit, expensive shoes. Good-looking in a square-jawed sort of way. Maggie has met him many times, of course. In his workaday mode, he strikes her as courteous, though brusque, someone who affects an air of distraction to obscure a constant state of irritation.

"How's everyone holding up?"

"We're holding," Maggie says. "That's about the best we can do." She cuts a look at Gunther, a prompt of sorts, watching as he untethers from his earbuds. How strange, she thinks, that the real world is weightless for him; his music, the place to anchor.

"How about you, Gunther?" Hopper touches Gunther's shoulder. "You doin' all right?"

Maggie wonders if Gunther hears how Hopper raises his pitch a little, drops his 'g'. It's how white men talk to him these days, she's noticed.

"I guess."

"It's a lot," Bruce says.

"It is, indeed." Hopper hoists his briefcase onto his lap. "And with what I have here, it's going to be a lot more."

Gunther groans lightly. "Oh man."

Hopper nods. "You wish it was over, I bet?"

"I wish it never happened."

"Yes. We all agree on that." Hopper pauses, tapping the briefcase with his index finger. "I've read Detective Peters' report, and I've been going through a great deal of evidence that was obtained yesterday through a warrant to search the Padrushky's house."

"Wow," Bruce says. "They've been through the house?"

"The team found Sean Jr.'s notebooks, his computer." Hopper turns to face Gunther. "It seems that Mr. Padrushky, Jr. had a coherent plan to—"

"Kill me." Gunther bolts upright, punching his thigh.

"That's correct."

"I told you, guys."

"Oh my god." Maggie winces. *We almost lost him.*

"I *told you.*"

Gunther looks so vulnerable and so angry; his tone of accusation, fueled by grief, reminds her of the afternoon when Gunther came home, raging, from kindergarten. A boy had teased him he said. He wouldn't say for what. The tantrum lasted for hours; Gunther kicking, screaming, throwing every object he could get his hands on.

Maggie remembers trying to hold him, trying to soothe him. For precious seconds, he would sink into her arms, a tired fawn, only to explode out of her grasp. She wanted to call Bruce, but she didn't dare take her eyes off Gunther. She had no idea how powerful the rage of a five-year-old could be; how destructive. Lamps, cushions, tchotchkes of various types flew; newspapers, books, toys whirled through the air. Gunther bore down on the house like a hurricane, leaving swathes of destruction.

Standing in the doorway to the kitchen, Maggie grabbed Gunther's wrists as he tried to pummel his way past her. She hung on as he flipped and twisted in her grasp, trying to slide through her splayed legs like a deep-water fish dragged on deck. Finally, he collapsed. Together, they sank to the floor.

Maggie reaches for Gunther's clenched hand. "You told us. You knew."

Bruce clears his throat. "I'm sorry."

Gunther closes his eyes, sinks back on his pillows.

"So what does all of this mean, Mr. Hopper?" Bruce asks. "What are you saying here?"

"I'm saying that from everything the evidence points to—plus what we've uncovered from his computer history—white supremacy chat rooms, other neo-Nazi affiliations—"

"Oh jeeze," Bruce mutters.

Gunther's eyes open. "I knew it."

"As far as Chief Rinehart and I are concerned, we have enough here to go to Judge Adkins to request a grand jury take a look at the evidence. We want to charge Mr. Padrushky, Jr. with committing a federal Hate Crime. That's a felony."

Maggie feels her stomach rise. "A racial attack? *Planned?*" What did that boy say to Gunther in kindergarten? Why didn't she insist that he tell her?

Bruce shakes his head. "Oh my god."

"The grand jury would have to move to indict. If they do, Padrushky, Jr. may be looking at twenty-five years in federal prison, no chance for parole. None. It means that Gunther will have absolutely no worries for a very long time. How does that sound?"

Gunther is silent, digging at an itch beneath the rim of his cast.

"Gun?"

"That kid should be in jail," Gunther says, "for the rest of his fucking life."

TWENTY-TWO

No worries, the DA said. Good luck with that. The man has no idea. His parents, either. Worries crawl through his brain; twitch under his skin. They always have.

His parents have left with Hopper. They're going to a press conference that, thank god, he doesn't have to go to. The conference, Hopper told them, was their chance to get the story out before the Padrushkys did.

"Let me explain something," Hopper said. "The law is the law, but there's another piece to this—the public's perception of the case. No matter how clear the matter appears to us, hate crimes are tricky. The grand jury will decide this case based on what I think is strong evidence, but on some level the public decides this as well."

His mom frowned. "You want us to play nice. We're good folks."

"You got it."

"Fuck that," his father said. Patches of red flared on his neck as though he'd been slapped there.

Gunther blinked hard. His dad dropping the F-bomb.

"That kid tried to kill my son."

Hopper was tapping the brief case again like he was the steno, not Gun's mom. "Absolutely true, but I'd like your permission to say that the Cannon family is very grateful that Gunther is alive and that they thank Gunther's supporters. And, at the same time, they wish the best for his assailant's recovery."

"Spin," Gunther said. He got it even if his parents didn't. It's only been a day and already the incident was being mixed and re-mixed on-line, a dozen different beats spliced in, a dozen different angles. "I agree with Mr. Hopper. If we don't spin it, they will."

So there was nothing more for his parents to say. His mom kissed his head and his dad squeezed his shoulder, and they all left.

As soon as the door closes behind them, Gunther gets out of bed and goes to the window. He's been getting snaps from Woody and Ryan and Sam and a whole bunch of other friends, but he wants to see for himself. His room, at the back of the hospital, looks down on a parking lot and beyond to the river where he and his friends like to fish. Now the lot is filled with police cars and vans with TV cameras aimed up at him like bazookas. His dad called it a circus, but it looks to him more like what he's seen in videos, the aftermaths of shootings where the survivors scatter and only the police are left in neon gear and twirling lights like a swarm of pissed-off bees.

In the bathroom, he sets his phone on the metal shelf above the sink, turns to the toilet. He didn't want to take a leak in front of his parents for some reason, even though the door slides shut. His phone buzzes like a pager, like it's annoyed at being ignored. He picks it up, scanning the messages that fill the screen. *Be strong. Praying for you. Love ya, man.* The scribbled shit of yearbook pages, some of it sincere; some not. Still, he can't believe how many there are—a hundred at least—friends, teachers, coaches, Mr. Johnson, his Boy Scout leader, and Mr. Denardo, his boss at Safeway last summer, all of the most popular guys in his class, and the girls, too.

A long time ago, before track, he used to want to be a celebrity; he used to want to be Michael Jackson or Jay Z or Lil Wayne. For Halloween, he dressed *gansta* and gave his mother a heart attack. He was eleven. He didn't know why she had to act so upset. But now the thought of all of the attention he's going to get makes his stomach kink. Soon he'll be back at school, and he'll be having to face all of these people, and he'll be having to tell them his story over and over again. The pain chops him. He's on the toilet, quick.

Ants in your pants? his teachers used to say when he was a little kid and couldn't sit down. They thought it was excitement, a little current jumping in his veins that said, move, move, move. But it wasn't that. It was dread. Like now. Someone was going to tell him something, something he knew but didn't want to know. Billy Creighton in Kindergarten coming up to him at recess, poking his forearm hard like it was Playdoh and asking why he and his mom didn't match? Mrs. Budrey, his fourth-grade teacher, telling him with tears in her eyes, that she'd thought of him when she voted for President, because she wanted children of color to know that someday they could be President, too.

After shock, what hit him was shame. Shame that something so obvious had never occurred to him. How could anyone be so dumb? He'd let the truth sneak up on him, take him by surprise like the wolf who ate grandma. It made him angry—at Billy Creighton, at Mrs. Budrey and at all of the people who took it on themselves to tell him who he was in their eyes. But, most of all, he was angry at his stupid self for batting the truth away, for pretending it didn't sting.

The day after Billy poked him, Gunther cornered him on the playground to show him the slick pink gully between his upper lip and gum. "We do so match," he said. What he should have done, he thinks now, was punch Billy.

Getting up from the toilet, he cups his hands under the sink faucet, then leans close to the mirror and stares. Is this him? There's a scrape above his right temple that he doesn't remember, a neat little grid, already scabbing in dark red beads. And a smeary bruise on his cheekbone that looks like faded glare paint against his skin. That's funny. His football career only lasted a few weeks, the worst experience of his life—until this. The rest of his face he knows: his eyes, his nose, his mouth, his chin. His mom tells him he is handsome, but he hasn't believed her since he was little. Handsome—*hot*—means tall, blonde, blue-eyed, the obvious, white.

Back in his hospital bed, Gunther slides deep beneath the sheets, pulling the blanket over his head. In the cool dark, the tears trickle in thin streams down the sides of his face, first hot, then cold as they reach his jaw, curve under to his neck. When he was little, his mom and dad assured him a million times that they were his real parents no matter what kids said. He shared their history, they said; he was part of it now, and he was the future, too. He had a birth mother, they told him, and a birth family. His birth mother had loved him so much she had given him to them, because she knew she couldn't keep him safe. That kind of love was super-duper love his mom told him. Suppa-duppa, he'd echoed. He was three years old, and he thought his mom was telling him that his birth mother was Super Woman fighting the bad guys, while he stayed safe with his mom and dad. He called his birth mother, "suppa mama," but he never learned her real name or the name of his birth family. The adoption was closed.

In the cave of sheet and blanket, he sees the truth. No matter what his parents say, he does not have their eyes or ears or mouth or nose. He does not have the length of their thigh bones or their tapered toes; he does not have Maggie's double-jointed thumbs or her croaky laugh; he does not have the twitch under Bruce's right eye, or his hooking shot. He doesn't have one single musical bone in his body, and he doesn't have his dad's love of rules (*rules are made to be followed, not broken*), though he has tried. Most of all, he does not have the color of their skin, which they always said didn't matter, but he knows is a lie. Hopper told them so; Padrushky proved it. His color might not matter to Maggie and Bruce, but it always has to others.

TWENTY-THREE

SEAN, SR. KNOCKS ONCE ON THE DOOR, knocks again. "Shawnee, boy, you in there?" The police officer sitting on the chair outside the room looks away, pretending he cannot see and cannot be seen.

"Shawnee?" Sean, Sr. pushes the door open. His son is lying back in bed, his eyes closed, his arms tethered with tubes to the machines that surround him like mechanical guards. "Shawnee?" He steps closer to the bed, swallowing down the acid that rises in his throat.

His son's face looks as though it has been pummeled; his head is bandaged from throat to crown; his blonde hair shorn to stubble. None of the surgery has been explained to him; not completely. The bullet, Sean Sr. was told, plowed up behind the jaw, and out from past the ear, missing so many places to lodge it was a miracle his son wasn't dead. He could hear himself using those exact words to his buddies at the bar last night as he drank pint after pint, all free, pity pints, they were, but he wouldn't say no.

"Messed you up, didn't it? Messed you up, bad."

No sign that the son is listening to his father. Shawnee's wrists droop where they are tied to the bed's railings, his torso is concave beneath the sheets. Sean Sr. reaches over the railing, shakes Shawnee lightly by his shoulders. "Son. Wake up. It's your pop. Wake up now."

Shawnee's eyelid tics; the dimple at the top of his bruised cheek flexes. He used to kid his son about that dimple: *Must've tangled with a gangster…Or was it a grizzly?*" Shawnee's eyes stay closed. Is he faking? He was a good faker when he was a kid. Could drown him in ice, and he wouldn't give up his pretend. He should have played poker. That's what he used to tell the kid. With a straight face like that, he could be a shark.

The door opens behind him. A man's gravel voice. "Hey, Sean."

"Lyle." He straightens, remembering that he was supposed to call Lyle first thing this morning. He didn't. All he knew this morning was a hangover as big as a house, but that hadn't stopped him from getting to the hospital before Joanne.

"How's the patient?"

"Asleep."

Lyle is a big man. The suits he likes to wear to show he's somebody are too tight across his belly and his ass. Joanne's brother, the scumbag lawyer, done good for himself, though. Married up and moved to Albany. Got himself a McMansion and an in-ground pool, a fancy car and a fancy wife. No dogs.

"Your boy screwed up."

"Don't I know it."

Lyle is beside him, hanging his hands on the railing and staring down at his sleeping nephew as though he was a corpse in a coffin. "What a stupid ass."

"Easy now. If Joanne hears you—"

"Joanne will hear me. We got work ahead of us. A lot of work. Him blowing off Miranda and the new charge."

"The new charge?"

"Do you want to sit down?"

Sean Sr. shakes his head, shoves his hands in his jeans pockets.

"The DA's calling for a grand jury. They want to charge Shawnee with a hate crime—on account of what he was yelling while he was chasing that boy, on account of what they found on his computer and in his notebooks. The dumb fuck."

Sean Sr. drops into the chair. The machines around Shawnee are beeping like broken alarm clocks. He'd like to smash them.

Lyle glares at him. "You don't know nothing about this?"

"Nothing about what?"

"The Hitler shit? The White Aryan stuff?"

"What the fuck?"

"Come on, Sean. The room isn't bugged."

"Ain't this a free country anymore? You telling me you can't hate who you want to hate, and this is America?"

Lyle snorts. "Hate whoever you want to hate, but don't keep a fucking notebook about it; don't make a plan to take out the only black kid in the school; don't fucking chase him with a .22 and shoot him. By the way, I know about the souvenirs even if no one else does."

"What's that supposed to mean?"

"Are you a Nazi or something?"

"Who the fuck are you? It's a hobby, that's all. Like I told Joanne, it's history."

Lyle straightens. "It better be before the police find it."

Sean Sr. holds his head in his hands. "I can't believe this shit. I don't know what happened to this kid."

"Don't you?"

"I didn't tell my son to plug a nigger if that's what you mean."

"You bullshitting me? As long as I've known you, you've been telling the same story of how you got kicked out of school because the dean was black, and you were white."

"It happened. I didn't make it up."

Lyle snorts, pushing off the bedrails with a light shove. "Is my sister going to be here soon? We three need to talk."

He looks up at Lyle, Mr. Suit with his too perfect hair and his baby-soft jaw. It was the last week of school; he was getting ready to graduate. *The last week.* He and his friends celebrating a little early pulled a prank; come on, no one got killed or anything. Nobody hurt too bad. Except it's not the way the Dean sees it; the black dean. "She's coming—as soon as she cleans up the dogs."

TWENTY-FOUR

YEARS AGO, IN THE CITY, Maggie studied t'ai chi. Her teacher, Greg, was a former boxer; the studio, a makeshift room carved from a loft. The plunked melodies of Intermediate Ballet, played on an out-of-tune upright, wafted through the flimsy walls like an oversweet perfume. But what comes back to her now is a memory of a place in the form, a crossroad of sorts, in which one is stepping in one direction, then pivoting to face the diagonal opposite, then stepping again to face an unexplored corner and again to its opposite diagonal. She remembers the experience of turning, turning, turning, arms raised, hands pinching or pushing, arms lowering, raising. The idea, she remembers, was to keep one's balance in the midst of change. She wasn't good at it.

Still, the image stayed with her after her first miscarriage, her second. It stayed with her on the morning in a doctor's office when she learned that she would never conceive a child again. Turn, turn, turn, she told herself, as she felt herself dissolve into an infinite cavity of grief.

But here, now, sitting beside Bruce in the hospital's auditorium, on a stage that usually hosts visiting doctors, specialists in this field or that, she has another thought about that image. She sees an image of battle, of the pivoting figure, wrist raised, flinging away her attackers. *To help someone not to hurt you*, she remembers Greg saying. *That's the practice.*

Hopper is at the microphone; she and Bruce sitting behind him, shielded only slightly from the audience of reporters. The lights make it impossible to see individual faces, and yet, Maggie realizes, those on stage can be seen. She wonders what sort of expression she should wear, not wanting to convey indifference or fear. It's Hopper's conference. She and Bruce don't have to say a word. But all eyes will focus on them—the parents of the victim.

Maggie laces her fingers, sets her hands on her lap. Beside her, Bruce is ramrod, resisting for once the curvature of his upper back, his tall-man slump. She looks petite beside him. Neither of them noticed their difference in height until the morning they picked up her wedding dress at the tailor's. There, waiting for the dress to be boxed, they'd turned, simultaneously, to the full-length, wall mirror. "Is that us?" Maggie said. "Are you really that tall?" Bruce blinked. "Are you really that short?" "We're freaks," Maggie said, and Bruce concurred, "Wedding off." They laughed.

Now her husband is staring at the crowd in the room, frozen, as though he has stage fright. Maybe he does. Or maybe he, too, has donned his armor, is girding himself against an onslaught of intruders.

A reporter, standing, knocks his pencil against his pad. "Is there bad blood between these boys? A grudge? A girl?"

Maggie flushes, furious, at the litany of rationales, escape hatches, for someone trying to kill her son.

Hopper shakes his head. "Nope. Gunther barely knew his assailant. They go to the same high school; they share a class or two. Everyone knows everybody at a school this small, of course, but Gunther and the assailant have never exchanged much more than a 'hello.'"

Instantly, the audience is rustling, stirred to flight. From the waving hands, Hopper points to a woman, a voluptuous brunette, whom Maggie recognizes from the evening news program out of Albany.

"You say evidence was recovered that may point to a hate crime. What kind of evidence? Can you tell us more about this?"

Hopper smiles briefly. "Great question, Melody. No. I can't." The other reporters chuckle lightly. "But I can tell you, as I said, that the evidence of a hate crime is strong enough to warrant us requesting Judge Adkins to appoint a grand jury investigation."

Murmurs break out, again the frantic hands. A reporter shouts, "Do you anticipate the Padrushky family requesting a psychiatric evaluation? Could this be a case of insanity?"

Insanity. In the funhouse, a trap door springs open, a skeleton tumbles out. Hopper didn't mention insanity. Maggie's gaze swerves to Bruce, thin-lipped, frowning. Would insanity absolve Padrushky?

Hopper holds up his palm to quiet the audience. "I imagine a psychiatric evaluation will be requested. In the meantime, given the evidence—"

"What would an insanity plea mean for his case?" Melody asks. It's Maggie's question, too.

Hopper pauses before releasing his breath. "That question is for Mr. *Padrushky's* lawyer," he says.

That's not how Maggie sees it. As soon as they leave the stage, she's after Hopper, clever man, who cleaves the throng at the side door, shoots past the elevators to the stairway door. Maggie blows past confused-looking Bruce, past the reporters and security guards. Hopper's down a flight when she reaches the landing.

"Wait," she calls. "Please."

The light in the concrete stairwell is the light of a locker room, of a jail cell. It bleaches Hopper's face turned up to hers. "What is it?"

He sounds annoyed, but Maggie doesn't care. "What happens if they decide to plead insanity?"

"'Not guilty by reason of insanity.' They'd be nuts, no pun intended."

"Why?"

Hopper rolls his eyes. "One, it means admitting guilt. Two, it's damn expensive. Three, Padrushky didn't kill your son, so they're not facing capital. Four, what we have in evidence, in Padrushky's own writing, is a clear and cogent plan. No way they prove that he didn't know what he was doing."

"So, we're safe."

Hopper exhales abruptly. It's the sound her father used to make when she asked what he considered a stupid question (all of them, it seemed to her). "You work in the courts, Maggie. You know that nothing's guaranteed if it comes to a jury trial." She sees his grip flex on the briefcase handle. "We'll see what a grand jury comes up with, of course. But I'm feeling confident."

Maggie hears the door to the parking garage clang shut behind Hopper as she heads back up the stairs. *If it comes to a jury trial.* What is Hopper really thinking? What is his plan?

TWENTY-FIVE

JOANNE SITS AT THE DESKTOP COMPUTER in the first floor den. She has only a short time to do something. She doesn't want Shawnee to be alone with his father or his uncle in the hospital room. From now on, she will be awake.-She will make up for the ways in which she has so obviously failed. She will listen and watch like a hawk.

She powers on the computer, and when it signals that it's ready for her commands, she is suddenly stymied. These days everyone's life is supposed to be an open book, the deepest secrets available at a keystroke. So how does she find out what's happening in her son's life—what was happening between him and Gunther Cannon that caused him to snap—how can she find the truth? She does not belong to the cyberworld; she prides herself on that. Her customers sometimes mention that she should start a "home page" for the kennel. No thank you, she prefers word of mouth. Her only memberships pertain to dogs. Occasionally, she has been known to post in chat rooms on the topics of unfair discrimination against Staffordshire terriers or how to house-train puppies. She and her husband share this one computer; she hasn't needed her own.

Her fingers pause on the keyboard. She doesn't even know, she suddenly realizes, if Shawnee's on social media or plays video games. She doesn't have a clue what he does—*did*—all those hours alone in his room. And it occurs to her that right now a detective is opening her son's computer, searching through a history of which she is oblivious. For god knows how long, she has been shut out completely from her son's secrets, his real life. In a matter of minutes or hours, this detective will know more about her son than she has ever known.

TWENTY-SIX

THE MINUTE MAGGIE SAYS she's taking off, Gunther seems relieved. Bruce has gone back to work for a few hours, and Gunther's friends, Woody, Ryan, and Sam have just arrived. Though polite, they are clearly dying to share their news out of her earshot.

Part of her, for sure, wants to listen at the keyhole. She has friends who feel that spying is essential to good parenting, but she and Bruce have always taken the high road. No looking at texts, no checking his computer history. Occasionally, she wonders what she might have missed, but then she reminds herself that as long as Gunther is keeping up his end of the bargain—decent grades, no drugs—he is entitled to his privacy.

The elevator takes her to the top floor of the hospital and from there Maggie follows the nurse's directions to the roof, the same nurse who tipped her that there's a gazebo up there where rogue doctors and nurses sneak off to smoke cigarettes.

She pushes the steel door open, grateful for the fresh air, the sky, the smell of something daring to blossom early, forsythia, maybe? The gazebo's empty except for an ashtray clad in metal, so sturdy-looking it could double as a bear-barrel, and a low wooden bench nailed to one wall. She pulls out her cell phone. Hesitates. Her heart is speeding; her palms growing damp. She's got to call Bev. She's the only one who can help. But how can she call? It's been a year since Bev left town for London, a year in which they both have been pretending that the friendship is not over, that it's just a matter of being in different places now, of their being busy. That's a lie. They are broken up. The break was her fault. The mending, up to her. Yet she's held back on apologizing. She's a terrible person. A bad mother. A bad friend. *Some say the world will end in fire, some say in ice.* She would like to melt, but instead stays cold.

TWENTY-SEVEN

At first it is awkward. Everyone standing around looking at their cellphones like they were teleporters: *Beam me up, Scotty.* Like it's Gun's funeral and he's already dead or something. He's not. He's alive, and that's something to celebrate, to whoop about and get crazy with. He's fucking alive. But no one says much except, "Hey." Ryan is backed up against the door, an earbud wire hanging like a strand of dental floss; Sam's flicking out moves with his damn yo-yo that—amazing as they are—everyone's seen before. Only Woody plops in the chair next to the bed.

Then a knock at the door, and the pizza delivery man comes in with two big boxes, and a big bottle of Coke, too. He smiles and touches the brim of his cap. "I hope you feel better." He hesitates, gazing at the floor, like he's forgotten something. Only after he leaves, does Woody say, "Shit, I think he wanted a tip."

Somehow even though that's not really funny at all, they're cracking up, and the room suddenly smells so good, filled with the thick, sweet smell of hot cheese and the spicy heat of pepperoni—Gunther's favorite—and everyone is suddenly happy, diving into those pizzas like they haven't eaten for a hundred years.

"So good, man," Woody says, drawing the tip of his slice into his mouth like a frog inhaling a fly. Then he's screaming, "Oww," and again, everyone laughs.

"You're famous, bro." Ryan's leaning over Gunther's shoulder, trying to show him his cellphone screen.

"The shit's gone viral," Sam says, joining him, "Have you seen the tweets? You see hashtag 'Gun Lives'?"

"You got any girl you want," Woody says.

Any girl, nice, but his mind isn't on girls right now. It's not like before when, like his friends, he could hardly keep his mind off them. "Not with this." He holds up his cast, lets it drop.

Ryan blinks. "Are you kidding, man? Girls are into that shit. They'll be signing it—"

"With their lips," Sam says, puckering. "You are The Man."

Gunther props himself up against the sagging pillows, his heart beating fast. "Did you see it? Did you see what went down?"

The silence is awkward; not like someone farted, worse, far worse, like someone had the bad manners to die right in front of them, or say, 'I love you.' Then Woody points to a helium balloon bobbing up by the ceiling light, "Happy Birthday" scrawled across a cartoon cake. "Someone's confused." The boys look up, Gunther, too. "It should say, 'Happy Fucking Alive Day.'"

"It should say, 'Happy I Survived Day.'"

Gunther laughs. "Happy I Didn't Die Day."

Yes, they all agree, and that breaks it open.

"I was scared shitless," Ryan says. "When I saw the fucker's gun."

"Shit, me, too." Sam's snapping his yo-yo double-time. "I was like, *outta* here. Gun, you were booking it."

Woody nods. "Three-minute mile. You lost me."

"World record." Ryan thrusts his knuckles toward Gunther who touches them with his own, lightly.

"We couldn't catch you—" Ryan starts.

"We heard the shots—"

Gunther swallows. "Did you think he got me?"

"Honestly, we were like *what the fuck?* By the time we got to Main Street, the place was going crazy—police, sirens—" Woody digs his hand into his pants pocket. "I got some pictures on my phone if you want to see it."

Gunther blinks. "Nah. Not now, man. Maybe later." He wipes the back of his hand across his forehead; just the thought of looking at Woody's snaps makes him sweat.

"Sure, hey, but listen—" Woody waggles a thin metal box in front of his eyes. "When you get out of here, I got a blunt that's going to blow your socks off."

"Shush, man. They got cops all over the place."

Woody ducks his chin, tucking the box back into his jeans. "When you need it. That's all I'm thinking."

That's all Woody is thinking. But Gunther is thinking of a cliff, straight drop to the bottom, no idea what he's going to do when he gets out of here, goes back to school. His life is messed up. No practice, no meets, no team. Even less of an idea of who he is anymore.

TWENTY-EIGHT

Holy Saturday Mass is a rarity, perhaps a once-in-a-lifetime occasion. The altar is draped in storage cloths. There are no flowers, no candles. The only smell that reaches Charlotte, seated in the corner of the farthest back pew, is the smell of floor wax with its comforting tang. She is glad that she is here among her people, worshipers who have known Shawnee since he was a baby. To them, he is still Scrawny Shawnee, the beanpole of an acolyte; the teenager who played organ for Sunday mass; a quirky kid, sure, but not *that* quirky, at least Charlotte hadn't thought so and nor had the others. No, she had to be here this evening with the rest of the St. Vincent congregation, in this place she knows so well, because in a crisis, you find succor with your own kind.

Charlotte opens her program, skipping to the highlighted rectangle on the right-hand page.

We ask for your prayers in this time of need. Help Shawnee to find strength and forgiveness in the eyes of the Lord.

May peace be with you,

Joanne and Sean Padrushky, Sr.

Charlotte bows her head and offers a quick prayer. Does that make her a traitor? She and Maggie have worked together for years. They aren't BFFs, but they belong to the same book group and regularly grab a Friday afternoon drink to blow off steam. Charlotte hasn't talked to Maggie since the incident, but she sent a sympathy text right away and a "Get Well" balloon to Gunther's hospital room. She wants Maggie to know that she has her back.

It is Shawnee's father who has always given Charlotte the heebie jeebies. He's a little hothead. A squirt. One of those guys who is always over the top about something, even if it's nothing. Potholes screwed up his axle, and the town owes him; or the town snowplow ripped his culvert, or illegal immigrants are taking over the country. Everyone and everything are against him twenty-four seven. She and her older sister, Marilyn, never understood how Joanne Carullo could have married that ape. Joanne was always considered smart, even if she was farm poor and came to school still smelling like the barn she'd no doubt cleaned earlier that morning. She wasn't a bad kid, just one of those people who liked animals better than humans. It made sense that she went to vet tech school. But marry Sean Sr.?

Charlotte glances at her watch, wondering if her sister Marilyn is going to make it after all? The music is starting up. Mary Morgan at the piano, not the organ, of course, playing the opening chords to which Father Lambert will soon enter the church. Charlotte settles herself, bringing her attention forward. She loves this moment just before the priest arrives, the curtain opens.

"Scoot over," her sister whispers, tapping her arm, perhaps a little harder than necessary.

Charlotte shifts her thighs, then her butt, giving up some inches. Her sister smells of dish soap, a pleasant lemony scent, and something else that Charlotte can't determine. "You're late," she shoots into her sister's ear, happy to feel superior.

Marilyn nods, squeezing next to her. "Remind me to tell you something," she whispers back, "as soon as this is over."

Just like in the old days when, as girls they used to chatter stiff-lipped like ventriloquist dummies during dull services. Then it was boys and someone's scandalous behavior. What's on Marilyn's mind now? Charlotte wonders.

"All rise." Father Lambert, dressed in purple robes, gestures upward and then they are standing and singing, and then they are kneeling and praying, and it all seems more serious than ever, given the bare altar, the draped candles.

A single light shines down on Father Lambert at the podium, making his skull cap gleam. "We do not know what could have compelled such a serious believer to act in violence against another boy and toward himself, but we will pray for answers and for God's forgiveness of his sins."

Charlotte nods in unison with Marilyn and the rest of the congregation in the nearly-full church; her heart swells, grateful for the reminder of God's mercy. It is one of those rare times, Charlotte thinks, when your spiritual life and your everyday life seem suddenly to merge and make sense, as though you have discovered a lining stitched to your coat, the silky seams matching, creating deeper protection than you ever thought you could have from the cold.

After the service, there is milling and hugging and chatter. When Charlotte turns to Marilyn, she is gone, caught up in conversations further up the aisle. What was Marilyn going to tell her? she wonders. Then lets it go. Her stomach is rumbling. She's got to eat before her blood sugar gets low and she starts to shake. Stepping into the aisle, she casts her gaze over the packed sanctuary, the congregation still heated up with talk. No Marilyn. She shrugs lightly and leaves.

TWENTY-NINE

SEAN SR. TAKES THE BOTTLE of soda Joanne hands him, twists off the cap and guzzles. Then he wipes his mouth on the sleeve of his suit jacket and hands the bottle back to her. From the look on Joanne's face, he can tell she isn't too happy about that; she isn't too happy about the way he acted just now, telling the town's Easter Bunny, some clown wearing a shag rug and ears at tax-payers' expense, standing outside the drugstore, waving a basket of Easter eggs in his face, to fuck off. But too bad. She's right to keep her mouth shut about it. One word and maybe he'll pop her one if she acts smart. Already this morning he's done what she wanted. He got himself dressed in this monkey suit and went with her to early Mass. All right. She had a point. Father Lambert has come through for them; their e-mail was flooded with messages of support last night and this morning. The Church is there for them, not like the rest of the morons in this town. Okay. He's grateful. He put on the suit, went to church; he was good as an altar boy; he kneeled and prayed and shook hands. Just like she ordered.

Still, he's angry. He can't explain to Joanne; he can't even explain to himself. He feels like a killer whale going stark raving mad in his tank. Everything is too close—this suit, this day, this town.

"Goddamn," he says, slamming his fist into palm. "That kid is going to talk."

They have reached their truck, their old one, because the new one, thanks to the police, is still on display in the park where Shawnee ditched it. He hasn't seen the truck, though he should just to make sure no one's ripped off his mirrors or keyed the sides. He ought to, but he can't. It would be like going to the morgue, having to identify the body of someone you loved. "He's going to tell me what the fuck was going through his head."

"Leave him alone," Joanne says.

"The fuck I will." He puts the key in the ignition, revs the engine. "It's Harter. I know it. He kicked him off the team."

"He quit."

"He wasn't the same after." He remembers even if Joanne doesn't. That's when the kid started locking his door; that's when the black curtains went up.

"Are we going to the hospital now?"

He snorts. "What do you think?"

Joanne looks at her watch. "He quit," she says. "He hated playing football, and you couldn't do a thing about it."

"Bullshit." As usual, she's got it wrong. It was the beginning of August when he called Coach Harter, tipped him off that he'd heard last night at the bar that the cops were going to raid his still. Now you can do me a solid, he told the coach. Next day, Shawnee was on the football team. And for a while that worked beautiful. In two weeks, he had biceps; three, abs. He was becoming a man.

Then one day when he should have been at practice, Shawnee was in his room, on his computer. The door was locked, but Shawnee opened it for him.

"What's doing? Why aren't you at practice?"

Shawnee shrugged, turned back to the screen.

"You look at me when I'm talking to you, son."

Shawnee spun in his chair; he looked like he might laugh.

"Something's funny?"

The boy blinked. "Kind of."

"Are you sick?"

"Yeah."

"The Coach send you home?"

"That's one way of putting it." Shawnee spun away from him, back to the screen.

For some reason, he couldn't bring himself to ask any more questions.

As soon as they turn into their driveway, the reporters come flying up to their truck, two or three on each side, like vultures diving for fresh kill. Without thinking, Sean Sr. reaches for the glove compartment. Joanne grabs his wrist.

"Are you kidding?" she asks.

"They're trespassing. I have a right." But he draws back his hand. He knows he has to listen to her even as his brain crackles with rage. If he hadn't listened to her over the years, he'd probably be dead.

The reporters are knocking on their windows, using their polite enough voices to ask if they can just talk to them for a minute, just a minute. They want to get their side of the story. They want to be fair.

Sean Sr. freezes his face, presses the remote control. The garage door opens more slowly than he likes, but by this time, the dogs are all jumping and barking, doing their best to seem ferocious. A plus for raising Pits, he thinks. As soon as the door is fully lifted, he guns the engine and shoots forward, scattering the reporters. Behind them, the garage door lowers, cutting off the sounds of the reporters' shouts, sight of their waving mics. Beside him, Joanne is clutching the dashboard, but when the door finally closes, all she says is, “Good work.”

THIRTY

LYLE DOESN'T THINK SO. Lyle is on his case as soon as he calls to tell him about blowing off the reporters the way he did.

"You're not getting this, pal. We're managing media right now. We need to get control of our image. We got to get out in front; spin them before they spin us."

"Someone running for office?" he asks. He is on the landline in the kitchen, but he's pulled the cord into the living room.

"Yeah. You. And Joanne. And Shawnee. It's a popularity contest. You against the Cannons. You better start working on winning Miss Congeniality. Shawnee's a saint who flipped. You and Joanne are hard-working, god-fearing, tax-paying citizens. And then there's the smear. We got to find angles. We got to find the weak links and put pressure on them. By the time we finish, it's got be Gunther Cannon is so despicable that maybe, just maybe, crazy Shawnee did the right thing."

Sean Sr. sucks in a deep breath. Lyle is back in Albany having

Easter dinner with the family. Before all of this, he and Joanne and Shawnee would have been there, too, stuffing themselves with glazed ham and Cindy's coconut cake molded in the shape of a lamb.

"Tall order," Sean Sr. says, but his mind is already jumping with ideas about how they can use leaflets and the Internet to control this thing.

Sean Sr., still on the phone, steps back into the kitchen where Joanne, at the kitchen counter, is stirring up some kind of special dog formula for the new pups. From where he stands, the stuff looks like buttermilk and smells like it, too. He wishes she'd keep her dog activities away from the human area, but he knows she'll never listen. "You think you're going to persuade your sister to come on board with this?" He can tell Joanne is listening by the way she keeps her gaze fixed on the dish.

"Does Joanne want to see her son locked up in maximum for twenty-five years? I don't think so. My sister will be on board or she'll keep quiet."

THIRTY-ONE

THE LOBBY OF THE ASSISTED LIVING CENTER, The Plantation (the name would irk him even if his son wasn't black, Bruce thinks), is decorated in the same beige and tan blandness of a doctor's waiting room or a chain hotel. Laminated coffee tables boast perfect fans of AARP issues; brass floor lamps with pleated shades hug the corners. Bruce thinks that his mother, too, has acquired a sort of patina of elegance since she moved in to the place. In her pink, quilted jacket and slim pants, his mother does not look like the mother he knew who once devoted her time to running the family farm and keeping the books for his father's hardware store.

When she sees him, she folds her magazine and rises from the depths of her wingback chair. "How's Gunther?" she says, leaning to kiss his cheek. "I wanted to come by the hospital, but I thought you all were probably overwhelmed."

This is true, Bruce thinks. It would have been a nuisance to have her there, and yet he is irritated. This is his mother, cautious (or is it considerate?) to the point where she seems uncaring. At least that's how Maggie sees it. Whatever the truth, he has given up defending her. Maybe Maggie is right. "His whole arm is in a cast; his left." He pauses for a moment, wondering if his mother remembers that Gunther is left-handed. "But otherwise, he's okay. We were lucky."

His mother slips her arm in his. "He's alive. That's what we need to focus on. How is Maggie?"

"In shock. We all are."

"You send her my love. Gunther, too, of course." His mother's stride is quicker than he expects; she tugs his arm like a small fierce ferry as they head down the carpeted corridor to the dining room.

"Everyone is talking. They're all asking me about what happened as though I am somehow the expert. You need to be prepared. You and Maggie and Gunther are celebrities."

"Great."

"It's the Tower of Babel, really. Thank God it's Easter. A lot of them are off with their families. Last night, one gentleman had the nerve to come over to my bridge table to ask why in heck you and Maggie adopted a black?"

Bruce halts. Watch out, he tells himself. You're on edge. "And you said?"

His mother looks up at him. Her gaze, he notes, is as sharp as ever. "I said it wasn't my business, and I doubted it was his."

"A decent answer."

"To be honest, I really don't know. I couldn't have answered the question even if I'd wanted to."

Bruce swallows. "Would you like me to tell you again?" He can hear his tone hardening. If only his dad was here. He understood.

"Not in that voice," his mother says stiffly, withdrawing her arm.

"We adopted Gunther because he needed us. He needed loving parents and a good home. And we needed him. We weren't martyrs."

At the entrance to the dining room, a waiter in a white shirt and bow tie greets them, and Bruce's mother gives her name and announces that they have a reservation. No doubt everyone seated would have looked up even without his mother's voice ringing out the information, still Bruce wishes she could have spoken more quietly.

As they make their way to a table in the corner, the diners greet Bruce and his mother with half-waves and "Happy Easters" and diminished smiles, which reveal to Bruce their embarrassment (he'd feel it, too, in their shoes) as helpless bystanders.

The table is well-chosen, besides being in the corner, there is a potted fichus tree (in decent shape, Bruce notices) that almost completely hides them from view. The waiter hands them menus with the Easter dinner choices printed in a large font.

"Don't go," his mother says, halting the waiter. "I studied the menu at lunch. I'll have the lamb. The rack. Rare. Then the mousse cake. I don't need a first course. Too much food. How about you?"

Food. Bruce hasn't thought about food for forty-eight hours. All he has eaten is the piece of pie and a sandwich grabbed from the hospital cafeteria and junk food from the hospital vending machines. He is hungry. Very. "I'll have the same, and a salad. Bleu cheese if you have it."

"Do you want a drink?" his mother asks.

"Do they serve martinis in this place?"

"What do you think makes everyone so happy?"

"All right," he says, turning to the waiter. "You have our orders. Plus two martinis."

"How would you like the martinis, sir?"

"Dry with a twist," says Bruce's mother.

Bruce will have his martini wet.

After the waiter leaves them, there is silence. His mother picks up each piece of the plated silverware and inspects it. Stalling, Bruce thinks. Which is fine with him.

She places the knife back where it belongs at the side of her plate. "I am very concerned for Gunther. I'm hoping that you and Maggie are thinking about what's best for his safety from here on out."

From here on out? Until Gun graduates from high school or for the rest of his life? "Stop."

His mother's mouth opens. "I was only going to suggest—"

That he's failed his son? "Don't." Of course, he and Maggie had weighed adopting a black child, had weighed the pros and cons of raising that child in lily-white Lake Village. What they'd decided in the end was that it might *help* Gunther to feel confident, as an adult, in the white world. Until yesterday's incident, they thought they'd got it right. He was a happy kid. A decent student. Reasonably popular. He loved running track. "Let's eat this dinner and not talk about it."

His mother reaches for her water glass, her hand trembling. It is not the hand Bruce remembers. The discipline hand. The brow-smoothing hand. It is a hand that has grown a topography of ridges and valleys, of mottled patches of purple mixed with more alarming splotches of red, an old hand that shakes as it encircles the glass, causing the water to spill over the brim as she brings the glass to her lips. And at her lips, pursed and tentative, the hand shakes again, shaking the glass. Drops of water spill onto his mother's chin and onto her satin blouse.

Bruce folds his own hands in his lap. "I'm sorry, Mother," he says.

THIRTY-TWO.

EASTER DINNER IS AT MARILYN'S PLACE, a double-wide in the nice trailer park, cozy, just the two of them. Charlotte and Marilyn could have travelled and spent the holiday with more family, but that seemed like a lot this year. Their other sisters lived west, in Pennsylvania. Two were married to coalmen and a third to a roofer, the brother of another's husband. Those sisters all had kids and in-laws, so it made no sense for them to come back to Lake Village, even if it was their former home.

"You were going to tell me something," Charlotte says, setting the Blue Willow, dried and shining, on the counter. (She held back the question until after dinner, knowing that Marilyn liked to concentrate on her food.)

"Hm?" Marilyn is growing a little deaf in her right ear, but Charlotte knows better than to mention it.

"Last night. Right before Mass. 'Remind me' you said."

Marilyn dips a soapy plate in the rinse tub, then lifts it out, letting the water run off the surface. It's not the way Charlotte likes to wash plates, but since it is her sister's house, and she wants Marilyn to spill, she isn't going to mention it. She and Marilyn get along better than anyone else in the family, and that is because Charlotte knows when to keep her trap shut.

"I was going to tell you something I learned, but after everything that's happened, I'm not sure I should."

Charlotte rolls her eyes. Her sister's 'holier than thou' phases can last a week, sometimes a lot longer. As a teenager, Marilyn just about convinced herself that she wanted to be a nun until her crush asked her out.

"Fine," Charlotte says. "Don't tell me. There's enough gossip going around this town already to satisfy me until Christmas." From the corner of her eye, Charlotte sees Marilyn fish around the bottom of the soap tub for the silverware. "By the way, did I thank you for dinner? The lamb made me think of Grandma Nonni's. It was that tender."

Marilyn pulls the forks from the rinse water and hands them to Charlotte. "Your string beans were nice. You used Mom's recipe."

"I think I put in too much garlic. I can taste it."

Marilyn shakes her head. "I missed the mint jelly. Even with a list, I forgot to pick it up. Senioritis."

Charlotte wraps the cloth towel around the forks like a bunting. "Come on, Mooshy. Tell your little sister what you were going to say."

Marilyn grips the edge of the dish tub and tips it on its side, so the grayish brown water rushes into the drain. Without a word, Charlotte hands her a piece of paper towel to mop up the basin.

"We'll sit down after I put everything away," Marilyn says, pressing the pedal on the garbage can and tossing in the wet paper towel. "I shouldn't say anything, but I guess because it's you, I'll tell it. But it's not going anywhere, right?"

"Of course not."

"I'm telling you because I don't want to tell anybody else, and the way I feel I might bust and tell the wrong people and that would be a shame."

At the table, Marilyn pours sherry into two small glasses. Charlotte and Marilyn always drink sherry on holidays.

"All right," Charlotte says, pulling a chair, "tell me."

Marilyn raises her glass to her lips. Miss Prim and Proper, Charlotte thinks. Only you wouldn't know it, looking at her large broad shoulders; her stout, strong legs. Marilyn is the tallest of the sisters; the prettiest, with her wide Irish face and deep blue eyes. It isn't clear to Charlotte why she didn't marry.

"I belong to a chat group."

"You do?"

Her sister frowns. "Father Lambert suggested it, actually. It's a website for Catholics."

"A dating site?"

Marilyn glares. "Did I say that? No, it's Catholic folk all across the country who want someone else Catholic to talk to. Most of us live in small towns in out of the way places. It's nice."

"What do you 'chat' about?"

Marilyn looks down into her sherry glass, a faint blush rising through her fair skin. "Once you get to knowing people—"

"Okay, Mooshy, what is it?"

Her sister blinks, still thinking. "All right, then, so the conversation got around to priests."

"To priests."

"I guess a lot of us have been through some very difficult times. I don't have to tell you."

"Abuse?"

Marilyn's mouth works up and down. "Yes, abuse, and other problems. So, someone was mentioning that their priest had been sent off, kind of disappeared, and no one knew exactly why, and I chimed in (or typed in) that exact situation had happened in my church—"

"Father Rand."

Marilyn nods.

"Did you use his name?"

She nods again. "That was stupid, I know. But I did, and you know you forget how widespread these sites are. You think you're talking to a few people, and you might be talking to thousands—"

"Someone knew Father Rand." Charlotte feels a light dizziness as though she has been blowing hard on a cheap balloon. "What did they know?"

"They knew where he was living. It was the same place their disappeared priest turned up."

"Where's that?"

"A monastery in Nebraska, in a place that made Lake Village sound like the big city."

"What was Father Rand in there for?"

Marilyn shakes her head, then drains her sherry. "Rest and relaxation."

"Why was your friend's priest there?"

Marilyn sighs. "For exactly what you're imagining."

THIRTY-THREE

RETURNING TO GUNTHER'S HOSPITAL room, Bruce is glad to see that Woody is visiting. He and Gunther sit side by side on the bed, their eyes glued to the cellphone that they hold between them like an oracle they are bent on deciphering. Woody's a good kid. And on Easter, he's the only one of Gunther's friends who has no other place to go. Jolene, his mother, lives in a run-down trailer on a piece of land about a mile from the Cannons' farmhouse. She has a shed in back that she calls an antique shop, and when she "goes picking"—which is about every weekend—Woody stays with the Cannons.

"You've been gone a long time," Maggie says, putting down her newspaper.

Her tone is faintly hostile, the tone he remembers her greeting him with after long days of being home alone with a toddler, the tone that implied betrayal, though he'd done nothing more than go to work, *so she could stay home*, he would remind her later after Gunther had been put to bed and her true anger burst. "Sorry."

She is expecting him to explain, he knows, but he can't. Not in front of Gunther. After he left his mother, he drove down to the edge of the lake, to a spot where he and Gunther used to go fishing. On the shore, they baited their lines with worms they'd dug from the garden compost, tempted sunnies to rise among the cattails and loosestrife. Now and again, they caught a trout, cause for much whooping and celebration. After leaving his mother, Bruce thought that the spot would soothe his thoughts. It didn't. Looking out at the plum-colored water, darkening as the sun went down, his anxieties kept tumbling in his mind, spilling out variations of the past and future.

"Did you see them, Dad?" Gunther's gaze is still pinned to the phone.

"See who?"

Maggie twists in her chair to give Bruce a warning look.

He raises his eyebrows, signaling her back. *Warning about what?*

"The Padrushkys."

"Oh yeah. The Padrushkys. We tossed back a few drinks together at the nurses' station."

"Not funny, Dad."

"I'm sorry. No Padrushky sightings, but Grandma Louise sends her love. To you, too, Maggie."

Maggie cocks an eyebrow. "How is your mother?"

"She's a celebrity."

"Speaking of celebrities, we've been watching TV."

"Anything good on?"

"Something we weren't expecting."

"What was that?"

"A news bulletin. A hook for the ten o'clock news."

"It's about me, Dad," Gunther says. "And *him*."

"Gun's the man," Woody says.

Bruce feels the muscles tighten around his mouth and down his neck. "How do you feel about that?" It is a shrink's question, he knows, though he's never gone to a shrink; he's never even thought about going.

Gunther shrugs. "I thought the dude was going to say Padrushky died or something."

"No shit, he almost did," Woody says.

"Let's cool that," Maggie says, frowning. "The facts are bad enough."

"The ten o'clock news. Channel 5. That's a big chunk of viewers." The last pocket of air before they drown, Bruce thinks.

Maggie stands. "Do you guys need anything?"

"Chips," Gunther says.

"Please."

"*Please.*"

"Thanks, Mrs. Cannon."

Maggie's fingers alight on Woody's shoulder before she leans over to kiss the top of Gunther's head. "Anything else?"

"You're going to be back before the news, right?"

"Of course."

"Bruce?" Maggie waits at the door. "I'd kind of like to talk to you."

Bruce watches the boys for a moment longer. He would like to stay with them. Maybe, with Maggie out of the room, Gunther might confide in him. Instead, he gets up. "Okay, guys, no girls, no booze."

Gunther rolls his eyes, while Woody chuckles, once, politely.

In the hallway, Maggie grabs his arm, propels him down the corridor to the vending machine alcove. "The news is all about the hate stuff," she tells him. "I can't believe how fast they've run with it. It's mind-boggling. It's like Hopper says. We need to stay out in front."

In front. In front of what? What is Hopper already seeing? What does he know about the toxins about to be released into their world? Deep in his front pocket, his fingers find the remains of the spotted maple wings he shoved in there on Friday. Since then, he has barely had a chance to sleep, let alone change his clothes. Or think about black tar spot and how he's going to keep the fungal spores from spreading. "What's the hush-hush? Why are we out here?"

"I'm not sure you get it."

"Believe me, I get it."

"What? What do you think?"

"We're about to be buried alive."

THIRTY-FOUR

His parents bring back potato chips and sodas.

"Nine fifty-eight," his dad says. "The news should come on any second."

Woody climbs off the bed to grab a slice of pizza, Easter dinner, while Gunther's parents pull their chairs close to the sides of the bed.

Then all of a sudden, the music starts, a rapid combo of snare and horns like a marching band on steroids. The news program's logo bursts onto the screen, a globe spinning like a basketball atop the tip of a finger. Gunther's stomach is suddenly churning, and he has an urge to grab his mother's hand like he did when he was a kid on his first roller coaster ride, but she is already holding his dad's hand so tight, he can see her knuckles bulge. Woody freezes behind them, looking up at the screen.

The spinning logo stops, and the call letters appear and the male announcer booms "Action" as if it's a movie.

The anchorman's hair, dark amber, slicked with spray, juts over his forehead like a scab ripe for picking. After wishing the viewers a "Happy Easter," he's lowering his voice, drawing them in with the promise of tragedy. "A happy Easter for many, but not for some…" Snapshots of Lake Village jump one after another: the bluestone façade of Foxwood hospital; the taped-off entrance to the Police station. A male reporter, holding a microphone, stands in front of Padrushky's cordon-offed truck and looks straight at the viewer. "On a perfect afternoon, on a perfect day, in a perfect village, a 'most perfect village' as Lake Village was recently branded, the tragic near murder of an African-American youth by a white youth, has rocked this community's world…Law enforcement is already speculating that this terrible incident may have an even more horrifying dimension. Racial prejudice may have been the motive for a white teenager, a student at Lake Village High School, to shoot his black classmate. If so, this would be the first hate crime to take place in this village since its charter in 1794."

The news cuts to a commercial.

"Thank god no names; no photographs." His father reaches over to squeeze his shoulder.

"That's the law," his mom says.

Gunther puts down the remote and sinks back onto his pillows. The mute is on, but the television images still flicker, stupid-looking people flapping their silent mouths in their stupid television world. "They're calling me an 'African-American youth.'"

His mom reaches for his hand, which he snatches away.

His dad, frowning, moves closer to his mother. "It's a label. It doesn't mean anything."

Wrong. It means everything. It's the way the white world sees him, while *he* goes completely unseen. He closes his eyes, remembering a different time when no one saw him. He was seven or eight, playing in the lake, holding his breath underwater as long as he could, until his lungs burned, and the air gave out. It was like holding a match and watching the flame's blue bud, so soft-looking, so harmless, work its way down to your fingertips. At the last second, you tossed the match away. The pain in his lungs was too much. He tightened his stomach and flipped his feet hard to propel himself back to the surface of the lake. Only this time, he felt a tug, a skeleton's fingers. The hem of his swimming shorts had caught on an underwater branch. He remembers looking up, up through the green, dusty water, up through the stream of silver bubbles. Above him, he glimpsed the pale, blurred faces of his parents. He could see them, but they couldn't see him. They were laughing, unaware; they didn't know he was drowning.

At the last moment, he shed his shorts, popped up, choking and puking, naked. His mom and dad grabbed him, pulled him to shore. He's always thought that his parents saved his life that day, but now it occurs to him that the color of his skin made him invisible to his parents that day. His brown skin blended with the lake bottom's murky water. He was visible yet invisible to them. Then, now, his life is his own to save.

THIRTY-FIVE

OPENING HIS EYE, his one crusty lid, he spies him—Father Lambert, weird old wolf in his granny clothes, sitting beside his bed. Who'd you devour today, Mr. Holy Moly? If the world would leave him alone. If the world would let him die. (Oh, he could be crucified all right, ha-ha, but not allowed to die.)

Father Lambert is whispering close to his ear. He can smell the layers of dying leaves with each exhale. "You must repent your actions, my son. You must show gladness that God has spared Gunther's life and yours. With a mighty arm, He directed your bullets away from fatal injury and therefore, your soul from mortal sin. Show your gratitude for God's protection, for His love, by repenting this day your sins."

A millimeter to the right and he'd have killed himself. God saved him, and Satan swore, because he was going to take him and roast him, cut him in pieces for his feast; in Satan's fires, he'd have burned to ash. Which is what he wanted. And eternal love? And sacrificial love and Father Rand turning his back on him to save his eternal soul, he said. Whose soul? His? *Father Rand's*? Oh, how he had believed in God's love and prayed for God's love and then Father Rand came to the church and his prayers were answered. Father Rand was God's messenger; Father Rand had told him that. He was God's messenger, telling Shawnee that he was one of God's children, that he was loved. That hand on his back; that breath in his ear: count, count, remember to count. How could he remember to count enveloped in the smell of Father Rand's clean, freshly-shaved jaw, in the sweet smoke of the censor that clung to his robes? How could he count when the shafts of light piercing Christ's breast on the cross were piercing him, too, filling him with an ecstasy that lifted him to the brink of crying out? He fought himself and played the music, played the music, the Passion of Christ, Bach's Passion for Christ. Ha-ha. He played and he played, not for God, the Father, HAHA, but for Father Rand.

"Talk to me, Shawnee. I would like to hear what is in your heart, what you need to repent. Then we can speak the words of the confession together and ask God's forgiveness."

Talk to me, his mother said. His father said, don't talk. You already talked. Talked he had; he'd confessed. Ha-ha. He'd confessed to the police like he was taught. He told them his plan; he wasn't ashamed. Only that his plan had failed: the targets survived, both targets were still breathing. He thought his father might understand. In the old days, didn't he talk about how the whites were being outnumbered? Didn't he talk all the time that in a few years the blacks and Hispanics would be running the country? Didn't he like to tell the story of how a black man done him wrong, how a black man threw the book at him because he didn't like the color of his skin? *And the son shall avenge the father.* Ha-ha.

He thought his father would want to pin a medal on him, one of his *souvenirs*. That's what his father called them. His collection of souvenirs. Usually they were covered up. But once in a while, when his father was in a good mood about something, he took them out to show him. A special treat. He laid the souvenirs out on the coffee table in the TV room on a velvet tablecloth; the medals on heavy ribbons; the brightly enameled pins, with their black spider legs against a bright white disc against a field of red. When you hold these, you're holding history, his father said. His father let him hold the medals. Cold at first, they warmed quickly in his palm. His father bought the souvenirs online. They arrived in padded envelopes, in boxes that could have held jewelry. No, not *jew*elry. HAHA. His mother did not like his father's collection. What do you want that trash for? She frowned and clamped her nostrils as though she was smelling something worse than poop. His father ignored her. It's history, that's what you can't understand, he said.

"God does not make mistakes. I want you to think about this. No mistakes. Can you do that? It's all I ask."

The souvenirs were kept under glass, under the velvet tablecloth. He remembers as a little boy, putting his nose to that cloth and breathing in its smell of old closets, the closet he liked to hide himself in at church, a closet in an old dressing room, rarely used. Dust and mold and the ancient sweat in the priests' old robes. Who was he hiding from or what? He can't remember. Once he'd fallen asleep in there, and Father Lambert had finally found him. His mother was worried, the priest scolded him. He was a naughty boy. But in his pocket, was a lollipop for him that tasted like pink frosting.

"Show your gratitude for God's protection, for His love, by repenting this day your sins." Father Lambert holds the chalice in one hand; the Host in the other, waiting.

What would Satan do? Trick him. "I repent," he says. Not. By devouring Christ, they become one. Ha-ha.

In the chat room, he calls himself Nos fo Natas, and they say that he is one of them, there is no messing with him. They will protect him. They will be looking out for him. Any minute, he thinks, he will hear the sound of his Aryan brothers' bikes roaring up the drive; he will hear their salute. They will be at his door. A posse come to save him. Then he will rise up. Like Lazarus. Like Christ. Ha-ha. And go with them.

◈

"Are you ready to confess, my dear?" Father Lambert rests his hand for a moment over Shawnee's, palm down on the blanket. Then he swings the long arm of the side table across the bed. On it are a chalice, and a wafer on a linen napkin. "I would like to hear what is in your heart, Shawnee, what you need to repent."

Shawnee is sitting up against the pillows. His eyes are closed; his wrists, untied. Joanne and Sean Sr. draw a breath in unison and hold it. From where they stand, just inside the door, they can hear monitors beeping in distant rooms; phones ringing. Every nerve is tight as they bend themselves toward Shawnee, listening for his reply.

Father Lambert's voice is a whisper. He is praying, his soft voice caressing the Latin like water over stones, but is Shawnee listening? Father Lambert sighs, takes up Shawnee's hand in both of his. "I will say it again, Shawnee. God does not make mistakes. I want you to think about this. No mistakes. Can you do that? It's all I ask."

Confess, confess. Accept God's *love, if not mine,* Joanne prays.

Sean Sr. takes a step toward the bed, but Joanne blocks him with her forearm. She presses her fingers to her lips; then touches her ear. *Listen.*

If their son is speaking, they cannot hear. But looking up, they see Father Lambert lifting the chalice to Shawnee's lips; they see his chin lower. A linen napkin flutters to the floor.

PART II

GRAND JURY

ONE

GUNTHER KEEPS THE ONLY PHOTOGRAPH he has of his birth mother in an old leather wallet tucked behind his socks in the drawer of his pine dresser. He's not religious; he's not even sure if he believes in God, but there are times when he just wants to look at her, to talk to her. He knows it's weird, but he can't help himself. Even though he doesn't know her, and she doesn't know him, he likes to pretend she does.

The photo is a school photo, wallet-sized, scarred through the middle with a white crack where someone folded it horizontally in half. In it is a teenaged girl with a shiny, black flip, and cheekbones so high they make him think of pizza dough resting on knuckles. (*His* cheekbones, his mother has told him.) She is smiling an easy, gap-toothed smile and in the glare of the photographer's lamp, her kohl-rimmed eyes seem to be asking the viewer to share a sad laugh.

"Gunther?"

Hearing his mother's shout, Gunther quickly slips the photograph into the wallet and shoves it back behind the socks.

"Are you almost finished up there?"

Finished? He's just getting started.

"John Hopper is on the phone. He'd like to talk to you."

Gunther clears his throat. Even the mention of Hopper makes his stomach clench. "I gotta brush my teeth." He steps across the hall and into the bathroom even as he hears his mother's footsteps thudding up the staircase. A few seconds later, she is knocking hard on the bathroom door.

"Gunther—" From the tone of her voice, he can tell she's as nervous as he is. "You need to take this. Today's the day, you know."

As though he could forget. Leaning close to the mirror, he grins at himself, hard. He has his birth mother's gap between his teeth and her slightly tilted eyes; somehow, today, this thought comforts him.

Outside the bathroom, his mom hands him her cell phone and heads back downstairs.

"Hello, sir, this is Gunther Cannon." His own phone pings in his palm as it has all morning. Snaps from Ryan, Sam, Woody, his teammates, but also the super popular kids like, Lara Sanders, captain of the cheerleaders, waving from the top of a cheering pyramid.

"How are you feeling this morning? Nervous?"

"Yeah, a little." A lot.

"That's normal. But you don't have to worry about a thing. Between the journals and the hard drive, Padrushky was explicit. By Federal law, this was a pre-meditated hate crime. No matter what his defense might like to think."

"Like he's insane?"

"Don't worry about that. Padrushky can be nuts and be considered perfectly sane by the law. It's complicated, but you're a perfect witness. You've got nothing to hide."

"Thank you, sir." The words are reflexive, words he's been schooled to say by his father and his mother since he was little. Only now, since his voice has dropped, he can work the pitch, drop it low and even, imitating his dad. White men like it. Something comes across their faces when he talks to them like this: *Kid's got respect; Kid's got something on the ball.* And what that is, he knows, is how to play their game.

As soon as Hopper hangs up, Gunther's phone pings again. Mandy Slicer, Lara's BFF with a kissy face. Ping again. Two hearts tied with a bow. Susan. The daughter of one of his mom's book group friends. Ever since he's been back at school, it's just like Sam predicted. Every girl acts like she wants him; everybody calls him "bro." Even the teachers bend over backwards to be nice to him. It should make him feel good, but it doesn't. It feels weird. Like someone turned a spotlight on him that follows him everywhere. He's got to be on stage every minute, acting a part—grateful for his friends, grateful for everybody's support, wounded but not scarred for life. He's got to play his self before the incident, Mr. Be Happy even when he's not. Has he ever been? That's the question he's been asking himself.

His mom calls up the stairs that breakfast is ready—everything he likes, eggs, sausage, and toast. "Okay," he says, only as soon as he smells the food from the landing, his stomach starts cramping and knotting, then dropping fast. He springs back into the bathroom. Sitting on the toilet, he clutches his gut, his cast pressed hard against his abdomen.

◈

"You have nothing to hide," Hopper said on the phone, but that's not true. He has a secret, something he's been hiding for a long time, something he's been hiding since it happened. Something he hasn't told anyone, even Woody. It was September, his favorite month, favorite because that's when cross-country began, and the air grew cool. Sometimes the heat hung on while the leaves changed color, and the grass seemed to burn even brighter green.

Some days, the sun gilded the hills while the sky was dark, and it seemed as if the whole landscape had been set in flames. He loved running on those days, running as far as he could, as fast as he could. He was a hurdler, a sprinter, but he also ran cross-country to build his endurance for spring track. He had it all, Coach Bruin used to say. It wasn't true. The school was small, the records not all that difficult to break. Still, he was proud that no fewer than five of the trophies in the glass case that lined the main hall from the entrance to the principal's office had his name on them.

Coach Bruin's enthusiasm was contagious. He made Gunther believe that he was good and that he was as proud of Gunther's speed as Gunther was himself.

Which made it doubly weird what happened in September.

Mr. Harter was the opposite of Bruin. Harter was the PE teacher and the football coach, a Lake Village High grad who got recruited for Division 1. Gunther had never liked him; the dislike was mutual. It started way back when Gunther didn't try out for Peewee or Junior Varsity; when it was clear that Gunther was instead going to go through school as Bruin's athlete, not Harter's. It started when Gunther beat Harter's pet, the quarterback, in a push-up contest and a sprint during Field Days.

So, it surprised Gunther when, a few weeks into the season, Mr. Harter came up behind him in the locker room, threw an arm around his shoulder, squeezed and punched his arm as if they were pals. Harter's touch made him want to jump.

"Was-sup?" Coach Harter said.

"Was-sup with you?" Gunther replied. His arm stung a little where Harter had knuckled his bicep, but he wasn't going to show that.

"Hold up a minute. Let's talk."

Gunther felt something shift in his stomach. He'd never been in Harter's space before. He'd never even talked to him. Something about the man repulsed Gunther. His pink skin; his loaf-like head shaved up the sides and back leaving a waffle-top of bright blonde hair. His piggy eyes.

"Shoot," Gunther said, stuffing his hands in his pockets. He was due at cross-country practice. He didn't like to be late.

"We're down a man. You probably know that."

He did. Pete Huntingdon had smashed his head the last practice game. His parents, both doctors, were pulling him off the team. "How's Pete?"

Harter hissed. "All parents want to do these days is keep their kids in diapers."

Gunther coughed lightly. He hated agreeing with the guy, but he did. His parents treated him like he was still a little kid as far as he was concerned. "Text us when you get there," "Curfew's eleven." Still, Coach Harter was an asshole.

"So?" He could see the cross-country kids, in their t-shirts and shorts, jogging toward the track. He had to get moving.

"I'd like you to suit up; join us for practice today."

"I'm a hurdler, Mr. Harter."

"Exactly. You got the speed and the agility. You're the key."

Gunther took a deep breath. Keep your cool, man. You do not want to be on the wrong side of Coach Harter. "I wish I could help, Sir, but I don't have time for two teams."

"Sure you do. Make us champions in the Fall; do your thing in the Spring."

"I got cross-country."

"Pussy stuff. You want conditioning? Practice with us. You'll be rock solid and sprinting like a tiger."

He started shaking his head, confused. Football instead of cross-country? From across the fields, came the sound of Coach's whistle. Fuck, he was late.

Mr. Harter was squinting at him. "Tell you another thing. I don't run the team; the team runs me." He leaned forward, doing the slapping, pinching thing again. "The team wants you, Gunther. They like you. They think you've got the stuff. Our school's reputation is on the line. What do you say?"

He couldn't say anything. The shifting in his stomach was now a churning. His forehead was damp. "Later," he managed as he turned away.

He started toward the locker room. Fuck. He had to talk to Coach Bruin.

The locker room was empty except for the football players, Hank Roman, Handler Shaw, Carson Bradley, and a bunch of juniors, even a few sophomores, because even before Pete dropped out, the team sort of sucked so far this year.

It was Handler who came up to him. "Dude, you're joining the team, right?"

"That's lit." Carson Bradley, the richest kid in school, nodded in Gunther's direction.

"My man." Hank Roman spun away from his locker, held his palm down low for Gunther to slap.

Gunther paused for a moment, before slapping it. Otherwise, just awkward. "I'm not—"

"You are," Handler said. "Because you're fast. And we need fast. Shit, you're the key, bro'."

"What's with that." Carson pointed to a kid opening his locker down the row. "Is Harter fucking nuts?"

"Son of Blubber got hisself recruited."

Gunther could not help looking. Shawnee Padrushky was sticking his face into his locker as though he wanted to hide, but even so, you could see a roll of fat bulging over the band of his sweat pants, and the thick hand gripping the edge of the locker door. When did that happen? The kid was thin last year.

"You got a black boy and a fat boy," Gunther said. Why couldn't he keep from making a joke?

The boys erupted, snorting, laughing, slapping each other and him. He was an instant hit, and an asshole, he thought. Shawnee Padrushky. They had a class together. Global. He'd borrowed the kid's pencil once and never given it back.

The talk with Coach Bruin did not go as Gunther expected. The Coach was in his office, and when he told him what Harter wanted, he shrugged.

"As long as you don't blow a knee," he said, "you do what you want. But I need you for Spring."

He nodded. It felt like the Coach had decided for him, like he was pushing him a little. It stung.

Woody thought Gunther was punking him. "No fucking way you're joining the Zombies," he said. The Zombies was what he and Woody called the football team as they watched them marching down Main Street in the heat of late August, sweaty and disgusting and blank-faced like their souls had been stolen.

"I know," Woody said, "you can be like a double agent or something. You can sabotage the operation from inside."

Gunther looked at him. "What do you mean? Like throw the games?" Woody was into some video game that took place in World War II. Half the time, he was planning secret missions.

Woody shrugged. "I don't know, throw something. You don't want to let fucking Harter control you."

True. On the other hand, being on the football team meant he would be popular—party with the in-crowd, date the hot girls, wear the jacket.

His parents, like Woody, weren't into the idea. Football was dangerous, his mom said; his father agreed. Like Coach Bruin, though, they told him it was his choice.

The tunnel between the school and the football field is a giant culvert, a shortcut from the lower field to the upper. The kids think it's cool, but mostly they stay away. The tunnel is the football players' territory; you trespass, you're dead meat. From time to time, a few of the younger kids dare each other to blast through, and that's what they do—run as fast as they can, screaming at the top of their lungs. Make it to the other side; you die laughing, winded, pumped with the victory of making it through alive. But of course, you don't do it when the team's around: Now, that would be suicide.

How long had he been practicing with the team, two weeks, three when it happened? They hadn't played a real game yet, just a couple scrimmages, which they'd lost badly, thanks to everyone's screw ups, but somehow Harter had made it seem like Padrushky was the most to blame. The other players didn't mind that. Gunther had felt relieved. They'd been razzing Padrushky since the beginning, but mostly ignoring him.

Then one afternoon on the way back to the locker room after a bad scrimmage, the players ducked into the tunnel and the whooping began, "Fu-u-ck," they screamed, making the tunnel echo. "Fu-u-ck," the obscenity spiraled down the cement cylinder as they pounded their bare knuckles against its ceiling and its sides. The light cut in at a slant, dark here, light there. Gunther wanted to get out of there fast, but he was caught in the pack. Ahead of him, Padrushky with the same thought, pressed his hands to his ears, hunched his shoulders and tried to make a break. That was it. The other players were on him like hawks on a mouse. They'd been watching, waiting for the slightest tell.

From behind, Gunther couldn't see who made the tackle, but he heard Shawnee's head thunk on the concrete floor. Shawnee was down, struggling and kicking, his belly exposed in the dim tunnel light, a white mound of soft-looking flesh, a target.

Shit, Gunther thought. Run. He couldn't. His legs were frozen; his heart pounding; he couldn't unclench his jaw. Behind him, the tunnel opened on the sunlit fields, the shouts and whistles of a soccer match; ahead, the tunnel was blocked.

Then Handler Shaw was dropping his pants, mooning the globes of his white butt, and then he was squatting, squatting on Padrushky's face. "Lick 'em," he growled. "Kiss my ass." The guys were hooting, whistling their appreciation; Padrushky was crying, his sobs braying in long hee-haws of pain. With his arms pinned, he couldn't hide his twisting features, the squinted eyes.

Then someone said, "How 'bout we give him a taste of prairie balls."

"Prairies?"

"You know, something black and hairy."

The laughing was harsh.

Gunther swallowed, then spun. He flew.

TWO

GUNTHER AND HIS MOTHER AND FATHER sit alone in a small room across the hall from the grand jury room. The clerk told them to wait there until it was time for Gunther to testify. "How long will that be, Vicky?" his mother asked. (Of course, she knew the clerk. She knew everyone in the courthouse.) Impossible to know, Vicky said. The grand jury had several other cases to review. "Like what?" his mother asked. She was like that; she was someone who liked information. "Drugs; fraud; nothing as big as your son's case."

Since then, they have been waiting for an hour, and Gunther is already so nervous he can feel the sweat pricking in his armpits; soon it will flood his new shirt, a white button down, super preppy, on purpose. Touching the stiff points of the collar, he thinks all of a sudden of the cootie catchers the girls used to make in elementary school to tell their fortunes and who they were going to kiss at recess. He loved teasing girls on the playground back then, dragging his toes like he was catchable, then taking off like lightning to get away from their smacking lips.

The suit, too, is new. They got it in Albany when his mom realized the last suit he wore was for eighth grade graduation. That suit, hanging in the back of his closet, looked like it was sized for a midget. Seeing the empty sleeves, the brass buttons glowing on the navy cloth, he wished for a second that it still fit and that the scariest thing he had to do was to shake the principal's hand in front of the school.

"How you holding up, Gun?"

He shrugs, not trusting his voice.

"You're going to do great," his dad says, reaching to touch Gunther's shoulder. He sounds calm, but his thigh is jiggling like he's late to get somewhere.

"Thanks," he mumbles. His forearm itches wicked inside the cast. With the eraser end of his pencil, he digs in, and gets a whiff of the smell, foul as toe dirt, that leaks from the cuff. The doctor said he could switch to a sling, but Hopper told him to hold off. The cast is a good prop, he said. It reminds the grand jury that he was badly hurt, and that after all of these weeks, he is still suffering from physical harm.

"Should he wear glasses, too?" his mom had asked Hopper.

"Does he have a pair?"

He and his mom exchanged a look. So, she knew he still had the glasses in the back of his sock drawer. Wire-rimmed, gold rectangles—a style a chemistry teacher might wear. Fakes. When he'd looked at himself in the mirror atop the carousel, he'd been shocked. He looked smart, he thought. Like a doctor or a lawyer or an engineer. He looked white. He begged his mother to buy him the glasses. He was ten years' old.

Glasses wouldn't hurt, Hopper had said. Good idea.

He is also wearing the tie that Hopper recommended, red and white stripes to go with the blue suit. The message was too obvious, Gunther thought. Like those politicians who couldn't have their pictures taken unless they were standing next to a flag. Hopper disagreed.

Believe me, he said. We can't overemphasize that you're a patriot, an Eagle Scout, a good citizen.

Even though I'm black, he thought bitterly, but kept that to himself.

His dad has stopped his leg; now, he's waving a pencil. "You're going to ace this thing. You're a pro," he says.

"Right, Dad. I'm a pro." His dad always says this to him before a meet to boost his confidence. It doesn't work. It actually makes him more nervous, but he doesn't have the heart to tell his dad that.

His mom pats his shoulder. "Like Dad said. You're going to be great. Keep it simple. Speak clearly. Breathe."

"You've said that a million times."

"Have I?" His mom tries to smile, but she can't quite pull it off. "I wish I could say something useful, but I can't think of anything." She shoots a look at his dad as though he might bail her out.

"You can't think of anything, because Gunther knows everything. He only has to answer the questions as clearly and honestly as he has done before. He only has to tell the truth."

His mom nods. "That's right. All you need is the truth."

The truth. Right. The light coming through the tall windows casts a bright stripe across the painting on the opposite wall, a judge with white hair and large, black robes. His skin is a vivid, sunset pink and his dark marble eyes are glittering. "What if Padrushky *was* bullied, would that change things a lot?" He gazes at the table, wanting to sound normal, but his voice soars to a place that sounds like he sucked on helium.

His dad clears his throat. "What you mean, exactly, Gunther?"

He looks up. Both of his parents are staring at him like he's a different kid than they remember. "I don't know. Forget it."

"No, you've brought something up; let's discuss it." His mom straightens in her chair, reaches for her water glass.

"Forget it."

"We're not going to 'forget it', Gun. Something is on your mind.

What's going on?"

"I was thinking, that's all. I mean, let's say Padrushky *was* bullied and lost it, does that mean he didn't commit a 'hate crime?'"

His mom squints, frowning, into her empty cup, but it's his dad who speaks. "I'm not a lawyer; obviously. That's something a lawyer would have to answer. But if *you* didn't do the bullying or weren't part of something like that, I guess it would still be the same motive."

"Clearly," his mom says, abandoning her cup and turning to him. "Why are you thinking about this?"

"I was *curious*. That's all." He's blown it.

His mom shifts in her chair so that her knees are almost touching his. "Listen, honey, Hopper and the police detective have been looking for evidence of bullying since the incident. There's nothing. No reports filed with the Principal or the Superintendent. Nothing reported to the police or to any other authority."

"Nothing in his journals, either," his dad says.

His mom nods strongly. "If Padrushky was badly bullied, bullied to the point that he snapped, they'll have a hell of a time proving it. No matter what, you were an innocent victim. Detective Peters asked you—'any bad blood?' And you answered 'no', and that's the truth, so forget everything else.

"I'm so sorry you have to go through all of this, Gun, but you're handling it so well. We're very proud of you—and I know you don't believe it, because it's hard to believe—but some day this nightmare will be over."

Gunther shuts his eyes. His parents have his back. He's grateful. But he can't stop thinking about the shit in the tunnel. His parents are wrong; he isn't innocent. He didn't haze Padrushky that afternoon; he didn't try to save him, either. The only thought he had that day when he heard Padrushky crying on his back in the dirty tunnel, his sweats yanked past his knees, was *run*.

There is a knock on the door and then the door opens. Sergeant Somebody-or-Other in a tan shirt and pants, a badge on his breast pocket. "Don't worry, folks. I'll take good care of your boy."

When Gunther stands, it feels to him like a ton of rocks have dropped into his legs; he can barely move them. Did Padrushky tell his lawyer about the hazing? Did he tell him that Gunther was there?

His dad pats his back. "Stay strong, son."

His mom hugs him, forgetting that his shoulder is still sore. "Just breathe," she says.

"You keep *saying* that."

Her cheeks tense in apology. "I know," she says, "I can't think of anything else to say."

◈

The jury room is the size of his homeroom at school, and it is set up like a classroom with rows of folding chairs, but no desks or blackboard. Hopper told him that there are twenty-three grand jury members, and it's not like TV. This isn't a trial. The grand jury isn't judging whether or not Padrushky is guilty. Their only job is to decide if the evidence points to the *charge* of a federal hate crime.

Hopper will be presenting evidence (that's why Gunther's there), but Padrushky will not be there; his lawyer will not be there, either. All the grand jury is interested in is evidence, and there's plenty to prove that there needs to be a trial.

Even knowing all of this, Gunther feels as though he has come on stage for a play. The room smells of coffee and men's cologne and something that stinks like hairspray or fresh nail polish. When he and the Sergeant enter, the grand jury members stop murmuring and watch him take a seat on the platform facing them.

A step down sits his mom's friend, Charlotte, the other court reporter, typing away at her steno machine, pretending she doesn't know him. Hopper, too, is acting like a stranger. This is how the play works. Hopper stands at a table and shuffles some papers; his back is to the grand jury, and though he is now facing Gunther, he doesn't make a sign that he sees him.

When Hopper does look up, he is all abrupt and professional-sounding, asking Gunther if Gunther Cannon is really his name and does he live at such and such place and go to such and such school? Gunther Cannon. It's a name he's been teased about all of his life. *Cannon balls. Cannon farter. When ya gonna shoot your load, Cannon?* But recently, he's been liking that his name is an arsenal. No matter which weapon, a gun or a cannon, he can blow you away.

The jurors lean in, staring at him like he's a member of a species they've never seen before, an endangered species, which he is, Gunther thinks: *in danger,* a species marked to die. Some are taking notes like they are students in a class they have to pass. Others are pulling sips from lidded coffee cups. One woman yawns, then covers her mouth, looking guilty.

Gunther presses his palms down on his thighs; he can't stop his shaking knees. He forces himself to lift his chin. *You don't want to be ramrod, but whatever you do, don't slump. Don't look down; make eye contact; show the jury you're confident about your version of the truth.*

Through the fake eyeglasses that he forgot to polish, the faces of the jurors look a little blurred. Still, he can see that they are mostly women, mostly people his parents' ages and older, and he can see that everyone on the grand jury is white—as usual.

"So, Gunther," Hopper says, "please tell the jury members what happened on the afternoon of Friday, April third. Please tell them exactly what you told Detective Peters of the Lake Village Police later that day." Hopper waves a file folder at the jurors. "You are welcome to review the transcript of that interview, conducted shortly after Gunther was admitted to the hospital."

Gunther takes a deep breath. There's a rustling in the room as the

Jury members ready themselves to listen; someone blows his nose; a few others, cough. Though he's told the story many times now, he still has to tell himself to calm down, to breathe. He wishes his heart didn't sound so loud in his ears; that he could change his already damp shirt; start over again.

"Gunther?"

Find someone in the audience to make eye contact with. Stick with that person for a few seconds, find someone else. He squints, then locks his eyes on a man in the front row, rocking cargos and a black t-shirt tight across a muscled chest. Instantly, the man's gaze levitates to meet his; Gunther blinks and cuts his eyes away fast. *What the fuck? Coach Harter.*

THREE

As soon as the door to the waiting room closes, Maggie turns to Bruce. "Okay. What the hell is going on?"

"Look, Peters is the detective, not us. I'm going to believe Gunther. He's telling the truth."

"He's hiding something."

"There's nothing in the school records; nothing in Shawnee's journals."

"Something's wrong."

"He's not a bully."

"I know that. There's something else."

Gunther's cellphone buzzes on the table. He left it on vibrate, even though they told him to turn it off.

"His fan club," Bruce says.

Maggie looks at the phone. Only a few weeks ago, her book group went off on a tangent, discussing whether it was okay to read your kids' texts. Some of the women claimed it was necessary to make sure their children were safe; she disagreed. Now she wants to pick up that phone. What if the Padrushkys had searched their son's history? They might have stopped him.

"Don't," Bruce says, reading her mind. "We trust him."

"I need to know."

Bruce's reach is much longer than hers. His reflexes, quicker. In an instant, he has clamped his hand over the cell phone, swept it up, pocketed it. Then he is out of the room, slamming the heavy door behind him.

FOUR

LYLE HAD TOLD JOANNE HOW IT WORKED. How the grand jury will be reviewing several cases this morning before Shawnee's. His case will be last up, Lyle had said, because it's the biggie. They'll probably start Shawnee's case after lunch—one-ish and God knows how long it will take. This morning, Sean Sr. headed up North at dawn, leaving her alone at home with the dogs to wait for the grand jury's decision. She wanted to kill him.

She is washing the dogs' bowls in the kitchen when the doorbell rings. Frowning, she glances at the wall clock. Two-fifteen. Who in heck? A reporter? The police? Whoever it is can wait until this last bowl is washed. The bell rings again, an insistent burr, nothing singsong. Joanne shuts off the taps, tips the metal bowl onto the others piled atop the dish drain. She is still wiping her wet hands on her jeans as she peers into the peephole in the center of the door. A man in brown uniform, a UPS man, not the usual one. This man is black. A real *black* black. Not a drop of brown in that color. Someone once told Joanne that the really black ones came from Africa, direct. She opens the door.

"Good morning," the man says. He's holding a cardboard box. Must be the puppy collars that she ordered.

"Good morning," she says. Only it isn't morning. It is the afternoon. "What happened to Frank?" Frank is their usual UPS man, a young, round-faced kid who always has treats for the dogs.

"On vacation," the man says. "I'm his temporary replacement."

Temporary. That's good. "All right. I guess everyone needs a vacation." She thinks she sounds polite enough, but she isn't sure. A black man at her door. Today of all days. It startled her more than she wants to let on. Is God testing her?

"Beautiful dogs," the man says.

Her two house dogs are with her, Sallie and Stubby. If you knew anything about pits, you knew they'd been named after two heroes of the breed—one, a civil war soldier; the other, the only dog that ever won a Purple Heart. *That* Stubby smelled mustard gas before the trench soldiers could, barking until they put on their masks.

"Don't I sign something?" Joanne asks.

The man smiles, showing white teeth in a largish jaw and hands her a tablet and a stylus. "Do you breed Staffordshire terriers?"

Staffordshire. Who is he trying to impress? Still, she nods. He must have read the kennel sign at the end of the driveway. "My spring litter is already spoke for. There's a waiting list. Minimum deposit, three hundred, and I require references."

The man laughs. "I don't know if I'm in the market. But my fiancée told me the other day that she's always wanted a blue."

Sallie and Stubby shift in their sit stays, but they are well-trained dogs. They await her command. "I don't breed that kind of trash."

The man looks genuinely surprised. "My fiancée read somewhere about a 'blue-nose pit bull'. I thought—"

"There's no such thing," Joanne says. "Blue is a dilute and recessive of black. To get 'blue,' you breed recessive gene to recessive gene over and over, black fades to gray, fades to inky purple. You get 'blue' all right, and you get deformities, and you get blindness and you get aggression and you get disease. Guess where those 'blues' end up? In cages, waiting to die. Those dogs aren't quite right, but some human made them that way. If you find a breeder who promises a 'blue,' run as fast as possible."

"Wow," the man says. "I hear you."

Joanne shakes her head. "Nothing but trouble. For you and your fiancée and even worse for the dog."

The man steps back down the stairs, thanking her again for the information and apologizing for taking her time. Joanne clears her throat and nods. She hopes she hasn't come across too abrupt, but really what she told him is for his own good and the good of the breed.

The delivery truck is parked at the bottom of the driveway. When the man reaches it, he turns to wave. Maybe he felt her eyes on him. Maybe he was more nervous than he had let on.

That's when Sallie noses the latch. Joanne forgot how good she is at that. How quickly Sallie can get to wherever she wants to go. In a flash, she is streaking toward the delivery man; Stubby, too, though he is slowed up these days by a little arthritis in his left hip. Even from this distance, Joanne can see the man's face change. His smile vanishes, and the whites of his eyes suddenly glisten with fear.

"Sallie! Stubby!" she calls. "Drop." From a dead run, they halt and collapse themselves to perfect downs. Joanne's heart is thumping hard, but she is proud of her dogs. They showed their training. One bite, and they'd be taken away, executed, by law.

The man sinks into the driver's seat and starts the engine. Standing by her dogs, Joanne watches him pull his boxy truck onto the road. In a second, he accelerates, the big tires spitting stones, raising dust.

When Joanne gets back to the house, the telephone on the kitchen wall is ringing. She stares at it; frozen; the dogs close in beside her, anxious, it seems, for her to pick up the telephone. Sallie keeps twitching her gaze; Stubby whines. Joanne crosses herself as she reaches for the receiver. The clock on the oven buzzes lightly as though an alarm has been set. Two-thirty. Too early for a verdict, Joanne thinks. Way too soon.

She reaches for the receiver. Lyle, on the other end of the line, is choking out words. Joanne rests her palm on the counter for balance. Is he crying or so angry he cannot speak? She takes a deep breath and looks down at the dogs, whimpering around her knees. Her dogs. Her beautiful dogs. She sinks to her knees, cradling their heads, one under each arm. The receiver is still tucked between her ear and her shoulder.

"We'll fight it," Lyle is saying. "You tell Sean and Shawnee not to worry. We will fight this fucking indictment tooth and nail."

She cannot speak. Her voice has snuck away. From her knees, she sinks sideways onto her hip, then rolls onto her back, her legs stretching out in front of her and her arms down at her sides. Her dogs nose her; one, at her neck; the other, at her ear. On the cool linoleum of the kitchen floor, she is playing dead.

She can tell by Sean's voice on the phone that he is drunk. Angry drunk, not weepy drunk. That will come. His drunks are like phases of a launch, the spent-fuel casings crashing to the earth in his wake. Now he is at the height of his buzz. His bursting contrails of mania drive Joanne to stop her ears and look away. "Shut up," she says. "Shut up, shut up. And listen." Because she cannot bear any more rantings about this asshole and that, his plan to slaughter all the bastards of the earth, the righteous crusade he will lead against the wrongs perpetrated against their son. If only. If only he were that shining knight; that crusader who could slay the foes. "Listen," she says again. "I'm hanging up."

He pauses for a moment.

"Can you drive? If you can't drive, I'll come and get you."

"I can drive."

"Turn down the radio."

"I can drive fine, I said."

She thinks for a moment. If he crashed and died on the way back, would that be so bad? "All right. But grab something to eat if you have to. Spray something in your mouth. We got to get to the hospital. I want Shawnee to hear it from us, not a TV."

"Shit, didn't you just tell me to get something to eat?"

"Okay, eat something. Get here in one piece. Don't take too long."

The pizza revolving in its plastic case on the counter looks like it has been there for hours, maybe even days, the way the pepperoni slices swim lightly in their own slick craters of grease. It doesn't matter to Sean. He tells the girl behind the counter he'll take two slices. The greasier the better, he thinks. He watches her gloved hands breaking the slices from the rest of the pie, concentrating on the task as though she were a surgeon.

"When was that cooked?" he asks. He doesn't care. Stale would be better for soaking up the alcohol in his gut. But he can't help but needle her.

She looks up. Blue eyes in a pink, pudgy face. Farm girl, no doubt. Making cigarette money at the Quickway. "Fresh baked every morning, sir."

He puts the bills on the counter. The wall clock reads four. "Fresh, all right."

The girl frowns, sweeps up the money, holds it in her fist. "You don't want it?"

Her eyes have gone hard on him and all he was doing was making a joke. "I'll take it. I don't have a problem with old pizza. Tastes better the next day, anyway."

The girl nods, pushing him out of her mind, like she does most customers, he can tell. "Drink?"

He puts his cans of Mountain Dew on the counter beside the stacked slices. "There's enough to cover it. Keep the change."

The girl rings him up, drops a quarter in the tip jar without saying, 'Thank you.'

Okay, if that's the way she wants to play it. He is stepping back from the counter when he notices the TV mounted above the cigarette display. A woman reporter is standing in front of a courthouse, talking into a microphone, while a ribbon of news runs below her. *Grand jury indicts Sean Padrushky, Jr. for felony hate crime and attempted murder.* Sean freezes.

"Hey, turn it up. That's my son. Sean Padrushky, Jr."

The girl looks at him, confused.

"Turn it up, goddammit."

The girl fumbles under the counter for the remote; hits a button. A head shot flashes on the screen. It's Shawnee, before the incident, looking sleepy, looking like the last thing he wants is to be photographed. Then it is Gunther Cannon, wearing eyeglasses and a suit and tie. He is waving at a crowd of people, bunched around the steps to the courthouse, holding signs, "We Love Gun."

"That's your son? The guy who shot the black kid?" The girl is still watching the screen, but the news has changed already to a commercial for some kind of diaper. She pivots back to him. "Why'd he do it? Was he jumped? My dad shot somebody once. Self-defense, but the dude wasn't black."

"Fuck if I know why he did it, but someone's got to clean up the mess."

The girl nods. "Sometimes you can't take it no more. I been there.

My boyfriend's pulling fifteen because someone pissed him off." She pulls two napkins from the metal container beside the register and tucks them into the paper bag with the slices, then squeezes the top of the bag tightly before she hands it to him. "Drive safely now."

Sean nods. She's on his side, after all, he thinks. It warms him.

◈

The phone is ringing again. It's been ringing all afternoon. Reporters. She hasn't been answering. But this is Lyle again. "Did you reach Sean?'

"Yeah."

"I imagine he's not taking it so good."

Joanne snorts. She doesn't have to answer obvious questions. "Listen, Lyle, I've been thinking. I'd be lying if I said Shawnee wasn't a quiet one."

"Quiet? It's like he's taken a vow. Maybe he's learned his lesson."

"They didn't read him Miranda. I'm sure of it."

"They did, Joanne. He signed a paper. He talked like a girl on a gabfest."

"I don't believe it. How could he talk straight? He was in pain; he was messed up."

"He waived Miranda; he confessed, and they've got his journals. I have a copy for you."

"I can't look at them."

"Don't," Lyle says. "Spare yourself."

"But he was crazy when he confessed; he was off his rocker, right? He's not the only one in our family who's crazy. You know what I'm talking about."

"Button it, Joanne."

"All right," she says, but that doesn't stop her from thinking of the genes. Some families got retarded people; the Carullos got suicides.

"Listen," Lyle says, "Call me if Sean Sr.'s not back in an hour or so.

I don't want you to be alone."

"I'm never alone," Joanne says. "I have my dogs."

On the counter is a pan of lasagna. From it, Joanne cuts two large squares which she puts on a square of tin foil and sticks in the oven on low. Some church ladies brought the lasagna by yesterday with a tin of cookies and a hand-written note: *We're praying for you and your family.* Several names were scrawled beneath. She read the note over and over again, each time slathering herself anew with shame. They'd become *those* people; the ones people prayed for, the beaten down, the disfigured, the basically untouchable. She crumpled the note and threw it in the garbage, so that it couldn't make her feel like that again.

Her son has been indicted for a hate crime. Hate. Hateful. Hate-filled. In her mind's eye, she sees Shawnee, age five, holding puppies under each arm. He is wearing foot pajamas and giving his "babies" rides. She is anxious, the puppies are whimpering, but Shawnee's eyes shine as brightly as theirs. He loves Tino and Jojo, he says.

Since then Shawnee's been in charge of naming the pups. Names got changed, of course, by the new owners, but Shawnee always loved the job, and she was happy to find a way to include her son in her kennel business. When Shawnee was in elementary school, there was Mario and Roy and Barnaby, and as he started getting churchy in middle school, it was Jesus, Paul, Matthew, and Mary. As a teen, he began to share his father's love of history: Ava, Ernst, Lazlo, Hermann.

This past fall, her champion bitch, Helen, had littered. Five pups. Four pure white females and a coal black male. One of the females, born with a bent leg, she had to cull. No use to a breeder or anyone else. The other four were healthy as hogs.

What do you want to name them? she remembers asking Shawnee.

"Hitler," Shawnee said, pointing to the black male.

"*Hitler*?" She had not liked it, of course. "No 'Hitler'," she said.

"Why the *hi-eell* not?"

His father got the joke right away, but she did not. They had both smirked. And she had wondered when her boy turned mouthy?

"Listen to your mother," Sean said, but she could tell he wanted to laugh.

"Tar baby." Shawnee scooped up the male, that was really too young for handling, and danced it away from her. "Blackie."

Sean Sr.'s laugh was ugly, a sound he'd bottled up that now came gurgling like sewage through a drain pipe.

She left the room.

When the lasagna is ready, Joanne pulls it out of the oven, watching the steam rise from the melting surface of cheese. Through the window above the sink, she sees the lights of Sean Sr.'s truck swing up the driveway. Good. She settles the tin foil on the counter and slides a square of lasagna onto each waiting plate. Sean is getting out of the truck. He closes his door firmly, without a bang. That is good, too, she thinks. He might be back to normal. He might be in good enough shape to go to the hospital with her to tell Shawnee the news.

FIVE

As long as Gunther can remember, he's wanted to be the best at something. It didn't really matter what. It could be playing a sport or inventing something, something big like electricity or cell phones. As a kid, he rigged up an automatic bed-maker with pulleys and paper clips and laundry line rope. But the ropes got tangled and the clips that held the sheet and blanket together always came off. It was faster, he learned, to tug everything in place by hand.

It isn't about the money, or the girls, not completely. It's because of the way the best people handle themselves. People like Usain Bolt, Gunther thinks, don't take the world too seriously. Except for the things that *are* serious—being the best, getting the job done, never giving up.

Sometimes he dreams, though he's never told anybody this, that he's holding a press conference, sitting at a banquet table on a stage just like this one, and he's handling it so well, just like he's seen Bolt do on TV after a meet, smiling and sometimes joking with this reporter and that, and when the question is right, Usain's shifting gears, deepening his voice, showing the interviewer exactly how much he knows about his sport; how smart he is.

Now, looking out at the roomful of reporters, Gunther feels dizzy, like he might even barf. The air smells like floor wax and something sour, maybe his own sweat. From where he sits, the room is a sea of noisy people shifting in their seats like school kids excited before the start of the show. Beside him, Hopper removes the microphone from its stand, squares his shoulders, clears his throat; the room goes quiet.

"As you all know, the grand jury has been deliberating this afternoon on the State of New York versus Sean Padrushky, Jr. to determine whether, based on the evidence, there is sufficient reason to indict Mr. Padrushky on the charges of attempted murder in the second degree and attempted assault in the first and second degrees as felony hate crimes. A hate crime is defined, I remind you, as a crime motivated entirely or in part by intolerance of another person's race, color, religion, or nationality. Today's grand jury, convened by the Honorable Judge Adkins, has unanimously voted to indict Mr. Sean Padrushky, Jr. on all of these federal charges."

In an instant, the reporters are on their feet, waving their hands, with the *pick me, pick me* urgency of third graders. Hopper points to a woman in the front row. Her skin, smothered in foundation, is the deep pumpkin color of a TV reporter. "Ms. McClosky."

"Congratulations on the grand jury's verdict, Mr. Hopper. You all must be pleased." Her smile expands for a second, then retreats. "But I have a question for Mr. Cannon."

Gunther clasps his fingers; his right eye blinks double-time. *Be chill*, he tells himself.

"Sean Padrushky, Jr. has been charged with a hate crime directed toward you, Gun."

Gunther frowns. *'Gun' like she knows him; she doesn't.*

"How do you feel about that? Do you hate him back?"

The row of TV cameras homes in on Gunther. Microphones rise from the audience like snakes' heads, eager to slurp down his words. Gunther cuts his eyes to Hopper. They practiced this question. Of course, he hates Padrushky. The fucker tried to kill him. But this isn't an honest equation. This isn't tit for tat. He takes a deep breath, levels his gaze at Ms. McClosky. "I hate what Padrushky did to me; he made me think I was going to die. But I don't *hate* him. I feel sorry for him."

Hopper squeezes his shoulder hard. Out in the audience, his parents are smiling and clapping. Everybody is smiling and clapping. Of course, they are. He's saying all the right things. He's saying, like always, what they want to hear.

◈

Outside the courthouse, they dip into the brilliant sunshine, sunshine as bright as it was the day he was shot, he and his mom and dad linking arms and running toward the waiting car. On either side of the red-brick path, the police have put up barriers to hold back the cheering onlookers and the press. Hopper instructed him to raise his suit jacket over his head, but his father said, "No, my son is not the criminal."

At the car, reporters are waiting with cameras and microphones, each hoping to be chosen as the one the family will speak to, but he and his parents disappoint them all, sliding into the car and pulling the doors closed swiftly as though they are disappearing into a submarine and submerging.

SIX

WHEN SHAWNEE OPENS HIS EYES, his mother and father are sitting by his bed. With their heads bowed, they look like they are praying, and maybe his mother is. She is wearing an open-necked shirt, sleeveless, and a clean pair of jeans and yes, she is fingering her rosary. His mom, he knows, hates to wear dresses and actually he's never seen her wear one, not even for his Confirmation. He guesses she probably wore a wedding dress when she got married, but maybe not, because he's never seen any pictures of his parents' wedding. There aren't any pictures in a frame or in an album like he saw at his aunt's house the one time they visited in Pennsylvania somewhere. The whole visit his aunt was showing off her pictures—her wedding, her husband's family. On and on she went, saying, "Remember this?" while she flipped pages in an album with covers that smelled like formaldehyde and new car seats. His mother didn't remember any of the people in the pictures, because she wasn't there.

He watches his parents some more, wondering when they will get bored. Neither of his parents likes to sit much. They are always doing, doing, doing. His mom is always cleaning kennels, walking dogs, grooming dogs, breeding dogs, raising dogs. His mom has ants in her pants, his dad always says and when he was little, he believed him and thought that explained it.

He is like them, but different from them. He always has been. Like them, he likes to be by himself. But he likes to be by himself without any animals. He doesn't like dogs, not really, which his mother doesn't understand. If anyone understands him, it's his dad, sort of. His dad likes history like he does. That's about it. His dad is the person who told him about World War II, and his dad was the one who gave him the philosophy that the fittest survive, even though it seemed the opposite of what he learned in church, Jesus' philosophy, "The meek shall inherit the earth." His father doesn't buy that crock, as he puts it, and he doesn't either, not anymore. If a person knows even a little bit about history, a person knows that a philosophy like Jesus's is dangerous and will get you nowhere—or dead—fast.

He shifts in his bed because he has to, but he doesn't want his parents to know he's awake. As soon as they know he's awake, they will want him to talk. He hasn't ever liked to talk except to Father Rand. When he talked to Father Rand, Father Rand listened. Father Rand taught Sunday School, and when he was six, he told Father Rand that he thought Jesus was as beautiful as a girl, and when he grew up he wanted to marry Jesus. If he had said that to his dad, he would have gotten soap to chew on, and so, even though he thought it for a long time, he didn't let anyone know until Father Rand.

The classroom in the church basement was cool, lit with the flickering light of fluorescent tubes. On one wall, a pulldown map of the world covered the blackboard. Patches of purple marked the places where Catholics lived and worshipped, contrasted with gray patches, the territories of non-believers. When Shawnee looked at the gray territories, he imagined vast deserts boiling under an unwavering sun. He imagined Hell.

When he told Father Rand that afternoon of his intention to marry Jesus, Father Rand smiled and spread out his fingers. "What do you see?" Father Rand asked. "A ring," he said. It was a gold band like his father's and mother's, only a little shinier.

"I am married to Jesus Christ," Father Rand said. "You can marry Him, too, one day."

That night he dreamt that Jesus was his wife and that He held him in his arms and kissed him like a wife. As he grew older sometimes the dream changed, and Jesus was Father Rand and he was kissing him, and Father Rand was telling him that he did not have to be afraid. Because he was afraid. He was afraid all of the time. He was afraid of his father, and he was afraid of his mother; he was afraid of the dogs and of the trees.

When he went into town, he was afraid of the cars and of the people on the sidewalks and in the stores. He was even afraid of the buildings. What kept them from falling down?

He told Father Rand about his fears, and Father Rand told him that he could love Jesus and he would never again have to be afraid.

In the meantime, Father Rand and he played the organ together, and they prayed together, and they loved Jesus together, and some day, he, Shawnee, would marry Jesus and that would mean, he thought, that he would be married to Father Rand, too.

His dad can't keep his eyes shut; can't keep his mouth shut, either. "He's awake, Joanne. He's up." His dad switches on the light that angles over the bed like an anorexic arm. "Shawnee, boy, son. Can you hear me?"

He freezes solid. Of course, he can hear him. He can also smell him. The mint spray over his whiskey breath. His dad, all right. And he can hear the sound of his mom's rosary, clicky-click, as she coils it, sets it on the side table.

"Are you talking today? Are we going to hear your voice?"

His mom is a stubborn animal, he thinks. She might never give up.

"Don't talk to him like a baby, Joanne. There's nothing wrong with him." His father is shifting foot to foot like a kid who's been locked out of the bathroom. "Okay, son, I, for one, love you, and I am here for you, no matter what these a-holes try to do to you, you understand?"

In the room, they all swore allegiance to their Leader and to each other to take the sword.

"Sit down, Sean. We haven't even told him yet. You wanted to tell him yourself, so tell him or I will."

Tell me what? He opens his eyes, lifts his eyebrows. *I'm not dead, people.*

"Look. He's telling you to talk."

His father's face hovers above his; his pupils look big behind a glaze of tears. His breath is warm. "You've been indicted, son. The grand jury, bunch of pinko bastards, declared you're guilty of a hate crime. Premeditated, the whole bit—"

"Are you stupid? They didn't say Shawnee was *guilty*, they said the *evidence*—"

His father rears back. "I am trying, Joanne. I am trying not to blow my stack."

But he's blowing it; that's clear. His father is purpling, and his eyes are growing bright. He thinks he's scaring someone, but he's not. A long, long time ago, when he was a little kid, he was scared. His father's anger could make him pee his pants. No more. First Jesus saved him; then, his Brothers. Who don't take shit from no one; who will someday rule the world.

He can feel the laugh taking shape in his gut; growing in size and density, like the snowballs of packed snow and ice the kids used to sling at him at recess, screaming, *cry baby*. He has to let it go, even though it sets his jaw on fire; shoves a spike through his skull; he has to laugh, no matter the pain, and laugh he does; it spurts up from his belly through his lungs out his nose, long and loud and hard, spraying snot everywhere.

SEVEN

"Father Lambert," the reporter says, thrusting her microphone at the car window like a torch or a baton that she aches to hand off to him. "Maureen McCloskey, Channel 2 News. May I ask you a few questions?"

He has just pulled into the space marked "Reserved for Pastor." The reporter and her camera man must have been lying in wait. He lowers his window. "A few, I suppose." This moment was inevitable. He might as well get it over with now.

"I understand Sean Padrushky, Jr. is your parishioner?"

The seat belt across his chest holds Father Lambert so tightly, he can hardly breathe. "Shawnee and his family are members of our church. I've known Shawnee since he was born. He's a good boy."

The reporter nods. "Feeling that way, you must be very upset at today's grand jury indictment of Shawnee for pre-meditated murder and a hate crime. Do you think Shawnee Padrushky is a racist?"

The blush starts beneath his collar, flooding his neck and face crimson. His mother used to say that his complexion had marked him for a priest. God would not allow him to tell a lie.

"Excuse me." Father Lambert releases his seat belt and opens the car door, forcing the reporter to step back. "I've told you, Shawnee Padrushky is a good boy. He is not the boy they're portraying. That is not the boy I know. Clearly, he was bullied; he was pushed to the point where he snapped." Maureen McCloskey's eyes fly open. They are green, very, very green.

"Shawnee Padrushky was bullied? Are you saying Shawnee is a victim? Was he bullied by Gunther Cannon? Please, Father—"

He pivots away from the microphone and scurries up the gravel path to the rectory. Behind him, he hears the crunching sound of the reporter and her camera man hastening to catch up, but he is too fast. At the rectory door, he shoots his key into the lock and is inside.

Once in his office, he pours himself a small cup of water from the cooler. Trickles of sweat run behind his ears. The blush pricks his neck. Never before in his life has he shut and locked a door in someone's face.

His hand trembles as he brings the tiny pleated cup to his lips. He has to sit.

At his desk, he bows his head, brings his palms together. He closes his eyes and listens to the rapid beat of his heart. *Oh, dear God, what did I say?*

EIGHT

LYING ON HIS BED, Hopper, propped against his thick pillows, sips his Scotch, neat, and awaits the 6 o'clock news. What a day. It was textbook. Perfect. All he had to do was present the evidence, let Gunther speak, and the grand jury delivered the goods, wrapped up in a bow.

Back at the office after the press conference, everyone stood up and cheered. He was the hero of the day. The man with the flag, entitled to a fanny wiggle in the end-zone; a glass of Scotch. Dunk.

The network's logo bursts on the screen. Next, a shot of the Cannon's arriving at the courthouse with a voice over of a reporter summarizing the events that led up to the grand jury investigation. Hopper turns up the volume. "Penny! It's starting." She's got to see this. "Penny!" His wife appears in the doorway, and he pats the space next to him on the bed, welcoming the warmth of her shoulder against his; her slender thigh.

"Exciting," she says, and he nods, silencing her with a finger to his lips. The camera is inside Town Hall now, sweeping the packed audience, then zooming in on him at the microphone.

"I could lose a few."

"It's the TV. Everyone gains a few pounds."

Hopper nods, squeezing her knee. "Listen to this. The kid's great."

Then McClusky's asking her question; Gunther's answering.

"Poor kid. The world's been foisted on his shoulders. He's not complaining exactly; he's grieving."

"You can't coach that," Hopper says, raising his glass to Gunther.

Penny shushes him. "Who's this?"

On the screen is Father Lambert behind the wheel of his parked car. His window is down, and his expression is flustered as the reporter, Ms. McClosky, points her microphone at his mouth.

Hopper sits up so fast he spills his drink. "What the fuck?" McClosky's asking the priest his opinion of "Shawnee Padrushky" (low blow, Carullo, feed her the kid's nickname, warm and fuzzy) and now the camera closes in on the priest's furrowed brow, his stern and careful words, as though they arrived from God's mouth to his hallowed ear, "This boy was bullied until he snapped."

McClosky looks surprised. "Is this something you have special knowledge of? Are you suggesting that Shawnee Padrushky was bullied by Gunther Cannon?"

Father Lambert rolls up the window, leaving the suggestion hanging in the air, and the clip ends, leaving Maureen McClosky to address the TV audience, "Was it bullying or was it hate that drove Shawnee Padrushky to pursue Gunther Cannon? The grand jury says 'hate', the pastor who counsels him says 'bullying'. But it will be up to a trial jury to decide."

"Wow," Penny says, "'*Counsels*.'"

"Son of a bitch." Hopper slams his glass on the side table. As the grand jury filed out of the room, several members stopped to tell Hopper that though they had voted to indict based on the evidence, they hoped that Sean Jr. would receive psychiatric care, and he assured them that though it may not seem like it, he had Padrushky's best interests in mind. Not anymore. If Lyle Carullo had the gall (and the strings) to put the priest up to that horseshit, the gloves were off.

NINE

SEAN SR. CHECKS HIS WATCH, nine o'clock. Nine o'clock and the light in the rectory is still on. Nine o'clock and even an asshole like him knows he should go home to his bed. Go home or go back to the hospital. He should be there for someone, for his wife or his son. But every time he thinks of either one of them, it pisses him off. It's Shawnee laughing. It's Joanne, setting her jaw like one of her damn dogs and telling him, "Don't bother to come home tonight unless you're sober."

Who says he isn't? What does she know? He went out for a few, sure, which was better than what he wanted to do.

"That's it," she said. "I hope you roll in a ditch."

He had near done that, on the back road, taking a turn too fast. He might have wrapped himself around a tree except that the new tires had held good.

Back in town, he circled the hospital, looking to find his son's window like a star in the galaxy. That wall of hospital windows was dark, though. His son must be sleeping. Still, he could have gone up, sat beside his wife on the two-seater in the brightly lit lobby. No. He couldn't, he couldn't face his son again tonight, or his wife. His knees trembled, thinking about it; he felt nauseous. Blow in a paper bag, his mother told him. He used to blow into his brown paper lunch bags, then punch them hard to make them explode. He laughed when his mother jumped, or the cafeteria lady screamed. Now he was the scaredy cat.

He turns his truck into the church parking lot, parking straight, he thinks, thanks to the glow of the white lines beneath the security lights. He gets out, trying not to slam the door, but it slams anyhow. Not a mean slam, but solid. Not so bad.

He pats his truck. Damn good truck. Saved his life only a few hours ago. Damn good tires, worth every penny that Joanne said he'd wasted.

The lot is empty except for Father Lambert's Lincoln. The path to the rectory door crunches under his boots. He might have called first, but who knows where the fuck his cell phone got to? He reached for it on the passenger's seat and discovered it was gone. He opened the glove compartment and a million items poured out, but not his phone, and when he slammed the compartment door closed, it opened again and again, and he found himself cursing the very truck he loved. Not you, he told his truck, patting the dash: just your goddamn glove compartment.

He rings the bell. Father Lambert won't mind. Father Lambert's his hero. What he said on the news. He loves Father Lambert for it. It's too early for crickets, but spring peepers are trilling in the air. The church has a garden in the back with a little pond filled with carp and lilies. He rings the bell again and the door opens slowly. He wasn't listening for footsteps, he was listening to peepers.

Father Lambert wears a maroon bathrobe and heavy slippers. Bits of white stubble gleam along his cheeks in the light of the security lamp. "Sean?"

"I hope I didn't wake you up, Father." He glances at the father's face and thinks suddenly that he looks ill.

"Come in." He sounds tired, but not angry.

The vestibule smells of incense and mop water. Father Lambert presses a light switch and the chandelier above bathes them in its yolky light.

"My office?"

Sean nods, mute. The presence of the father has punctured something. In his mind's eye, he saw himself hugging the father and being held. The effect of the liquor is waning. Joanne once told him that when he drank he smelled like a little boy who pissed himself. He wonders if Father Lambert is thinking that now. All of a sudden, he feels ashamed.

"I'm sorry, Father. I—"

Father Lambert settles himself into the cushioned chair behind his desk. Sean sits across from him, pressing his forearms hard onto the chair's narrow arms.

"You saw the news, I guess."

"I did," Sean says. First, the yuppie bitch in the low-cut blouse yapping her version of the story, making it sound like she could hear all the suffering in the world, like she was some kind of priest herself. Next, the smirking Hopper in his pin-stripes, reading the verdict; beside him the nigger in a monkey suit. That's when his bottle of beer hit the TV.

He can feel a sob pushing steadily up his throat, a bulldozer-load of sorrow, and he wonders if he has the strength to push it back down. Looking around the room, he hopes to fix on something that will straighten him out, something that will help him get a grip. On the wall behind the father, a limp Jesus hangs from a dark wooden cross; to its right, a portrait of Mary, in shades of blue.

"I heard what you said about Shawnee—" Not until he switched on the radio in the truck, not until he was on the way home from the bar. Then he cut his tires and headed back to town. "I—" The sound that leaves his mouth surprises him, a high-pitched bleat like a sheep under the knife or a prisoner's last cry for mercy. "You know he's a good boy, Father. Please help me save him, Father. Please, don't let them take my boy."

PART III

CAMPAIGNS

Mayday

ONE

They come by at night, after work, although some, who are out of work, come earlier, four-thirty, five, which Joanne doesn't much mind. They are polite; they bring their own drinks; their own snacks; they aren't looking for handouts, though she usually rounds something up. Some dip and chips; a pallet of bottled water. And she makes coffee, an urn of it. That's how many there are once everyone's arrived. Sean Sr. moved the trucks out of the garage; set up banquet tables he borrowed from the Church; folding chairs, too.

It was not Father Lambert, but cousin Andrew, Lyle's teenage son, who created a website devoted to digging the dirt on Gunther Cannon and proving that Shawnee was bullied. Cyber-Turd is what Uncle Sean used to call his nephew by marriage, because until this brainstorm, he was the kid most-destined for genius according to his father and mother. Every Thanksgiving and every Christmas and every Easter, the Padrushkys got an earful on the Turd's achievements: He was captain of his school's robotics team; he was going to the Math Olympiad in

DC and so on until they could puke. The Turd was two years younger than Shawnee, and didn't have anything in common with him, it seemed, except that they both hung out on their computers all day and night.

Now Sean Sr. could have kissed the kid. Now Andrew the Angel, Joanne said, because she agrees with Lyle and her husband—they got to do something. And thanks to Father Lambert's interview, there are people out there, lots of people, who are willing to support their cause. Thanks to Father Lambert's Grace of God fund, there is more than enough to pay for the signs, the staple guns, the metal stakes.

It's amazing how fast the word spreads once the website goes live. There are distant cousins and church-goers and folks who say they are sick and tired of the government telling them what to do and how to act. There are people from groups that Joanne, personally, feels are somewhat skeezy, but it's hard to not appreciate folks who put their money where their mouth is; who know how to roll up a sleeve and come out for a cause.

Thanks to Father Lambert, Sean Sr. and she have met people who care for Shawnee, who want Shawnee to get help, who want to get him out of jail and into a hospital. Whoever these volunteers are, whatever they believe in, they are here for Shawnee. That's what counts, Sean Sr. says, and for once, Joanne agrees.

Tonight, and every night for the last week, the supporters have come to the Padrushky's garage to assemble the *Save Shawnee* signs. They have been stapling posters to metal frames, stacking those frames in bundles tied with baling twine which they toss in back of their pick-ups, stow in their trunks.

Everyone is jolly; the snack table is full; the coffee hot. There is great excitement in the air—so many like-minded folks, united for a cause—one could almost call it love.

For the first time since the incident, Joanne feels happy. She feels like something good is coming out of this nightmare. She wishes she could tell Shawnee, but the way it works in jail is the prisoner has to want to talk to you. It's like being at a school dance. She's a wallflower waiting for her son to put her on a call list. Taking her hand after mass last Sunday, Father Lambert assured her that this was a good thing, a sign that Shawnee will repent one day. "Can't you see, my dear? He's ashamed to face his mother." The father's hands cupping hers were warm. She could not meet his eyes. She wanted to believe Father Lambert, to have a faith in Shawnee as strong as his, but she did not.

The morning they moved Shawnee from the hospital to the county jail, Joanne was home with a sick dog. When she got to the hospital, he was already gone. It had never happened to her before like this; she looked at the nurse who delivered the news, and it was like a hand had reached up inside her, yanked her lungs out. They'd taken her son; they'd jailed him; she hadn't said good-bye.

That evening a clip of Shawnee was on the news; Shawnee, already in prisoner's stripes, hunched over his handcuffed wrists, ducking into the back of a police car. She felt sick.

Up and down the rows of tables, people look up to greet her as she passes. "Stayin' out of trouble?" "'Course not." "Hearing anything from your boy?" "Not much." Church people, bikers, farmers. Ted, one of the regulars, a bag of bones beneath his sagging overalls, looks up from his stapling. "How're you doing, Rosie?"

Rosie, though she's sure he knows her name. "All right." Joanne likes Ted, a neighbor they didn't even know they had until the *Save Shawnee* campaign. Now he stops by every day to help.

The garage smells of coffee and gasoline and sweat. Country music twangs from the radio atop the gun cabinet. The doors are open and as the sun sets, the ceiling lights flicker on, bleaching the volunteers to ghosts. *The Lord works in mysterious ways.* Father Lambert insists on this, and Joanne is inclined to agree. Look around, she tells herself, as she refills the coffee urn, unwraps a tray of devilled eggs someone has dropped off for the volunteers, there's good in people. It's something she never in life would have believed.

TWO

THROUGH THE EARLY MORNING FOG, the yard signs along Route 52 are blurs of red. Bruce does not give them much thought. Notices of some kind. A Rotary Club breakfast or someone is running for something. Precisely spaced and fairly low to the ground, maybe Burma Shave is back.

The car radio is tuned to the station out of Albany. All over the world, the news is not good. On every continent, it seems, people are killing each other by the tens, the hundreds, the thousands as though they are ants, not humans. It's a fucking mess, Bruce thinks. Just like home.

Last week after the grand jury's verdict, a *New York Times* reporter, a neat little man in khakis and a tweed jacket, showed up at May's Diner. If he was trying to blend in, he failed. The diner clientele picked him out instantly. It was too early in the season for tourists, and no one ever sat alone in a booth, scribbling on a notepad during the breakfast rush. According to Charlotte Walkman, Maggie's friend, in minutes, half the diner was crowding the reporter in his booth, all wanting to make sure he knew that their town was not racist.

Hopper called them that afternoon with the heads' up. The *Times* reporter had just called him for a quote, but he'd shielded them from being contacted. "It could jeopardize the jury selection," he told the reporter. He and Maggie were grateful, but worried.

The article appeared in the "Region" section three days ago, "Upstate Town: Home of the Free and the Brave?" The reporter described Lake Village as clueless about why a hate crime could have taken place in their "perfect village." Many residents were irate, the article claimed, at the notion that the town was in any sense racist, while other residents pointed to Lake Village's ninety-nine-point-nine percent white demographic to argue the town's implied bias. Rumors of bullying were rampant as the only "reasonable" explanation of why Padrushky, Jr., a would-be priest, would attempt to kill Cannon, a "likeable" black athlete. Others simply chalked up the attack to insanity.

◈

When Bruce was a boy, an allee of Dutch elms lined Main street. Those neatly spaced-trees with their high-reaching branches seemed to Bruce like protectors or guardians of the village. He still remembers riding his bike beneath their vault-like canopy, through a whirling confetti of light and dark and whooping out of sheer joy.

Bruce was a freshman in high school when the *Ophiostoma ulmi* found its way into the first elm. Soon the fungus flowed from the host elm to its neighbors. Down the allee it coursed through the elms' braceleted roots. Within a year, entire branches of leaves began to wilt.

Bruce remembers looking up into the crown of the first dying elm. Above him, the signs were unmistakable, the yellow leaves drooping along the branches, rags left on the clothesline, some still damp, some curling into themselves, stiff. He wanted to weep. There were interventions. The town tried them—sawing off the diseased branches; spraying insecticide to kill the beetles that smuggled the fungus under the bark. By the time Bruce graduated from college, every elm on Main street had died.

◈

The hate crime indictment, Bruce thinks, has spread amongst everyone he knows like a toxic fungus, like *Ophiostoma ulmi* once spread through the elms on Main street. "It's nothing personal," people say, "but why do they have to call it a *hate* crime?" If he answered the way he wanted to, he'd regret it, he thinks. "What do you think it should be called, a crime of 'brotherly love'?"

The day after the *Times* article appeared, Mayor Manchuso rebutted on the front page of the *Daily Journal*, "Why should we be tarred with the brush of racism for one crazy teenager's misdeed?"

Overnight, *one crazy teenager* has become Lake Village's slogan. At the Club, members greet Bruce with a pat on the back. They shake their heads, lower their voices, *one crazy teenager,* they say. *Be glad when this blows over.* Not one of them mentions the racial allusion in the Mayor's editorial. *Tarred,* Bruce thinks with bitterness. Not likely, since the residents of Lake Village are white.

After Gunther was attacked, the Cannons' friends and neighbors, even people in town they didn't know well or at all, showed their support through notes and emails. There was a rally at the high school to welcome Gunther back and a pledge by the school board to hire a diversity consultant. He and Maggie felt buoyed by the outpouring of concern for Gunther. They felt optimistic about Gunther's chances of moving on intact, knowing that he was loved.

That was before the indictment, before the article in the *Times*, and Manchuso's diatribe. Now he and Maggie and Gunther are the targets of open glares in the supermarket, at the gas pump, on the streets, as though *they* are to blame for the media attention, as though *they* are to blame, possibly, for the incident itself. The thought of it makes Bruce want to smash something.

The infected stems of a elm develop dark streaks that can only be detected by cutting through and peeling back the bark of a dying branch. Bruce's heart is streaked with rage; the fungus is in him. He has to fight back. But how?

Bruce slows the old Subaru, easing it over the heaving railway tracks at the entrance to the village. On the right is the Great American and just beyond the cheapest of the motels. From here to the lake is a stretch of elegant Victorians with expanded waistlines of wraparound porches and bric-a-brac eaves. Some are homes, most are lodging. Long ago, when this was still hops country, the freight train ran all the way to Albany; then came the blight, and now there's only enough track to shuttle tourists back and forth along the ten-mile stretch of the river between Leland and Lake Village. Still, the beauty of the lake attracts tourists all summer long and into the fall. Summer people—sailors, golfers, and strollers keep Lake Village afloat.

At the end of the street, Bruce turns left, then right into the parking lot of the country club, where the golf course snugs the lake. A ray of sun breaks through the thinning fog, catches the red letters on the cardboard sign planted in the verge of grass at the head of the parking spot marked, Reserved for Manager. SAVE SHAWNEE. Bruce jams into park, cutting the ignition. In a flash, he's out of the car, jerking up the lawn sign with its shivering spiny legs. It's the sign that's planted all along his route. He cannot believe it.

Moving quickly through the still rooms of the Club, Bruce dismantles security alarms, flicks on lights, turns on air. The rest of the staff won't be in for another half hour or so; first, his assistant, Amy, then the maintenance guys and the caddies. Usually, first thing, he'd jump on a tractor, drag a hose over the greens to knock off the dew, but today he goes into his office, shuts the door, dives for his computer. He's typing as fast as he can, the website address at the bottom of the SAVE SHAWNEE sign flashing behind his eyeballs like a news banner. Though the morning air is still cool, he's sweating.

In seconds, Gunther fills the screen—Gunther, age eleven, wearing aviators and a baseball cap on backwards; his bare chest is draped with bling; the shirred elastic of his boxers, visible above the waist of his sagging jeans. The caption under the photograph: *And they say he's not a criminal?*

Bruce blinks hard. His heart drums in his chest. He knows the photograph. Shit, he *took* it. Halloween night. Gunther trick-or-treating as Lil Wayne. Maggie flipped when she saw Gunther's costume; she ordered him to change, but he took Gunther's side. "What are you worried about?" he said. "It's *Halloween*." Gunther offered his fist for a precious knuckle touch.

Ohmigod. There's more. The Lake Village police coerced Shawnee to waive Miranda and confess; the grand jury's verdict was "rigged"; the judge showed bias moving Shawnee to Lawrence while awaiting trial, and finally, a request for donations to the "Save Shawnee" fund.

Outside the window, the sky is turning shades of apricot and lemon, the sly eye of the sun peeks through a bank of silver clouds. Bruce digs his fingernails into his forehead. Who *are* these people? Why do they want to destroy his son? Gun's a good kid, not perfect. Nobody's perfect. (He'd tell that to Gun when he was younger, beating himself up for some little mistake on the sports' field or a bad grade on a test.) But he's a friendly kid, a decent kid. An *Eagle Scout*. An athlete. And by the fucking way, *the boy* who was *shot*, not the *shooter*.

A memory blazes. The night he shared a story with his on-line, transracial adoption group. He was telling them that Gunther had a blast at his first Cub Scout jamboree, that the Scout leader came by the house to tell him what a great kid he had. In a second, a response popped up, Felicia from Queens: *Watch out, Dad. White folks love our black sons until they grow up.* The words shocked him, sickened him. He never entered the chat again.

Outside the crew and the caddies are arriving; the early bird golfers. Bruce wonders if they saw the SAVE SHAWNEE signs on the way to work? In the parking lot? Did they read them? Do they agree that Shawnee should be *saved* from going to jail?

On the wall across from Bruce's desk are several framed awards he's received over the years for Excellence in Golf Course Management. There are pictures of him standing in a chummy line of older men in golf shorts and polos; and a hand-painted list of the great golfer's attributes, a gift from a Club member. Why the fuck is he here? He doesn't care about golf, he cares about *trees*. He is a scientist, not a goddam golf course superintendent. He was all but PhD in plant pathology. Then out of the blue, his dissertation, "The Prevention and Treatment of Elm Disease," was rejected. "Insufficient data," the committee's report concluded. After five years of careful experiment. *Supervised* experiment. "It's all politics," a member of the committee confided. "Sucks."

A year later, his advisor published a paper in "Nature," using Bruce's "insufficient" data as his own. Bruce tried to appeal, but nothing came of it. A lawyer he consulted told him he didn't have a chance of winning his case. Then as now, there was no clear path for his rage.

He dropped out of his program, took an arbor maintenance job in the Parks Department, trimming branches, inspecting for disease. It wasn't a bad job, really. Some days he imagined himself a GP making house calls; each tree he examined, a beloved patient.

He met Maggie on one of his rounds. Unbeknownst to her, she was sitting under one of the last mature Dutch Elm in Central Park. He didn't want to disturb her, but he had to take bark samples. When she looked up, her large, dark eyes surprised him. He could tell that she'd been crying—either that or she suffered from bad allergies. No, it had to be tears. Her voice shook a little as she apologized for being in his way. No need, he said, offering his hand to help her get to her feet. She refused. She was nimble. She sprang, dusting twigs from her shorts, her trim legs, eager, it seemed to him, to contradict any impression he may have gotten that she was vulnerable.

To his surprise, she wanted to know more about the elm and what he was doing. He took out his penknife, broke off a twig, shaved a sliver, then held it to her nostrils. "Smell," he said. "No smell," she said. He sniffed. "Right. That's good. What else?" She ran her finger over the cut and that's when he noticed her fingertip's perfect length and shape. "Nothing. Wood." "Exactly. No streaks. No wintergreen smell. This baby's sound." He patted the trunk, and Maggie beamed. They decided to grab coffee, and he learned the reason that she was crying. It was eerie; meant to be. She, too, had been cut from her graduate program, a master's degree in Piano Performance. In a matter of months, they were living together in his studio in the Heights. Both of them, it seemed, had lost a leg, the leg, they were both convinced, that held the weight of their entire worth. When they found each other, it filled their deepest wish of being whole again.

There's a knock on the door and it opens. Amy. "Everything okay?"

"Did you see those signs?"

Her heavy blink leaves light tracks of mascara on her cheeks. "What the f—is that about?"

"They're smearing Gunther on a website."

Amy shakes her blonde head, kewpie sad. "That's horrible for you. I'm sorry."

He's known Amy for ten years, at least. He hired her, for god's sake, right out of high school, moved her up from secretary, to purchasing, to second in command. For *you*? Isn't it horrible for her, too? For the whole town? "I need to get out of here. I got to talk to Maggie, our lawyer, the police."

"I'll cover. What do you want me to tell people?"

"Tell them that white supremacists are trying to slander my son."

Amy is nodding, looking confused.

"No, just tell them that I had an emergency."

THREE

FRIDAY MORNING THE WAITING ROOM is full at the county jail, but Sean Sr. thinks he knows the gal at the window, though he can't remember her name. Betty Lou or Doreen or something. A girl who might be something to look at if the acne hadn't scarred her good. Now she looks up at him and asks his name and who he is there to see. Sean, Sr. winks. "You know goddamned well who I'm here to see. If you don't know, you've had your head up your ass for the last thirty-six hours."

"Jesse," the girl, Doreen or Betty Lou, says. "Jesse, will you handle this?"

Then a mean-looking bastard, must be six foot six, a fucking giant, a guy Sean Sr. has never seen before takes the girl's seat.

"ID," he says. "Driver's license."

Sean, Sr. reaches into his front pocket. He knows when not to mess. Still he can't help an eye-roll, though Joanne warned him, no eye-rolling, no sighing. No being human, he guesses. No freedom of speech. This is America. Her brother is on his case, too. You're almost as bad as Shawnee, he told him, and that made him mad. "I'll fire your ass to hell, Lyle, even if you are family."

He's on the edge and he knows it. First, Shawnee was denied bail; now he's being moved from county to state prison, pre-trial, for committing a so-called hate crime (since when are American citizens not allowed the freedom to hate someone?), for trying to shoot himself. According to the authorities, sticking a .22 to your throat and pulling the trigger is a *crime*, not an act of *insanity* that requires a head doctor.

Sean Sr. shoves his ID into the slot under the window and says his name so slow you'd think he was a retard, he thinks. The giant behind the window writes it all down on a form.

"When do I see my son?" His heart is beating fast; he could use a cigarette, but there is no smoking here like every place else. Another little freedom taken away by the good old government of the USA.

"When we call you," the giant says. "You can take a seat with the rest of them."

The rest of them. Sean Sr. looks around the small, dimly lit room. Trash, young and old, trailer park and worse. He knows where they are from. They're from places back in the hills a person can't believe, shacks of rotted out wood and broken windows stuffed with rags.

Joanne only two weeks ago put an ad in the paper to find some kennel help. A girl showed up. She loves dogs, she says. Mother takes in all kinds of strays. She was from Mortonville. The worst. A couple of shacks all owned by the same bastard, TJ Morton. A manure tub that place. Joanne was offering five dollars an hour. The girl says she's okay with that. At least at first. Then she started showing up later and later. Dogs were howling; kennels were filling with shit. Then one day, she doesn't show. He told Joanne, the hell with her. Joanne was worried. She liked the girl. The dogs had liked her, even Sallie.

The girl didn't have a telephone, of course. Not even a pre-paid cell. So, Joanne decided after a few days that she needed to drive over the pig sty way, take a look, make sure the girl was okay.

When Joanne got back, she was mad. She walked right past Sean, through the house, right on into the kennel. She did not say a word.

Only later, at dinner, she broke. "Whore," she said. "Two-faced bitch."

"Whoa, what happened out there?"

"She took a job at Connersville Vet. She said it paid twice as much."

"Was there an apology?" he asked his wife.

Joanne shook her head. "No thank you, either. Because you know who trained her. You know who picked her out of the trash."

They are calling names now over the loud speaker. So much for confidentiality, Sean Sr. thinks. One skinny-assed kid after another wearing a jumpsuit and looking like they should be working on cars not sitting in jail appears in the doorway. When Shawnee's name is called, he stands up fast. His son, wearing the stripes of an AWOL zoo-keeper, is flanked by guards.

One month ago, Maundy Thursday, the priest washed this boy's feet; nine months ago, he was a goddamn acolyte playing the organ at church. His son brings his chin up, narrows his gaze. He does not look happy to see his father; he does not look like he has any feelings at all. Sean Sr. feels his chest fill fast. He coughs and coughs again. His throat is full of phlegm and his knees are rubber. He reaches for something to hold onto, but there is nothing to grab.

"Need a hand?"

The voice belongs to a large woman who hoists herself from her seat to catch him as he stumbles back.

"I'm okay," he says, waving the woman off. His son is looking at him. It's impossible to read his face. Curiosity? Disgust?

The visiting room looks like a bank lobby or a betting parlor, a row of windows fronted by a counter, each with a chair in front of it and a telephone. The guard ushers Sean Sr. to a window on the far end.

They have the far wall for privacy. Visitors' jackpot. Sean Sr. slides into the bucket of the plastic seat. Shawnee sits hunched on the other side of the window. His hands are free, but his ankles are cuffed. Sean Sr. clears his throat as he picks up the receiver. "What's up?" he says.

Shawnee ducks his chin. His head is shaved so close Sean Sr. can see the veins across his scalp, deep blue rivers travelling nowhere. "Not much."

"When's moving day?" To Maximum. Up North. No man's land. Not far from where he's surveying a thousand plus acres of conifer and scrub.

Shawnee shrugs lightly. "I dunno." The guard behind him stands stone-faced, his hands loose.

They are listening, Sean Sr. knows. Their conversation is being taped. It's no secret. Still he has to take a chance. "Have you had any visitors? Anybody I know?"

"Yeah. A couple."

"Like who?"

"My lawyer."

"Okay. That's good." Is it? Lyle didn't tell him he visited.

"What did Lyle have to say?" Sean Sr. glances up at the guard, old Hear No Evil.

Shawnee shrugs. "We might be making a deal."

We? "A deal? What kind of deal?"

"A plea."

"No one said nothing to me."

Shawnee looks at him. His eyes are bright now, and cold. "It has nothing to do with you."

Sean Sr. clenches the receiver. "Does your mother know?" Obviously, she and her brother have been plotting behind his back.

Shawnee shakes his head. "Nope."

"So, what is it? What's the deal?"

"It's not a deal yet. Lyle's got to ask for it."

"What's he want?"

"They drop the hate crime, but I got to state for the record that I shot the kid for a reason."

"They get it on the record, but you still go to the can?"

"Ten years, fifteen total, Lyle said."

"Lyle? What about the DA; what about the judge? Have they signed on?"

"Lyle's doing the right thing by me; he's trying to get me out the fastest way he knows how."

Sean Sr. bangs his forehead with the base of his palm. "Do you like Kool-Aid? Is that what this is? Anyone who comes along and tells you what to do, you do it?

"You were coerced, son. The statement you wrote; hell, the cops didn't even read you Miranda. I'm going to get you out of this mess. We don't need Lyle. I'm getting a goddamned psychiatrist to testify that you're insane; get you into a hospital. I don't want to think of you as nuts, of course. But I'm going to get you help, get you treatment, not jail time."

His son stares down at the counter on his side of the glass. "Nah. You don't get it. Lyle says that if I get committed to one of those hospitals, I might never get out."

"Lyle says, what about your father says?"

"Uncle Lyle's my lawyer."

Sean Sr. pounds his fist into his palm so hard it stings the bone. "Goddammit. People think because they're this or that, a lawyer or a doctor, they know something. They don't know jackshit."

"You know something?"

"Goddamn right, I do. I know that until today, Lyle's been saying you got to be insane to do what you did. The Mayor said it in the newspaper. You need help, a hospital, not a fucking jail cell."

The guard steps forward, taps Shawnee's shoulder, points to the clock, and Shawnee rises and follows him, an obedient child.

In a flash, Sean Sr. is on his feet. He can't stand it; his son being told what to do, herded like he is the man's property, his beast. "Hold up," he shouts.

The guard stops; Shawnee, too. They turn and stare at him like he is the one who is insane.

"I didn't get a chance to tell you what I'm doing for you—I got a whole campaign started—posters and a website. Here, I got a picture—" He holds his cellphone up to the window. "We're getting the truth out, son. We're going to save you. A fucking convoy went out last night, posting these. People care."

The boy looks at him, his eyes keen with a sort of menace. "I don't." Then he turns back to the guard and starts his shuffle toward the stairs.

Back in his truck, Sean Sr. pulls out his cellphone, speed dials his brother-in-law, direct, bypass secretary, bypass message tape.

"Hey," Lyle says.

"You're fired."

Lyle snorts. "Fuck you, Sean."

"You two-faced, bullshit-talking asshole. What'd you tell my son? Insanity, you say. Insanity's what we're aiming for, then you make a deal behind our backs?" Through the cab's windshield, he watches visitors entering the county jail, lumpy women hauling shopping bags; skinny punks pushing strollers. "What about 'Save Shawnee'? Wasn't that your idea?"

"Hold on, asshole. You're so goddamned stupid. You ever heard of strategy?"

"What strategy? The strategy was to get my boy into a hospital."

"Wrong. The strategy was to get the public, and by extension, Judge Adkins, to *consider* insanity; to plant a seed of doubt; to get the sympathy on Shawnee's side. We're never going to prove insanity, asshole.

You know what kind of evidence they got? But build the *doubt* about Shawnee's sanity, you got a chance at killing the hate crime—that's ten years off his sentence, jerk-off. Ten years more likely that your dumb-fuck son gets out of jail alive."

FOUR

CHIEF RINEHART, DA HOPPER, Mayor Manchuso, and Superintendent Jones are already seated at the table in the conference room off the Chief's office when Bruce and Maggie arrive. It's only May, but the heat has soared. The men have shed their jackets, loosened their ties. The air conditioning in the old police building is on the fritz; heavy-headed fans whir weakly, hardly pushing the humid air. Even with the windows open it is oven hot.

To Maggie it looks as though the men around the table would rather deal cards than talk. Yet to be fair, she thinks, they were willing to meet them on a moment's notice on this freaky hot afternoon.

Chief Rinehart half rises, extending his hand like an unsteady compass needle.

"Please don't get up," Bruce says. "We all know each other."

The Chief flashes a tight smile, drops back to his seat and the other men nod, grateful, it seems, not to have to exert themselves.

Maggie takes her seat next to Bruce. They have already decided that he should lead the meeting. He understands these guys. He can speak their language. Her job is to listen, to take notes, keep her mouth shut, which won't be easy. Not after what she saw on the website this morning. The Padrushkys have broken into their house, stolen their lives. They have snatched their family photos, twisted facts, distorted their life story.

The men grab their pads of legal paper like kick boards to help them to propel through the meeting. Maggie uncaps her pen and starts to write in shorthand, her cloak of invisibility, her refuge. All day long at her job, she observes and notes; types in the secret language of the steno machine. Spy and medium. She bends to her page.

"Let's begin this meeting." Chief Reinhart taps the eraser end of his pencil on the table as though it were a gavel. "Last night, or early this morning, some*one*, or some persons, staked signs throughout the area—" The table erupts.

"Any idea who did it?"

"How many signs?"

"Is this county-wide?"

"Are there any signs on public property?"

"Can we talk about the *website*? The cyberbullying?" Maggie pins her gaze to Hopper. "Is what they're doing legal?"

"'*They're*'? I don't believe we've identified the perpetrators." Sweat glistens in Chief Reinhardt's sideburns and along his hairline.

"Oh come *on*," Bruce says. "You know exactly who it is. The Padrushkys and their supporters. Father Lambert, and every other goddamn Neo-Nazi in the county. Maybe even the country."

The Chief crosses his forearms, bracing them on the table. "I get you're upset, Bruce, but hang on—"

"Goddamn right I'm upset. I grew up in this town. I thought I knew this place. I never expected anything like this."

"Well." It's Mayor Manchuso. "Let's say the obvious. None of us could have expected anything like this. One crazy—"

"Don't you dare talk that bullshit to me and my wife. I guess there's no other reason why a white kid tries to kill a black kid in your book. Only that's not what the grand jury believed. They only looked at the *real* evidence."

Mayor Manchuso blinks hard, the corners of his mouth bending into deep commas.

"Are there any signs on school property?" Maggie asks.

Superintendent Jones in his pink polo shirt and white shorts looks as though he's been pulled from his tennis game. "I haven't heard of any. I expect Principal Hadley would have let me know by now, but I'll shoot him a text."

Maggie picks up her pencil, turning to the Chief. "What's the radius for these signs?"

The Chief shifts in his chair; his temples and forehead are shaded the pink of a bad sunburn. "Look, everything on public property's coming down. It's just a matter of getting the resources. I only got six men; three cars. Everybody's on sick leave; vacation—"

Maggie turns to Hopper. "If the signs are on public property, can we file charges?"

Hopper frowns. "I'd rather not get into the legal issues right now."

"Why not?"

"We already have a big iron in the fire. I don't want to get side-tracked."

Bruce leans in. "Those signs need to come down right away. If you don't have the manpower, we'll get volunteers. Maggie and I will get the ball rolling if you don't."

The Chief shakes his head. "Whoa, Bruce. We're trying to cool down the situation. You understand?"

"No, I don't. Unless 'cooling the situation' means protecting our son."

Mayor Manchuso clears his throat. "I'll say it again even if Chief

Reinhardt doesn't want to. We don't know for sure that the Padrushkys put up the signs."

"The Padrushkys created the website. They're not hiding it."

"The *signs*, I'm saying."

Maggie rolls her eyes. "Oh, right. That couldn't possibly be the Padrushkys."

"Let's watch the tone here, please." Chief Reinhardt, pulling rank.

Superintendent Jones frowns. "Frankly, guys, the social media stuff is what I'm primarily concerned about. This is how the rumors get started and the kids get riled up."

"You're right, Superintendent," Bruce says. "The stuff on the Padrushkys' website is total, unbelievable crap. So, what are we going to do about it?"

Superintendent Jones is shaking his head. "I'm just saying, if you folks are thinking of starting up your own campaign, it's just going to perpetuate the craziness. I mean there are kids in that school trying to concentrate on homework, exams, soccer playoffs, Senior Week, you name it, but all anyone is talking about is the incident *still*."

Maggie and Bruce exchange a look. At the beginning, Superintendent Jones seemed entirely in their camp, but all that he's done so far is the usual preaching to the converted in the form of a high school assembly, featuring anti-bullying skits and t-shirts.

Chief Rinehart shoves his palms against the rim of the conference table as though he'd like to dump it, or the subject of the meeting, over a cliff. "Can someone here clarify? I mean is this going to turn into something larger than we can handle? Hopper?"

Hopper squares his shoulders. "My office will certainly be looking into the legality of the 'Save Shawnee' website. At the very least, we have to determine if the coverage is going to taint the jury pool."

Mayor Manchuso runs his hand over the crown of his head. "You know, given all the negative publicity, it wouldn't be such a bad thing to ask the judge to move the hullabaloo to a bigger place, a different county. To Connorsville even. Their police force is ten times our size."

Chief Reinhart, nodding, relaxes his grip on the table. "Good thought, Mike."

Superintendent Jones, too, nods.

"Wait a minute," Maggie says. "That's the Padrushkys' strategy. To get the trial moved away from Lake Village."

Across the table, the officials look at her with glazed, impatient eyes. And suddenly Maggie gets it. Once before, she was in this position. The Mozart competition. In the insular world of the Conservatory, word had gotten out that she had miscarried, then broken down. Not one of the judges was going to take her performance seriously after hearing the news. Their body language announced it; the abrupt manner in which she was greeted, asked to play. After fifteen measures, she was signaled to stop.

Chief Reinhart inhales deeply, sets his forearms with clasped hands on the table, shifting them slightly as though racking pool balls. "I got a force of six men. Bring in extras and we're talking overtime. With the publicity I gather the Cannons want to bring to the party, we're talking a security budget way out of our league." He angles his gaze at Bruce. "Like you say, you're from here. You appreciate how small a town this is. You get it."

Bruce lets his breath go with a light whistle. "This is what I get, Chief. The Padrushky trial is a hot potato that you'd like to hand off. But Maggie and I aren't caving. We're not letting Lake Village or the Padrushkys or your department off the hook."

In the parking lot behind the police station, the asphalt is sending up waves of shimmering air that smell like warm metal.

"Wow," Maggie says, "I thought Hopper would jump in a little more."

"It made me wonder."

"We go to the Unitarians. To the NAACP. We start a blog, a Facebook page, link it to Twitter, Instagram. My book club will help. The track parents, too. We are fighting these assholes."

"Have you talked to Gunther?"

"I texted him, but I haven't heard back"

"So, we don't know if he knows?"

Maggie shrugs. "I'm assuming he does."

Bruce sniffs, his nostrils flaring. "I don't know how I go back to the Club, I'm feeling so angry."

Maggie looks up at Bruce who is standing beside his car, tapping his keys on the rim of the roof. His eyes have become fish eyes, glazed and watery. She wants to throw her arms around him, but she knows he wouldn't like that, that he would prefer that she pretend she doesn't see. "Don't go back. Come home with me. Let's start this campaign."

Back at the farmhouse, the rooms welcome them with their cool stillness. In the summer, the old house keeps out heat; refreshes like a permanent shade.

"I need to lie down for a few minutes," Maggie says. It's like she's dragging a sandbag of fatigue; she can barely make it up the stairs.

In the bedroom, she unfastens her skirt, sheds her suit jacket; next, the stockings and the white blouse. It feels strange to take off these clothes; like shedding the day, the tension of the meeting, the enormity of the new events. At least the first act is over. Or is it the second? Where exactly in the action are they? When will this end and how? Will they ever recover? Will Gunther? In plays, the characters undergo catharsis, shift their attitudes. But the truth is that she is too numb, too scared, too shocked to know what her thoughts are at all.

Then Bruce's hand is on her back. His finger tip traces her spine, pressing hard. She yelps a little where he hits a nerve and it hurts.

"Sorry," he whispers. His hand comes around her waist, snugs her to his naked torso.

When did he take off his clothes, enter the room? "You're kidding, right?" Maggie turns to him. She loves his body, lean and muscled as a farmer's. Though they are ill-matched vertically; horizontally, they are a perfect fit.

Quickly, she slips off her bra; her underwear. "How can you be in the mood at a time like this?"

"It's a miracle."

On the bed, they roll as one. Her hips rise over his, her breasts settle in the hollows above his clavicles. Bruce's eyes are closed; the corners of his mouth slightly lift as though he has sunk into a pleasant dream. She feels his hands on her lower back, her buttocks, she feels his penis stiffen against her crotch. Images of the day flash in her mind: the photograph of Gunther; Bill Reinhart's flushed face. So much seems beyond her; way beyond. Stop, she tells herself. Shut it down. Let it go. She kisses Bruce's forehead, his mouth. The slightest scent of aftershave clings to his jaw, clove or cedar.

She is grateful that Bruce needs her, desires her. She needs him, too. She always has. The afternoon he found her in the bathtub, miscarrying, he scooped her out, called an ambulance. He didn't panic; he knew exactly what to do. They'd lost a baby for the last time, the doctor told them. She was lucky to be alive. And when she broke down in the white bed in the white room, Bruce was there.

FIVE

GUNTHER HASN'T BEEN ABLE TO GET himself to walk on Main Street since the day he was shot. Even the thought of heading downtown makes him sweaty and queasy. His mom told him that it's PTSD, the same as veterans get, which sort of helps to know, but also doesn't. Half the time, he feels like he's sneaking around corners or like there are ghosts sneaking up on him. His brain is always tense, always waiting. A kid pops a lunch bag in the cafeteria; the school bus misfires, a rock dinks the windshield of the car, and he wants to hit the floor.

"It's your fight or flight reaction," Dr. Bowman, tells him. "Your body's reacting in a way that makes good sense based on its experience. Your brain is trying to protect you. It will take a while for it to settle down and trust that you're safe."

Gunther has only seen Dr. Bowman, the psychiatrist, once before. He's an okay guy. Chill, like his dad, but fidgety like someone who would rather be doing something outside. If Gunther could get himself to talk, he would tell the man that that's the point—he doesn't know how he'll ever feel safe again.

This morning on the way to school, he saw the signs, and so did everybody else on the bus. By the time they got to the high school, everybody had seen the website, too. They'd seen his photo, Lil Wayne wearing a floppy hat and shades, his pants pulled low. All day long, the guys had teased, knocking his shoulder with their knuckles. "*Gansta—*"; "*You da man—*" Their mocking meant to show him that they had his back. That he was one of *them*. But he wasn't. They could joke about it; but he was fucking scared.

Dr. Bowman's office is in Connorsville, on a block not far from where Ms. Bev used to live. He hasn't told Dr. Bowman about Ms. Bev. He doesn't plan on telling him anything about her. But shit, sitting here in the leather chair that feels like a big baseball mitt grabbing you on all sides, he misses her.

"Gunther?" Dr. Bowman leans forward in his chair, presses his fingertips together. "Is there anything you'd like to say?"

Gunther considers. The doctor does not sound mad that he isn't talking. He seems kind of sad. Maybe he should tell him about Ms. Bev, but it's too much explaining. It's not worth it. One day Ms. Bev was his mom's best friend; the next thing, she wasn't. His mom never said what the fight was about. His dad, either. He wanted to ask Ms. Bev himself, but he didn't. And then she was leaving. She got a teaching job in London. He didn't know if he would ever see her again.

◈

Ms. Bev's house was in a neighborhood of small, tidy houses with pitched roofs and pastel siding. Each had a neat square of front lawn and a private, almost sacred square of backyard. The houses, Ms. Bev told him, had been built decades ago as places for the railroad workers to live. Most of those workers were Italian, some were Poles, but a few were black. On her living room wall, there were photographs of the black railroad men in overalls and caps. They wore easy smiles as they stood, gripping their long-handled shovels. Their dark skin shone.

"Black." At five years old, he had heard the word before, of course. Black was a color, the color of the words on the page, the color of night. Black was the crayon you used when you wanted to make things seen. He liked black. Black could be the color of mad. When he was mad, he snatched up his black crayon and pressed down as hard as he could, scribbling over the pages in his picture book. Black, black, black. That made his mother mad, too.

But the day in kindergarten Billy Creighton told him he was black, he looked down at his hand, expecting to find a slash of black paint, a streak of marker, but no, no smudge or stain, just the brown skin on the back of his hand.

That afternoon, he came home to Ms. Bev and his mother in the kitchen, drinking tea, and there's something he had to ask. "Am I black?"

His mother's and Ms. Bev's gazes hooking, unhooking, both reaching out to him as though he was about to fall. Ms. Bev snagged him with her arm, pulled him onto her lap. She ran her fingers through his close-cropped hair. "Black and proud, baby. Black and proud."

But that story doesn't stick, and when he's older, he needs to ask again. Who is he? Who the hell is he? He's heard by now all the other names for black, and he's heard some names for what some black people might think of him, and he wants to say he isn't a cookie, a color, a label.

He and Ms. Bev are picking beans from the lush tangles that grow up the trellis on the back of her house. He's ten or eleven, and he likes coming over to Ms. Bev's house some afternoons when his mom's still at work. He likes helping Ms. Bev pick beans. He likes hunting for the plump hard bodies of the ripe beans, the clean snap of their release, but he's been waiting all day for the chance to ask his question, and finally, it bursts.

"Am I all the way black?" His gaze is fixed on the green denseness of the vine in front of him. Still, he hears her sharp intake of breath, its release.

"You're black, but you don't know your story. Your black story. Your history."

His chin drops. Is it his fault? He thinks she is telling him that it is.

"You've got to read."

Read what? Shame ripples through his body. He doesn't know how to ask.

He takes the bus to Connorsville without telling his parents. He doesn't text Ms. Bev, afraid she will tell him not to come. It's a Sunday; the neighborhood so quiet, it's like somebody died. But it's only because the college is out for the summer, the students have all left.

When she answers the doorbell, she doesn't look surprised. "I'm still packing if you want to come in."

He does want to come in, but the tone of her voice makes it sound like it would be better if he doesn't.

"That's okay," he says. "I'm—" The word repeats itself, and he does not know where to go.

"I know."

He looks at her. She is not made up like her usual, and she's changed her hair, swept it up in a great swirl of braids tied with a wide band of printed cloth. He smiles. "I like your do."

"Something different."

A car swishes by, going too fast down the narrow street.

"I won't miss that," Ms. Bev says, squinting fiercely in the direction of the speeding car. "But I will miss you." She reaches for his wrist, bringing up his hand, so his palm faces hers.

It's kind of creepy, but he goes along. She is like an aunt to him, no matter if she wanted to be "Ms. Bev." Their skin is almost the same shade, a dark, blackish chocolate. She is older than his mother, but only the ripples around her knuckles tell.

"Look how long your fingers are now. I remember when they were tiny, tiny things. I remember those big brown eyes and those bitty white teeth, and your hair—" Ms. Bev laughs. "I felt sorry for your mother." She takes away her hand. "But cute. Cutest little guy I ever seen. And friendly. You smiled at me the first time we met, and I a complete stranger. You were showing off those teeth. King of the hill."

He tries to muster the answering smile she is hoping for, but it doesn't come. His throat is dry. He can't talk; he doesn't want her to talk anymore. He wishes he could hear her sing lullabies again, the way she used to when she was visiting, and he was little, and she tucked him into bed. Her singing, he remembers, was so different from his mother's, deeper, richer. When she sang of rivers of milk and honey, he thought that's what her voice really was, milk and honey, swirling, flowing, carrying him in its swift current to another land.

Ms. Bev heaves a deep sigh, like she's answering a question that he hasn't even asked. "It's a shame."

"What is?"

"You've been robbed, baby. Robbed in broad daylight. You know what I'm talking about?"

He nods, but he doesn't really.

"You heard of Birmingham? You studied that?"

"Yeah." They studied Civil Rights stuff in Unitarian Sunday School along with Multi-Cultural Diversity, a unit he'd found more embarrassing even than the unit on sex.

"I was ten years old when they murdered those girls. Even though we were living in New Jersey, I saw the whole thing in my mind's eye. I'm telling you, those girls were *me*. Their dresses were *my* dresses, their do's, *my* do, Peter Pan collars and ankle socks, and shiny shoes only on Sunday. I didn't sleep for years and years after they burnt that church. I lay in bed, my nerves kinked; my hearing, supersonic. Every creak of a branch or scuffling sound outside the window was a man in a hood, a bunch of men. I went from innocence to experience. That's how it was for me."

Innocence to experience. That's like it is for him, too. Though he didn't understand it that day when, no matter how hard he tried, it was someone else's life, someone else's story.

"Gunther?" Dr. Bowman touches his arm, startling him. "I can tell you've been off somewhere for most of our session, but I'm afraid our time is up. Maybe you'll want to tell me about it the next time I see you?"

Gunther blinks. Dr. Bowman's eyes are all crinkly with concern. He doesn't know that some of the hairs in his mustache are sticking out the wrong way. Gunther launches himself out of the deep chair, ignoring Dr. Bowman's outstretched hand. "Yeah," he mumbles. "Maybe." But he doesn't plan on seeing Dr. Bowman ever again.

SIX

The volunteers left the garage a mess—staples all over the concrete floor where they might puncture the dogs' pads; mangled frames; a trash barrel overflowing with beer cans and paper plates. After the pickups and cars were loaded, Joanne went to bed, too tired to clean up. Sean headed out with the rest of the crew.

This morning, high as a kite on no-sleep, he woke her, wanting her to come with him to visit Shawnee. To tell him all about the campaign.

"I can't."

"You'd rather stay with the dogs?"

"He won't see me. I ain't on the list."

"What did you say to that boy?"

"Nothing."

"I guess that was your mistake."

That did it. She flung off the blanket, grabbed the rifle leaning against the night stand where he liked to put it and, the way it came up, even Sean Sr. knew he'd stepped too far. He was halfway out the bedroom door when he paused to look back at her. "All right then. Cool off."

"Hell, I will," she said.

She should have let it go, but all through the shoveling and raking and scooping, all through the feeding and watering, she keeps hearing Sean Sr.'s words, *your mistake*. No kidding. Her mistake. One of many. Like marrying him.

He was headed for vet school. He had the grades to go on; he had done real good. Top of the class. Their ducks were all lined up. They were engaged to be married right after graduation, a small wedding. Neither of them needed much more to celebrate than a certificate and a bottle of beer.

A week before graduation, Sean and his roommates started celebrating a little too hard and a little too early. Began with the case of Blue, followed by Jack Daniels, followed by god knows what. The community college was in a small town. The bars (all two of them) closed at eleven-thirty sharp; the Seven Eleven at midnight. The boys were tanked and happy and the night was beautiful and clear and so they headed to the college farm, a place they knew they would have to themselves, a place to carry on with the party.

She loved that farm. Fifty acres; old, but decent equipment. The farm was where the Ag students got their practical experience, and where the vet techs, like her and Sean, got to work with large animals, cows and horses and sheep and pigs.

She learned the details from the police report in the town newspaper. Sean, Sr. had never totally explained, and she hadn't been the type to ask.

It wasn't a fire. The barn was still standing after what they did, the fences, too. But the gates were all opened. Not one, but two, three, four—upper pasture and lower—the paddock gate and the gate to the triangle that housed the bull. The cows, all milkers, did what milkers do—they came home, found their stanchions, all but chained themselves back where they belonged. All of the cows but Bessie. Old dry Bessie lost her bearings, got into something she shouldn't have and went down, out in the field and all alone that night.

The charges: trespassing, destruction of private property, animal cruelty. One week short of graduation, Sean and his friends were kicked out of school. Within twenty-four hours, the vet school that had accepted Sean Sr. told him to kiss off. She and Sean Sr. postponed their wedding because of the court appearances and the fines. She picked up work as a kennel cleaner to pay the lawyer's fees. She was nineteen years old; Sean Sr., twenty. She had only one thought in mind, the thought that's guided her day and night through her married life: stay loyal.

SEVEN

BY ELEVEN O'CLOCK IN THE MORNING, the rain is starting to pour, driving the early golfers in and giving Bruce a chance to focus on doctoring the maples. Traditionally, bagging the debris is the best method of containing the tar spot, but he's ordered a new product, a spray, that's supposed to be effective without damaging the environment.

He's about to leave the office for the maintenance garage when the phone rings. Amy.

"I thought you'd want to know that Joe punched in this morning and then took off. He's heading back out to the green. He flipped me the bird when I waved at him."

"What an asshole," Bruce says. "Not you. I'll grab him."

It's the third time this week that Joe has fucked off. His girlfriend's giving him whatfor; his mother's sick; the alarm didn't go off. The fucker knows Bruce can't afford to fire an experienced grounds man.

Strange thing is that Bruce envies him. More than once in the past month, he's wanted to walk off the job, hunt down Padrushky,

Sr. and kill him. It's Padrushky, Sr. who's the real lunatic, the mastermind behind the slander and rumors about Gunther's *gansta* ways; it's Padrushky Sr.'s twisted imagination and talent for propaganda that has succeeded in poisoning this town.

In the cart, Bruce heads up the hillock past the sand trap and down towards the woods. Joe's too sneaky to drink out in the open and besides, it's raining. Sure enough, from twenty yards, he can see Joe, sprawled on his back under a blue spruce; next to him a pile of empties. Bruce knows this spruce. It's one of his favorites. When he was a boy, he climbed just about every tree on the course. The butternuts and the sugar maples and the oaks older than his grandparents. He climbed those trees to hide from his father who wanted him to practice chipping and putting, twisting and driving. His dad practiced golf for hours, but he got sore after a short time, and bored.

"Hey Joe, what are you doing under there?" Bruce squats on his heels, peering into the shadows of the blue-needled branches. "It's Bruce."

Joe answers with a large bullfrog croak of a belch. "I'm drinking."

"I see that."

"You want one?"

"How about get from under there, clock out, and go home."

Joe groans, propping himself on his elbows. He is a strong kid, muscled from working on his parents' farm as well as this job. "Am I fired?"

"No. I need you. So get the hell out from under the tree and go home and come back tomorrow without the refreshment."

Joe sits up, his legs turned out like a dancer's, his hands wrapped around a beer can snugged to his crotch. "You're good people, Mr. Cannon."

"Thanks, Joe." Bruce keeps his voice even. Years of experience has taught him to treat drunks much like lunatics. You don't pick fights. You don't disagree.

"*Real* good. No matter what some people say."

Some people. Bruce feels his anger rise. Once he knew and liked everyone in this town. That has changed.

"Let's get up." Bruce offers his hand, and Joe clasps it, rising to a squat, so they are facing each other.

"I got nothing against black people," Joe says. "Black dude saved my granddad's life in 'Nam. He kept a photograph of him on his bureau. Wouldn't let no one talk bad about black people in his house."

The rain is thickening now, cascading down the back of Bruce's slicker and dripping into his shoes. "Enough bullshit, Joe. Get up." His voice dips into a growl. "Get up or I'll fire your ass."

Joe stands, hoisting the half-spent six-pack to his shoulder. "You don't get it, man. I stood up for you at May's this morning. I said, so what if he loves his nigger. That nigger's his *son*."

Bruce hooks a right, but Joe dodges him, suddenly nimble.

"Hey, I'm out of here. I'm going home." He turns away, tripping, catching himself, picking up a jog.

Bruce could chase him. He could run him down in the cart, herd him like a loco calf into the pond, but he does not. When he gets back to the office, he sits down in front of his computer and stares at the blank screen.

EIGHT

MAGGIE TAKES HER PLACE AT HER STENO machine to the right of the Judge's box. Then all rise and Judge Hanlin takes her seat. The low-ceilinged room is filled with the bleary, restless light of flickering tubes, and the air holds the musty smell of rec room carpet. Maggie hates this room; she hates Family Court. Every day she records stories of unbearable sadness. Their vocabulary sticks in her brain like plaque.

The worst days are like this one. Hearing after hearing of custody cases, of foster families who want to adopt but can't, because the absent birth parent miraculously appears; and on the other side, mothers and fathers in recovery, begging to be reunited with their children. And the children, themselves, some scrubbed, some not, nearly mute beneath the terrible lights.

Judge Hanlin is fair; she shows the children kindness and respect. She fixes the adults with a level, don't-give-me-bullshit look. But in her chambers, after court, the Judge confesses to Maggie that half the time her ruling is a crap shoot, she can only do her best.

Today, a woman wants her son back. She's off drugs, she says, and has the documentation to prove it. When she talks of her son, she breaks into tears. That's not enough Judge Hanlin says. The boy, six years old, has never lived with his birth mother. His foster parents, he considers to be his own.

Oh my god, Maggie thinks, even as she types. What if Gun's birth mother appears, wanting to take him back? What if she reads about the incident and decides she needs to rescue Gun? Even though the adoption's closed, with all the publicity Gun's case has gotten, it wouldn't be hard to track them down. The scene plays in her mind, cartoonish, bizarre. She and the woman tussling over Gun as though he were an object not a human being.

That day on the phone, Bev called Gun, *my boy*, and Maggie wouldn't share. But now it occurs to her that both of them were wrong. Gunther is not a possession; he can't be owned.

Judge Hanlin bangs her gavel. The woman sits down. Maggie won't know what's been decided until she reads back her report. It's like playing a fugue. She types and thinks her thoughts at the same time. It's the only way now that she can get through her day.

NINE

Friday evening, Hopper's telephone rings. His land line, not his cell, because where he lives, there are no cell options. It's that remote—a road to a road to a road, all unmarked, and up and up, and then in and in. His wife, Penny, reading in her chair by the window, shakes her head. "You answer," she says.

Only five people have Hopper's number at home: Penny's son, Pete, from her first marriage; their sons from their marriage; Hopper's mother, in Florida; and Bill Rinehart, the Chief of Police. So fair enough, Hopper thinks. The chances are the call is for him.

"Hopper, here," he says, picking up the receiver. His eyes are still on his wife. Like a good hunting dog on a scent, when she's in a book, nothing can distract her.

"Jerry Manchuso. Did I catch you at a good time?"

"Good as any. What's up?" He wants to scribble the name on a piece of paper, show it to Penny, but there's no pad, no paper.

"I'd like to meet with you. Me and Charlie Rothberg."

The Mayor and the President of the Chamber of Commerce. He takes a deep breath, keeping his tone neutral. "What about?"

"I think you know."

"I'm stupider than you think."

"Hope not."

"Try me."

"We want to talk some things over with you. Shoot the shit."

"Do you gentlemen have something more meaningful to contribute than shit?" At the sound of the word, Penny flicks her gaze back at him. She has been listening after all.

"Ha ha, Hopper. How about breakfast. Tomorrow. My camp."

"Does Judge Adkins know about this meeting?" Of course, he does.

"Why would he?"

Election's this fall. "What time did you say?"

"Eight-thirty. Can you find the place?"

"I believe I can."

As soon as he puts the receiver down, Penny closes her book. "And that was?"

"Mayor Manchuso inviting me to a pre-trial powwow at his camp tomorrow. Me and Rothberg."

Penny lifts her eyebrows. "Not Bill Rinehart?"

"I guess he's not part of the friendly persuasion committee." He watches Penny open her book again. "Hey, you don't have any outstanding parking tickets, do you? Any dirt you're hiding?"

Penny shakes her head. "I paid my library fines last week. I think we're safe."

TEN

Kathie Schecter lives in the center of town, in a large Tudor overlooking the lake and works as a physician's assistant in a pediatric practice. Maggie has always liked Kathie, who, though wealthy, is also down-to-earth and unabashed about her privilege. She is the book group hostess this month and has already let everyone know by group email that she's excited to show off her new kitchen, featuring a marble countertop quarried in Italy. From anyone else, such a declaration would be off-putting, but not from Kathie who is always in jeans and sweatshirts and wears her graying hair in a gender-neutral crew cut.

The book group is held on Friday evening, and Kathie has set out platters of thinly-sliced vegetables and bowls of green-flecked dip; cheeseboards and grapes on the kitchen's enormous island. Along the back counter, a row of wine bottles, red and white, and a display of delicate-stemmed wine glasses.

Maggie has been looking forward to getting together with the group, especially after Gunther texted that he was staying at Woody's, and Bruce assured her that he could use some time alone. She needs to air this latest outrage; she needs the support of sympathetic friends.

Yet so far this evening, no one has mentioned the signs; no one has mentioned the website. Have they seen them? Are they playing dumb? It feels not as though she's invisible, but rather that she's untouchable, her anger and hurt communicable, a disease from which they might need to protect themselves.

Holding her glass of red wine, Maggie listens to the women as they stroke the green and gray surface of Kathie's countertop and exclaim, "It's the ocean," "it's like weather," "glorious." She stares down at her reflection in the countertop. It feels as though she is looking up at herself from a glistening bog. The red of her wine a distant cranberry floating near her chin.

For years the group has served as a place to vent the wrongs done by coaches, teachers, school administrators, bosses, and wait staff. It's been a place to share life's "boo-boos," no matter how minor. The book group's unconditional love has been a relief and a revelation to Maggie, whose mother, stern, reserved, working hard to pass her CPA after Maggie's father died, believed in sucking it up. But now as the women shuttle from the kitchen to the living room, settle into leather love seats and chairs and sink to the plush rug, Maggie finds herself buttoning it, her mother's daughter.

Tonight's agenda, aside from admiring Kathie's kitchen, is to make up the list for the next six months of reading. Making the book list always involves a bit of jockeying. The serious readers, Maggie, Bunny Farnsworth, Kathie, make their cases for what they think everyone else in the group should read.

Maggie settles herself on one end of the love seat. Charlotte, who has come in late, plops beside her, flashes a sideways smile. Is it a signal?

"Catch me up, guys," Charlotte says. "What have I missed? Sex, drugs, and rock 'n roll?"

Jane, a petite blonde, who owns a real estate agency in town, laughs. "Not much. We're still getting tanked."

"That sounds good," says Charlotte. "I just assumed you all'd be discussing how we're going to hack the Padrushkys' website and start our own campaign. 'Save Shawnee.' What kind of bullshit is that?" Charlotte's face is flushed, eager. She takes a long swallow of wine.

The room goes silent, and Maggie feels her cheeks stiffen. She'd like to hug Charlotte, but everyone else in the circle freezes, staring into their drinks, gazing at their nails.

Maggie, too, looks into her glass. "We don't *have* to discuss it." Her defensiveness, after all, is impossible to hide.

Kathie clinks her wine glass hard on the marble coffee table. "We *do* have to talk about it. I agree, Charlotte. I just didn't know if you wanted to go there, Maggie."

"We thought you might need a break," Jane says, setting the others nodding.

"Oh, thank god," says Maggie. "I was getting paranoid. I thought maybe you guys didn't care. I'm dying to talk about it with my friends. I'm completely freaked out."

Now everyone is bursting with *sorry's* and *it sucks*. Kathie rushes over to her for a hug, *Of course we care*, and Charlotte squeezes her arm. The group breaks into pairs, burbling their condemnation of the events and their dismay at how their friend has been wronged.

All except for Bunny Farnsworth who flicks back a strand of her satin-smooth hair, and says, "I know it's important, but can we discuss this shit later and talk about books now? I've got an expensive babysitter."

Michelle Jones, the Superintendent's wife, who has just come back from a makeover with an expert at the Mall of America and is almost unrecognizable beneath a cascade of auburn curls, leans in toward Bunny. "Do you want me to pay for your fucking babysitter? Maggie and her family have been attacked."

Bunny sniffs. "I know that, Michelle, and, for the record, so have we. According to the *The New York Times*, we're all a bunch of racists. We're all ignorant hicks who shoot at black people without thinking twice."

"Jesus, Bunny." Kathie frowns.

"*Maggie's* not saying that," Jane snaps. She looks, as do the others, at Maggie, needing her to say something.

She can't. Electric wire wraps her head. The pain is searing. Bunny is speaking again, her words as shrill in Maggie's ears as a dentist's drill.

"Maggie's not saying it, but has she rebutted it? Has she written a Letter to the Editor of the *Times* or even *The Daily Journal*? I'm just saying, the Padrushkys may be way out of line, but the residents of Lake Village aren't."

Michelle nods. "My aunt in California called wondering if I live in the same 'Lake Village' she heard about on TV."

"It's not like the media makes it sound. That's for sure," Kathie says.

"I've been getting a shitload of emails from downstate realtors, and two closings were put off this week. Buyers aren't sure they want to move to *that* Lake Village."

Then everyone except Maggie and Charlotte is talking, shifting seamlessly from stories of justice to injustice, like a school of nervous minnows stirring with the pull of the swiftly moving current. When they finally settle, it is Michelle who asks in a tone straining to sound neutral, "Do you think we're racist, Maggie?"

Maggie opens her mouth; everyone is staring at her, awaiting her answer. How has the conversation gotten here? With the people only half an hour ago she thought of as safe? "Of course, I don't think you're racist. You're my friends."

The women exhale, "We love Gunther," "He's a great kid," "So polite," "You've done a great job." They sound as giddy as if they've been dismissed as targets of a firing squad.

Maggie will always remember that she heard quite clearly a voice in her head that warned her to stop, to hold off saying what she most wanted to say. She remembers just as clearly deciding to ignore that warning, needing like a stubborn child to prove for herself that flame truly burns.

She clears her throat, steadies her voice. "But let's face it. The town we all live in is white. We *chose* to live here. Do you ever think about why?"

In the stillness, the only sound is a faint thumping from a room somewhere in the vast house; the bass line of an electric guitar. One of Kathie's kids must be practicing. It could be a stand-in for the thudding in Maggie's chest.

Bunny Farnsworth snaps open her leather-bound notebook. "*You* chose to live here, Maggie. You and Bruce chose to be Lake Village's rainbow family." She raises her pen like a dagger above the open page. "Now does anyone have a fucking book to recommend?"

Standing is difficult. Maggie's legs wobble like custard. Her feet and every other sense organ have gone numb. From a distance, she hears someone asking if she's okay; if she needs help. It might be Charlotte; it might be Kathie, or one of the other women. The idea is to keep her head high, the tears in check until she reaches her car. She passes through the bright kitchen, the countertop's luminous particles shining in infinite, swirling galaxies. A hand on her shoulder stops her. Kathie's. "I'm really sorry. You could stay. We'll strangle Bunny. Let's plan another meeting. Strategy. We want to support Gunther."

Maggie's mouth tightens. She manages a brief nod. Focus, she tells herself. You only have to make it to your car.

"Okay, well, take a bottle. Take two." Kathie snatches two bottles of wine, slips them into Maggie's tote.

Maggie is halfway down the driveway, when she hears Kathie shout, "What do you want us to read?"

Without hesitating, she shouts back, "Native Son." In it, she remembers, a black man accidentally murders a wealthy white woman. All of their fears come true.

In the dark of her car, Maggie clasps the steering wheel, lets the tears flow. When she is done, she wipes her eyes with a wad of mashed tissue she keeps under the arm rest; checks the mirror. The funny thing is, Maggie thinks, Bunny Farnsworth is right.

ELEVEN

BRUCE STANDS IN THE UPSTAIRS hallway outside Gunther's bedroom and wonders whether to knock or barge right in? Maggie's still at her book group, and he's been on the computer, looking for ways to shut down the Padrushkys' site. So far, his search has been fruitless, unless he wants to go the Dark Web. He might.

Through Gunther's door, he hears the heavy metal blasting away; the howls and moans of the musicians' primal pain. He gets it, though he has never screamed in his life, not even in front of the TV, watching the Bills blow it. He'd like to scream now, though, at the thought of the Padrushkys getting away with their crap, their blatant lies. His inability to do anything about it.

He knocks with medium intensity. A greeting, not a warning or a threat. No answer. No lowering of the music even. He imagines Gunther in an ecstasy of listening; thrashing the strings of an air guitar, drowning out the day's events, the new stress. Gun had a shrink visit today, Maggie told him earlier. Then he went straight to Woody's. He hasn't heard from Gunther except for a text in reply to his: *Chill, Dad. It's going to be* O.K. His son looking after him. He could have wept.

He knocks harder, still no answer, so he turns the knob, deciding he wants in.

The room is dark, almost pitch black, thanks to the vinyl shades duct-taped to the window frames. Overhead, the constellation of plastic stars that Gunther and he put up years ago glow in luminescent lumps. They tried to create the major constellations: the Big Dipper, Orion, Cassiopeia, and the Cygnet. But Gunther at eight was not coordinated enough to draw a grid, to place the stars, big and little, in their correct locations. On the wall opposite the end of Gunther's bed is a poster of Missy Elliot in hot pants and fishnets. (Bruce doesn't want to think about its positioning.) On a shelf above Gunther's desk, though it's too dark to see them, is a cluster of trophies, golden boys, clearing hurdles (subliminal encouragement, Bruce thinks); below them, a corkboard pinned with track meet schedules and chore reminders.

In the middle of the floor, a lava lamp glows, the liquid shapes elongating and sinking, only to rise and form again. Gunther and Woody sit, cross-legged, staring at the lamp as though they are stoned. They might be. But in the light, a clear glass bottle gleams like a diamond.

"Dad. Shit." Gunther leaps to his feet, accidentally kicking over the bottle. Gin spills in a wide river as he dives for his cell phone, perched in a speaker on the bookcase. Woody peels his shirt, mopping frantically at the gin.

"Lights!" Bruce roars. *Action.* But there is already way too much of that going on.

Woody finds the dangling string of the ceiling light and yanks. In the pale light of the frosted dome, the room seems even more surreal. Piles of dirty clothes rim the room like glacial ridges; the red blobs of the lava lamp having lost their luster still form and reform mindlessly.

"This is what you're up to? This is how you're spending your time?"

Gunther, still standing, looks down at the floor. "Sorry," he mutters.

"Me, too, sir." Woody's fingers fly reflexively to the agony of pimples on his left cheek.

What a loser, Bruce thinks. Then checks himself. The truth is that Ryan and Sam have stopped coming over. Track meets; girlfriends. Woody's the loyal one. "I'm disappointed." He picks up the near-empty bottle and sniffs the top. The sharpness of the gin fumes stings the inside of his nose. "You stole my alcohol?"

Gunther and Woody exchange a look.

Woody clears his throat. "No, sir. My mom—"

"Your mom?"

"She gave it to Gunther today. It was a present."

Bruce blinks. Can the world get any more absurd? "A present?"

Woody shrugs. "She knows what it's like when the shit hits the fan."

Woody's mother, Jolene. A bottle of decent gin would have cost her something. "Wow."

Gunther's strategy after the indictment has been to go along with the friends' excuses, to act like he believes them when they can't come over after school or hang out on the weekends. Not Bruce. Especially after today, he doesn't believe a goddamn word anyone says to him, not what they say to his face anyway. Suddenly, Bruce wants to weep with gratitude for Jolene's gift to his son. Something tangible. Something that might dull the pain. He'd like to take a slug of that gin himself. But the boys are still standing there, looking scared, awaiting his response, he guesses. Tall, handsome Gunther; stocky, pimpled Woody. Mutt and Jeff aching to become men.

He can feel the laughter rising, through his feet, through his ankles, inflating the space between muscle and bone, expanding his belly, his torso, his chest. Now it is breaking open at the base of his throat, rushing hard. With his mouth open, he is laughing, laughing so hard, his gut hurts, he doubles in pain, laughing so hard, he drops to his knees, from his knees to his side. He curls, laughing so hard that his heart squeezes, unclutches, and then he is sobbing.

Somewhere at the edge of his vision, he can see Gunther and Woody looking baffled. He can hear them open the bedroom door, back through it. He thinks for an instant of the consequences of his outburst, he thinks of trying to control himself, but he can't. He is caught in a tide that carries him swiftly from laughter to grief. He is seeing all of a sudden, his father dropping like felled timber in the aisle of the hardware store; he is remembering the terrible injustice of being cut from his program; he is remembering the day they brought Gunther home, innocent to their deed. He misses his father, he misses the joy of being a scientist; most of all, he misses the days when he and Maggie and Gunther seemed a normal family doing the best they could in the imperfect world.

TWELVE

AT EIGHT O'CLOCK SATURDAY MORNING, Dick Romley and his cronies are holding court in the back corner booth at May's Diner, just where Charlotte expects to see them.

"Hey, Charlotte," Dick waves, and the others, Drake Lyman, Bob Donner, Andy Pates turn her way in unison, like someone jerked an invisible string threaded through their jaws.

"Hey," Charlotte says, climbing onto a round stool at the Formica counter diagonally across from their booth. She could pretend to consult the menu, but it's truly not necessary. Everything at May's is familiar. The cow figurines, each dressed in a different costume lined up on the shelf above the coffeemaker; the Wilco Insurance Company calendar depicting, no matter the season, a horse and sleigh piled with wreaths and gifts; the glass case of shivering cream pies.

May stands behind the counter, pencil poised above her order pad. She's a thin woman with boy-short hair and a boat tan. A gold cross the size of a matchbook lies on her freckled chest. "I know, 'two rubber eggs. And dry wheat toast and coffee, milk, no cream.'"

"The usual."

"You betcha." May rips the order off her pad. The door swings open to the kitchen, and Charlotte inhales the heavenly smell of potatoes deep-frying in hot oil and bacon sizzling on the grill—the smells that make her feel like life is good even when it isn't. Take the weirdness of last night's book group. After Maggie left, not one book got decided on, not one, because everyone was so worked up about whether the town is racist and whether Shawnee Padrushky should go to a mental hospital or to jail.

The mug that May plops in front of Charlotte has a graying rim, lightly cracked. But you don't complain to May unless you're from away and don't plan on coming back. Charlotte tips in some milk. "Thanks," she says.

"What's new over there, pussycat?" Dick Romley bellows from his corner booth. (Dick's Corner, people call it.)

Charlotte raises the porcelain mug and sips, savoring the coffee's warmth, its hint of bitterness. She'll acknowledge Dick Romley when she's ready, thank you very much.

"Charlotte?"

Patting her lips on the diner napkin, Charlotte turns away from the counter to face Dick's booth. "Something bothering you, Dickie?" She knows what Dick's after. She was the court reporter for the grand jury trial; she's Maggie Cannon's friend. He should also know that it's useless to pry anything out of her.

"Never a dull moment in this town."

"There used to be," Charlotte says. "It wasn't so bad. Right, Drake?"

Charlotte's known Drake Lyman all of her life. His family owned the pharmacy in town, a beautiful old place with wooden cabinets, a tiled floor, and even, way back, a soda fountain. Now Drake works behind the Lucite panels of the pharmacy in the supermarket, and

Charlotte drives all the way to Connorsville to make sure he doesn't know her prescriptions.

"I don't know, Charlotte."

"Sure you do. But some people will do anything to stir up a little excitement."

Whistles start up then; Bob Donner shoves his shoulder lightly against Dick's.

"Is something bothering you this morning, Charlotte? Woke up the wrong side of bed?"

"It's the only side I've been waking up on for weeks."

"Paper's out," Dick says. "Did you see it, Charlotte?"

Dick Romley, editor and publisher of the *Lake Village Journal*, an away person with enough dough—he bought the newspaper and the radio station five years ago, straight cash—that he thinks he belongs. "Something in *The Daily Urinal* I should read?"

"She's good," Bob Donner mutters.

May lifts the coffee pot. "If there's going to be a fight, take it outside or get this dumped on your head."

Dick slaps the table. "Fight? Nah. I just thought Charlotte might be interested in my editorial, that's all. You know Padrushky, Jr., don't you? I hear he was a sweet kid."

"He was."

"So, what happened?"

"Million-dollar question."

"He was bullied." A man who Charlotte hadn't noticed before is standing at the register as May hands him his takeout order.

"Oh yeah? By who?" Charlotte asks. She can feel her heartbeat kicking up to hummingbird speed.

"It's on-line. The black kid's a bully. That's the truth. None of this bullshit, *dis*-information you're getting on the news."

Charlotte has the man in full view now. Shaved head; tattoos wrapped like cartoons from biceps to wrists. "Now who's dissing who?" she asks.

"I'm not dissing nobody, but who do you believe—a con artist or an altar boy?" The man grabs the knotted handles of his plastic bag and pivots toward the exit. A hard jingle of bells sounds in his wake.

"Have a nice day, asshole."

"Charlotte? Warm-up?" May moves away from the register, picks up the coffee pot.

"I think she's plenty warmed up," Dick says, raising his open palm to receive high fives from the other men in his booth.

Charlotte presses her lips. Her head is suddenly filled with heat and her heart is thudding. Calm down, she tells herself. She can't afford to explode, not in front of Dick Romley and his buds. "Who was that jerk?"

May shrugs. "Might be one of the McCreery boys growed up. Hard to tell."

McCreery. Could be. Trailer trash at best. She went to school with a pack of them. One kid getting in more trouble than the next if that was possible. "Fun type."

"Uh huh. Eggs here." May sets a plate on the counter in front of Charlotte. "Anything else, Hon? As long as it's legal."

"Jeeze, that's no fun." Charlotte turns her attention to salting and peppering her eggs, then dousing them in hot sauce. "Texas eggs," her mother used to call them, though her mother never once stepped foot in Texas.

May hands her the check, and Charlotte slips a five-dollar bill under her plate to cover the tab; at the bottom of her purse she finds another dollar in change for the tip.

"Okay, Dick, what did you write that you're so pleased with yourself?"

From Romley's booth, the men look over at her with sly smiles.

"She's calling you out, Dick. She's tough."

"Yes. I'm tough. So, what is it?"

Dick smiles. "All I said was that Gunther was in the wrong place at the wrong time."

"What's that supposed to mean?"

"What I said."

"No, you mean something by it."

"I mean the kid was unlucky."

"No. That's not what you mean. You know it. I know it. The town knows it. You mean Gunther Cannon is in the wrong place, living in Lake Village."

The men on either side of Romley shift in their seats, some blinking, some examining the invisible contents of their coffee mugs.

Dick Romley tightens his smile; his eyes give off mean little lights. "Your words, Charlotte. Not mine."

There are things Charlotte wants to say but can't. It's like keeping a dragon in a Ball jar. It wants to leap out. But as a court reporter, she is sworn to secrecy. She can't tell Romley about Shawnee's neatly penned plans; his perfectly punctuated sentences; the parallel clauses that she'll never forget: *Find a nigger. Shoot him. Rid the world of undesirables.* Yes, it would be nice to have a simple answer as soothing as eggs and bacon and warm toast. God, she wishes there was one. But there isn't. Neither bullying, nor insanity can account for what the evidence points to—pure, unadulterated hate.

THIRTEEN

"Grab a seat," Jerry says. "You want some coffee? A pastry?" Jerry Manchuso, Mayor of Lake Village, is a thick-necked man with a stomach that sags over his belt like it's weighted with wet laundry. Rumor has it he made his money Downstate, garbage disposal or plumbing, wink wink, before moving Upstate to live out his days in peace. Some people love him because they don't have to pay him (he donates his mayoral salary to local charities); some because he plays well with others and doesn't make waves with the unions. Hopper doesn't hold a firm opinion; they rarely meet.

"Is that all you got? You offered breakfast."

To Hopper's surprise, Jerry looks embarrassed. "I'll fry up some eggs if you need them."

"Nah. Coffee. Black." He pulls out a chair at the oak table where Charlie Rothberg is already seated.

Charlie, white-haired, pink-faced, extends his hand. "Did Manchuso offer you a four-course meal or something?"

"He promised we'd be chewing on something other than horseshit."

Charlie clears his throat. "Thanks for coming. We don't want to waste your time."

"Good. So, what's this about?" Hopper doesn't mind Charlie much, though he has had a thought of investigating the Chambers' doings for the past year. He's heard some murmurings around town that Charlie's been skimming.

"Hang on," says Jerry, handing Hopper a mug of coffee. "We're waiting for—"

As if on cue, Father Lambert steps into the kitchen.

"Hello, Father." Hopper stands and offers his hand.

"Mr. Hopper."

Hopper is surprised by the firmness of the older man's grip, a courtesy and a warning as though they were about to fight a duel. He and Father Lambert have met a dozen times at this town function or that. And once as the priest was on his way to visit a young man in the County jail, a prisoner who to Hopper's mind discovered Jesus to relieve his boredom.

The others at the table murmur their greetings as Father Lambert seats himself, tucking his robes under his long thighs like an old woman afraid of chill.

"Let's cut to it," Jerry Manchuso says.

There's always an alpha, Hopper thinks. "Let's."

"Here it is straight. This is a small town. We got a weak economy even in the best of times, and god knows this isn't the best of times."

"More like the worst," Charlie Rothberg pipes.

Jerry nods but shoots Charlie a stare that tells him to shut up. "We got to squeeze every little bit of income we can out of those tourist dollars. We got to keep up to our message, our brand—"

"Cut to it, Jerry," Hopper says. "I need to hear something I don't know before my coffee gets cold."

"I'll say it." Charlie leans toward Hopper. "Padrushky's trial is going to focus national media attention again on Lake Village just when tourist season's picking up. We're talking now through Labor Day weekend and into Leaf Peeper season. All this racial stuff plastered all over the place. It's going to be a shark feed."

Hopper scoots his chair back a couple of inches, rests his forearms on the table. He is starting to enjoy this meeting. "I agree, by the end of the summer, there will hardly be anyone who hasn't heard of Lake Village, America's *Perfectly* Racist Town. But I read somewhere that bad publicity is as good as positive."

"Jesus, Hopper," Jerry says, "who rammed a stick up your ass?"

"Gentlemen." Father Lambert presses his palms together as though he might be starting to pray. "Please."

The men rumble their apologies while Hopper stays silent. Then Charlie Rothberg speaks again.

"I represent, as you know, the downtown merchants and the B & B and Innkeepers' Association. Everyone's in a panic. This trial could affect us for years. Ruin our town. And let's face it, why should these people suffer for something one lunatic did?"

Father Lambert clears his throat lightly but stays silent.

"You're saying what?" Hopper says. "Come on, someone spill it, or I'm taking my appetite down to Mickey D's and get me a real breakfast." He leans his weight on his palms, makes like he's getting up.

"Mr. Hopper." Father Lambert places his hand with the rosary on the table, his fingers still moving bead to bead. "What we're trying to say is we'd like you to offer Shawnee Padrushky a plea option. We'd like you to remove the felony charge."

"The charge of hate crime."

Father Lambert nods. "Yes. That."

"You don't know what you're asking, Father."

"I believe I do. I've been reading the law. I know how long Shawnee will be incarcerated if he's convicted."

"Oh, he *will* be convicted. No doubt of that. The evidence is clear—"

"Please consider, Mr. Hopper, if the boy receives the maximum penalty, he's lost a lifetime. His soul will die. He'll have no chance to rebuild his life."

Hopper feels his jaw tighten, his ears heating. Who gave Father Lambert the manual on the shelf life of a soul? "How about Gunther Cannon? Does *his* life count here? Most of the time we look to protect the *victim*, not the attacker."

Father Lambert is nodding. The others are frozen, not saying anything. The priest has sharp high cheekbones, an eagle's jutting beak. He might be a wind-beaten seventy or eighty, but there's nothing elderly about his eyes. Hopper's seen eyes like that, a gaze like that. They belong to the most confident of defense lawyers; the truly brilliant ones.

Father Lambert rummages in the pocket of his robe, shifting slightly to the left, going deep as he gropes for something in the material. On the table, he places a small, yellow notepad with a thin cardboard cover. He slips on his reading glasses then flips the cover back to peer at his own scrawl.

Yes, a real pro, Hopper thinks.

"I had an interesting visit yesterday afternoon." Father Lambert taps the notepad with his forefinger. "A woman came to see me in much distress. A good Christian woman, a regular congregant, a woman who's lived in Lake Village all of her life, respected, honest. Reliable. She's in a hurry. 'Now or never, she says. We go into my office and we sit. When her tears stop, she speaks. She witnessed something, she tells me. Something truly horrible, truly ugly, an offense against God is how she puts it.

"'What was that?' I asked her. She saw something through the cafeteria window at the high school last fall, she told me. Something she should have reported, but did not, because she was afraid. A boy, a football player, she said, went flying past her window, a dark-skinned boy, running like his life depended on it. She only took notice she said, because a minute or two later, the rest of the team came tearing, like *they was shot from a cannon*. They were coming from the cement tunnel that the kids sometimes take as a shortcut from one playing field to another. They're chasing him, she thought. But then, she saw something else. A couple of the boys were dragging something, some *one*. She was about to call out when a whistle went off, they scattered, and a coach took charge. The boy they left behind stood up. He wasn't wearing any pants. Completely exposed. It was Shawnee Padrushky."

Hopper feels his gut tighten. *Good one, Father.* "Did she identify any of the boys?"

"Their backs were to her; all she could see were their jerseys. Except the one. The only one she was sure she saw was dark-skinned. The only one."

"And Padrushky," Charlie Rothberg adds.

Father Lambert nods. "Yes."

Convenient. Hopper pushes back his chair and stands. "I'm leaving, folks. Thanks for nothing."

The other men at the table follow his movement with their eyes, their expressions grim.

"My parishioner is willing to be deposed if necessary. She's willing to swear an oath."

Hopper turns to face Father Lambert. "Listen, Father, what your alleged witness swears won't affect my thinking one bit. Don't even begin to get your hopes up. I appreciate you wanting to tend your flock, to 'save Shawnee,' but take a prosecutor's advice—stay out of it."

When Hopper gets home, he cuts the engine, letting the cab rock a minute. He's got to cool himself down or Penny will be on top of him to watch his pressure. Even with the walking and breathing stuff she's got him doing, his read is a mile high. But exactly how is he going to calm himself? An *alleged* witness, he reminds himself. To *alleged* bullying. A bullshit witness. Still, Father Lambert runs a good bluff. The collar doesn't hurt.

Penny is at the kitchen counter, twisting a tray of ice cubes into a glass pitcher. She looks up. "What?"

"Assholes. All of them."

"Here." She hands him a glass of iced tea, which he accepts, gulping it as though he's parched.

"They've got something on Gunther, they say. I'm sure it's bull. But what if Adkins is sending me a signal here? What do I do, Penny?"

"Call the Cannons," she says. "Set up a meeting. Let them decide what kind of risk they want to take."

"Yeah, but that's risky, too. I have to decide what risk *I'm* willing to take. This is a big case. If it goes to trial, I have to win it. I'm not going to admit to anyone but you—the 'Save Shawnee' shit? It's working."

FOURTEEN

In the police van, the prisoner beside him farts and the air is suddenly thick with sulfur; no one says a word. The farter is a heavy black man, his arms hilled with muscle; his jaw as solid as a pit's. If he wants to die, Shawnee thinks, he can say something right now, make it happen in minutes. This is his chance. The only thing he cares about is the Cause, and the best he can do for the Cause is to eliminate himself. He tried once, and he failed. We need a martyr, they said, and he was ready for that; he had been so ready. But he failed. No one understands how badly he failed except his Brothers, and he cannot talk to them. If he could, he would bow before them, put his neck on a block. He would sacrifice his life over and over again if he could. He can't. Not here where the eyes are on him. Here, the torture is they will keep him alive. When he closes his eyes, the Failure plays over and over again. He is running, he is taking aim, he is shooting, and missing. The target's head should have spilled its seed all over the bricks. But he missed. At short range. At no range. He should have been his father's bitch, not the priest's. He should have practiced shooting straight, not Bach. Waste of time, so the next thing he is running, then kneeling, then shooting himself and what the fuck happened that he is still alive? God's angel shoved his hand, his mother said. Like she knew. Satan, rather, laughing his guts out.

"Stinks in here," he says. He imagines the words hovering, finding their man, firing. He's not missing this time. "Stinks like monkey shit."

The other prisoners shift in their seats; someone behind him turns a laugh into a cough.

"Shut up back there," a guard shouts from the front seat. He glares at Shawnee in the rearview mirror. "Whoever's doing the talking, zip it."

Beside him, the farter is silent, but Shawnee can see his dark eyeball glistening, all pupil, like a lizard's. He is smiling the slightest of smiles, like someone waking from a good dream, a dream of eating something delicious or fucking someone deeply. He winks.

Yes, I'm going to die. Pure relief.

FIFTEEN

CHARLOTTE DOESN'T REALLY THINK that Maggie will accept her invitation for a drink tonight. But between Dick Romley's editorial this morning, the Padrushky's website, and Bunny Farnsworth's callousness yesterday at book group, she feels she has to reach out. It's the only decent thing to do.

To her surprise, Maggie texts right back. "I'm in."

The bar in the front room of the Woodfire Café is nearly empty. Most of the customers—students, professors—Connorsville-types, are eating out back on the Cafe's deck. That's where Charlotte would rather be, but Maggie needs to sit inside. She's nervous, she says, about bumping into people, even good people, tonight.

Charlotte picks up the bar menu, a narrow strip of laminated cardboard. The Woodfire is the last place she would have picked. Vegetarian. Over-priced. "I hope they serve real liquor."

"They don't. Beer and wine only."

"You tricked me."

"Sacrifices. But it's on me. You want to share nachos? Without sour cream?"

Charlotte rolls her eyes. "You mean the good stuff?"

"You can have it on the side."

The bartender hovers, his fingers splayed on his side of the bar. "Ladies?"

"A large order nachos. Sour cream on the side. A Corona for me—in the bottle—two limes."

"Same for me," Charlotte says. "One lime."

"I'm the picky New Yorker," Maggie says. "It's in my DNA."

"I'll say."

Maggie digs into her purse, pulls out her cell phone which she puts on the bar. "Rude, I know, but I might have to answer it. We're being bombarded again."

"It's okay," Charlotte says. She hasn't told Maggie yet about the head butt in May's this morning or the asshole at the register. On the way down to Connorsville, they kept the conversation to office gossip and the weather. Still Charlotte didn't miss that Maggie took the highway, the long route from Lake Village to Connorsville that bypassed the 'Save Shawnee' signs and kept the radio off. The elephant in the car was heavy enough to sink the tires.

The beer bottles arrive, plumed with slices of lime. Maggie squeezes one slice, then the other into her beer and takes a long pull without even a mock "cheers."

Charlotte understands. There's nothing to toast really. "Want to go there?" Charlotte's talking about what happened at book group, of course. She doesn't know if Maggie's read Dick Romley's editorial.

"Not really."

"Your call, you're buying."

"All I want to know is when did Bunny Farnsworth become such a jerk?"

Charlotte sips her beer. "There's always been potential."

"At least Kathie offered to set up a strategy meeting."

"What are you thinking?"

"Bruce wants to start a 'Save Gunther' website, but I'm not sure. I don't know if that would be effective."

"Eye for an eye."

"Exactly." Maggie belches lightly, her hand over her mouth. "Let's talk about something else. Any hot new men in town, looking for a good woman?"

"Do you mean a fat woman?" Charlotte steals a look at herself in the mirror that runs the length of the wall behind the bar. The woman who looks back at her has a round face, too round, she thinks, and piggy eyes too close to her nose. She takes a sip of her beer and turns her gaze away. Mercifully, the tiers of beer bottles cut off most of her body.

"Come on now. You told me you were exercising."

"I said it, doesn't mean it's true. I've given up. Exercise and men. The good ones are all taken"—her gaze dips. She's never told Maggie about her high school crush on Bruce, and she doesn't plan to now—"and the gay ones are great to talk to, but I need something extra."

Maggie nods. "I read about this app that works like a heat-sensing missile. You're sitting in a café and suddenly you've got the number of someone in the same place who's checking you out."

"Sounds dangerous." Charlotte hates it when her married friends act like they know what it's like to be single. "I'd rather take up horseback riding. They say it simulates the action."

"'Simulates' or 'stimulates'?"

"Maggie Cannon!" Charlotte laughs. Maggie with her hair down is fun.

"Excuse me. Hot plate." The bartender lowers a large oval plate onto the bar, then snags their empty beer bottles with his thumb and index finger. "Another round?"

"Not for me. I'm driving. Charlotte?"

"The price is right. Sure."

Maggie pulls off a hunk of chips puts them on her napkin. "We should do that."

"Go horseback riding?"

"Go down to the city, find you a hot—"

In the mirror above the bar, Charlotte notices a man enter the café. He's wearing a black Stetson and a long, leather jacket, a Marlboro Man come to life. "Maggie, don't move."

Maggie squints, following Charlotte's gaze to the mirror. "Oh shit. Padrushky."

"Stay calm."

"We've got to leave. Right now." Maggie dips her hand in her purse, opens her wallet, pulls out a twenty-dollar bill.

"He's coming over here."

"Now." Grabbing her phone, Maggie springs up, shoving the stool with her heel so hard that it topples backward, hitting the floor with a bang.

In a second, Sean Sr. is beside them, his eyes bright with triumph. "A little too much to drink, young lady?"

"Stay away from me, you fucker."

The bartender leans across the bar. "Do you ladies need help?"

Charlotte grabs Maggie's arm. "We need to get out of here."

Once inside the car, Maggie grips the steering wheel, then sticks the key in the ignition. "Ohmigod, look at my hand. I'm shaking. I got to call Bruce. This is crazy. Padrushky doesn't go to the Woodfire. He doesn't *accidentally* show up. He's trying to antagonize me, get me to do something stupid that he can post on his website. This is really scary."

Charlotte is silent. She's known Sean Sr. for years. Everyone agrees he's nuts, but is he dangerous? "You think he followed us?"

"Yes."

They are on the highway now. Maggie seems to be calming down. Her hands are steady on the wheel; her eyes are on the road; her speed is even, though a little fast.

"Shit. Is that the police?" In the rearview mirror, red and blue lights are twirling, ridiculously festive.

"Yes."

"I'm being pulled over?"

"Looks like it." Charlotte reaches for the hand grip above the door as Maggie swerves hard onto the shoulder and slows to a stop. In the moments of silence, before the trooper comes up to the car, Charlotte feels a strange peacefulness. She and Maggie could be two sea creatures in the dark, two immovable tortoises, slumbering on the beach.

The trooper knocks on the window and Maggie lowers it. Stone-faced, he probes their faces with his flashlight, next the car's interior.

"I'd like you to step out of the car, Ma'am. I need to see your license."

Charlotte hopes that Maggie will be quick about it, not get mouthy.

"You want me to get out of the car?"

"Yep. With your license."

"Was I speeding?"

"I watched you from down the road. Have you consumed alcohol in the past hour?"

"One beer. I'm not drunk. I wasn't speeding."

"From what I observed, I'd like you to take a sobriety test, or if you wish, a substitute, a Breathalyzer."

"Is this a joke?"

Charlotte chances a deep inhale. *Shut up and do it.*

The trooper squares his shoulders. "Step out of the car, Ma'am. Now."

Charlotte nudges Maggie's thigh. "Go," she whispers.

Maggie hesitates for another second then reaches for the door handle.

Charlotte lowers her window, breathes in the evening smells. Humid pavement and cool clover. Spring toads ringing like unchecked alarms. Through the windshield, she sees the trooper putting Maggie through her paces. The closed eyes, the nose touch. Then Maggie is leaning back and raising her arms like she is asking an orchestra to rise; then she is walking a straight line, heel to toe, no doubt counting her steps out loud like a kindergartner. Out there in the deep twilight, she is a one-woman circus, going through her tricks. She hopes to God that Maggie isn't legally drunk. It seems impossible, only one beer, but she's such a little thing.

When the trooper finally lets her go, Maggie sinks back into the driver's seat and closes her eyes. Dark is falling in tiny, peppery bits, minute pixels of black and white. Maggie reaches her hand toward Charlotte, dropping the car keys in her lap.

"Can you drive?" she asks.

"My pleasure," Charlotte says.

The phone is ringing as Charlotte comes through her back door into the kitchen. She thinks about letting the machine pick up; she is dead tired. Her body aches all over. Her plan is to run a bath, pour a drink, a whiskey. But these days, she makes herself answer the phone. There is so much happening it seems, and everything is urgent.

The caller is Marilyn. She sounds tense.

"What do you think I up and done?" she says.

"Joined the Army." Charlotte slides into the armchair by the telephone. All she wants now is ice cream, a big bowl of vanilla with hot fudge. Forget the drink.

"Confessed."

By god, this is too much for one night. "Confessed to what?"

She hears Marilyn heave a sigh. Her sister lives alone in a trailer next to the motel where she manages the night desk. Slow in the winter; busy in the summer. It complements her school job.

"It was eating me, you know. With all that's being written, with everything that's being said. The boy's been bullied, the boy's not been bullied—"

"Who'd you talk to?"

"Don't laugh."

"Dear Abbey?" Charlotte cradles the phone beneath her chin and heaves herself up. Is she going to tell Marilyn about tonight's adventure? First, she has to see if she has anything in the freezer.

"Father Lambert."

"You didn't."

"Like I told you, something was eating me."

"You didn't say what it was."

Marilyn lets out a sigh. "I saw those boys—those football players. I watched the way they were hassling Shawnee Padrushky."

"Not Gunther Cannon."

"The whole bunch. I was working the after-school program. I was putting away snacks, but I happened to look out the window. They were huddled like a pack of hyenas, headed for that big culvert, you know the one, the tunnel—"

Charlotte feels her gut clench. The tunnel. Yes, she knows it.

"I can see it from my window. They all duck in, Shawnee with them. They're sneaking a smoke or drinking a can of beer. I don't think a whole lot about it. What's it to me? All of a sudden, a kid comes flying out of the tunnel. I can't see the face, but I can see the color, if you know what I mean. And then the rest of that bunch comes out, running, and dragging something which they leave behind on the grass before scattering. It isn't a tasty bone on the ground, it's a kid. He's holding his privates and his pants are down, down around the ankles. It's a terrible thing to see. I'm reaching for my cell phone when Dewey Harter strolls up to the boy, strolls, mind you, like he must have been there all along or at least knew what could be happening."

"Screwy Dewy."

"No hand up, no nothing except a great big yank on the boy's pants."

"Up or down?" Charlotte feels her stomach turn. She remembers the warm spring night, the golf course in shadows, she and Dewey high on cough syrup, but that was no excuse for pushing past *No*. "Oh god, Marilyn, who was it?"

"Shawnee Padrushky was the boy. Gunther Cannon was in the pack. I'm sure of it."

"But you said he was running. Maybe he was scared of them, too."

"Maybe."

Marilyn is stubborn. You don't even try with Marilyn. "Why did you go to Father Lambert? Why not to the police?" Between the frozen pizza and the bags of peas, she spots a carton of cherry vanilla.

"This town's too small and life's too short."

Charlotte pries the lid off the ice cream. Forget the bowl. "What else didn't you see?" If there's one thing she has learned from her years as a court reporter—most witnesses get it wrong.

"I keep seeing your boyfriend—"

"Cut that out."

"His arm around Shawnee Padrushky's shoulders."

Charlotte puts her spoon down. She's eaten too much, too fast. Her whole head bursts with pain. She closes her eyes, and Dewey Harter's face appears, blood-filled and raging, his teeth clenched and his nostrils pulsing. Dewey Harter. Dewey Harter must have urged those boys on. Dewey Harter who on a night she trained herself not to think about, pinned her, spread her, raped her, on the wet ground.

"Charlotte?"

"Brain freeze. I'm eating ice cream."

"Have you been listening?"

"Every bit."

"Did I do the right thing?"

"Are you sure or *almost* sure you saw Shawnee Padrushky on the ground?" Her sister begins to hiccough. "Sip some water." Her sister always gets the hiccoughs when she is anxious.

"God only knows." She means this.

"Marilyn, how crazy do you think Sean, Sr. is? The father, not the son."

"What do you mean?"

"Would he hurt someone, do you think?"

"He hasn't killed anyone yet."

"Right. Okay." Charlotte stands up. She's trembling, her heart ramming the base of her throat. Even after all these years, she thinks, if she had a gun and good aim, she would shoot Harter, God help her. "I got to hang up now, sis. My head's pounding." In the silence, she knows Marilyn is contemplating whether to challenge the brush-off.

"Take three Advil," she says at last. "Two does nothing."

The only phone booth in town stands at the edge of the parking lot outside the county jail. Inside it, the air traps the smells of sweat and cigarette smoke and stale beer. Charlotte tightens her nostrils and reaches for the receiver, a thrill of distaste at the thought of touching an object so laden with strangers' germs. The telephone number, gleaned from the St. Vincent's roster of church members, is written in large numbers on a scrap of paper that she glances at now as she dials. Her index finger is trembling; her whole hand. It is as if she is dialing a secret code; a number which could unleash a nuclear force. If she misdials, she doubts she will have the courage to try again.

The receiver to her ear, Charlotte looks out. The moon is rising above the county jail, a huge bright moon, a pizza moon, pocked yet beautiful. She wonders if the prisoners can see it from their cells, if Shawnee can see it, then she remembers, he moved to State today.

That news, too, was in the paper. The phone stops ringing. A woman picks up. Charlotte starts to speak. She doesn't have a gun, but she knows someone who does.

SIXTEEN

THE KITCHEN IS FILTHY. Dirty dishes in the sink; bits of celery and onion, each in its own little puddle of grease strewn across the counter, and sitting on the stove top, a half-scraped skillet and a pot of slightly burned rice. Maggie's rage whistles through her skull, explodes.

She can hear the TV on in the living room; sports of some kind, turned up loud. "Hello?" she calls, moving toward the sound. "Hel-*lo*?" From the open doorway she sees Bruce and Gunther, a yoked team, bending toward the TV screen, cheering a player.

"Thanks a lot," she says, turning back to the kitchen, and its testosterone-fueled chaos. It looks like it's been a hell of a party without her. "Goddamn it."

"What's going on?" Bruce comes into the kitchen while Gunther hovers in the doorway. "What's wrong with you?"

"Everything. Every goddamned thing." She rests her palms on the kitchen island that Gunther assembled last Mother's Day.

"Like what?" Bruce asks.

Maggie shakes her head. The backs of her eyelids are burning. She doesn't want to cry, not in front of Gunther. She can see that he is already looking scared.

"Want some water?" Bruce pushes a glass under the faucet and opens the tap.

"Thank you."

"Okay. So what is it?"

Bruce hands her the glass, which she gratefully accepts.

"I was stopped by a trooper on the way back from Connersville."

"You were speeding?"

"No."

"You were *drunk*?" Gunther asks from the doorway, his voice rising in panic.

"I wasn't drunk, Gun. The trooper did the tests, and I passed them all."

"Oh, god." Bruce is shaking his head. "They tested you for a DWI?"

"I was completely sober." Maggie sets down her glass. Though she is telling the truth, she is suddenly awash in shame.

"Shit, mom. It's going to be in the paper. They'll make it *sound* like a DWI."

"I wasn't charged."

"So, what? Someone's going to post it, and everyone will believe it. It doesn't matter if it's true."

Maggie feels her gut flip. Gunther's right. It will be fodder for the Padrushkys. The occasion for more lies. "I'm sorry, Gun. It's horrible. I wish I could change it; I wish I could change everything." She moves toward Gunther. She needs to hug him, to show him how much she loves him and how sorry she is for all of the events that are out of her control.

But Gunther is already stepping back into the hallway, pivoting to head upstairs. "I got to go," he says.

"How about you help me clean the kitchen first?" Bruce says.

"I can't. I've got to check some things." Gunther's hand is on the bannister. He looks like he could launch himself up the whole flight with a single leap. "I gotta go—"

Maggie sighs. "Let him go, Bruce."

"On one condition—"

"Come on, Dad."

"No 'come on;' you do what you need to do in your room, then you move the laundry and you fold it."

"Okay, okay."

"*All* of the laundry."

"*Okay.*" Then he's up the stairs.

"Tonight," Bruce calls after him.

In the silence, Maggie and Bruce listen to the rapid thumping of Gunther's dash to his room.

"There's more," Maggie says, picking up the dirty skillet and lowering it into the sink.

"Jesus. What?"

"I think Padrushky sicced that trooper on me."

"Are you kidding?"

"He came into the Woodfire, and I got up so fast, my stool fell over. Next thing I know, he's in my face, asking if I'm drunk? I wanted to punch the guy."

"He would have charged you with harassment."

"I wanted to charge him with intimidation."

"Should we call Hopper?"

"Maybe, but I don't think this amounts to anything in his book."

"So, what do we do?"

Maggie hesitates. She hasn't told Bruce yet what happened at the book group. She's not sure why. "We need Bev."

"Bev? That's a switch, considering you drove her away."

"Do you have to remind me?"

"You had your reasons, I guess. I thought you were nuts."

"Okay," Maggie says. "I was nuts. I was an idiot. But it's done."

Bruce is in bed, the top sheet pulled over his ears, the fan blowing hard. He has left the TV on mute to provide Maggie with light to find the bed. It's amazing to Maggie that he can sleep after the day they've had.

Slipping beneath the covers, she reaches back, feels along the headboard for the remote, clicks off the TV. The room is bright with moonlight. It stripes their bed, illuminates the wall above her dresser, the framed photograph of her and Bruce, seventeen years younger, holding their newly adopted baby, Gunther. It is impossible, she thinks, that she and Bruce were once that young. She, in her big-framed glasses, and puff-sleeved dress; her curly hair layered in a near mullet. Bruce, with long sideburns, wearing his Parks Department shirt and slacks. Gunther, swaddled in a baby blanket, is no bigger than a football, tucked into Bruce's arm.

The beginning, Maggie thinks, when she and Bruce and Gunther lived in a one-room apartment, a 4th floor walk-up in the Heights, when she believed that the answer to the question, *Why do you want to adopt?* was incredibly simple: *We want to be parents.*

SEVENTEEN

WHEN THE TELEPHONE STARTS RINGING Saturday evening, Joanne is in the basement with the pups. They are her only joy now. She sits on the cement floor and the troops, as she calls them, come wiggling and racing toward her. She isn't sure why they come to her, but they do. Her good smells, her association with food. Then their warm plump bodies are on her and her hands on them, feeling their warm fat bellies, running her hands up and down their limbs, checking their joints, squeezing their paws. They are perfect, she thinks. A perfect litter. Not one flaw in any of them.

Sophie, the bitch, looks up from her bed in the corner, moves lazily toward her. When she reaches her, she sticks her muzzle up to her face and licks. Her way of showing appreciation, Joanne thinks. Thanks for taking the kids off my hands.

Through the ceiling, she can hear the telephone ringing in the kitchen, but no, she isn't going to answer it. If it's Sean Sr., she doesn't want to hear it. He left the house this morning after shutting himself in his study all night, chatting on-line with the "Save Shawnee" people, the SS, he calls them (though she warned him not to), working on new publicity angles, pitching ideas for the website. She's grateful for the support; truly, she is; but it's overwhelming, too, and she's afraid of it getting out of hand. That's Sean, Sr., out of hand and over-the-top.

She grabs a squeaky toy, a flattened squirrel, fake, of course, with spreading limbs and waves it above the puppies. Instantly, they gather, fighting each other for the toy, jumping and falling and struggling to right themselves. She's picked out the alpha; Rebel, she calls him. A brindle with caramel eyes. Already he's stouter than the others and knows how to use his teeth and his hips to shove in first at the food dish.

"Rebel." She reaches for him, pinching the base of his jaws. "Leave it." He does, and she rolls him on his back, ignoring his puppy growls, telling him to settle. Confident, yes; dominant, no. Her pits go out into the world socialized and friendly. If they can't achieve that, they go down.

She has always seen humans in the same light. That is why nothing now makes sense to her. Shawnee's behavior makes no sense. He has never been that alpha; he has never needed pinning down. Not like his father, god knows. So how did she miss the aggression in her own son when she can spot it in a dog like a bright red flag?

After changing the litter paper and giving the pups clean water and filling their bowl with kibble, Joanne heads back upstairs. The call might have been important, she thinks. Perhaps she should have run upstairs. At the kitchen sink, she washes her hands, then dries them on the terrycloth towel that hangs from the rack above the side board. The light on the answering machine is blinking. She'll listen, after all. Joanne presses the "play" button, her hip butted against the counter. A voice comes on. A woman's. Joanne frowns. Who is this?

Listen. I am not a friend; I am not an enemy, either. You need to know something. Your son was a victim; this fall, someone witnessed the

Lake Village High Football team under the auspices of Coach Harter, haze your son. It was bad, real bad. God bless. I hope Shawnee gets help.

Joanne straightens, grabs a pencil from the jar on the counter and a square of paper from the box next to it. She hasn't heard right. She hasn't caught everything. She pushes the button again, her pencil poised. "Victim," she scribbles. "Football. Harter. Haze." She stares at the words and her stomach flips, her head fills with rage. Dewey Harter. Shawnee's coach. Not for long. Shawnee quit football. He wouldn't say why, no matter how hard his father pushed him. He went back to his room. He wrote *Forboten* on his door in black Sharpie and got punished for it. He locked his door and didn't come out except for school. He grew thin again and mushroom pale; there were shadows under his eyes. Did she ever ask, is something wrong? No. She never would have asked something like that outright and in the open. That wasn't their way.

EIGHTEEN

MAGGIE CAN'T SLEEP. Every time she closes her eyes, she's seeing Sean Sr.'s gloating sneer as she leaps back from the bar; she's seeing 'Save Shawnee' signs spaced along the county road; she's seeing the state trooper's cold dark eyes and hearing his uninflected commands. Her limbs twitch beneath the thin sheet; she tosses, flipping side to side. It feels like her nerves have been switched to "on"; her veins course with energy. *Act.*

In a second, she is climbing out of bed and heading downstairs, through the kitchen and into the mudroom where she grabs her barn coat from the rack and throws it over her pajamas, shoves her bare feet into rubber boots. From the hook inside the door, she snatches her car keys, her purse. She's never felt anything quite like this before. Like her brain is running on the bright fuel of the moonlight.

Outside the air smells of iron, the clouds are doing strange things. There are places in the sky that look like piles of ash, like the dregs of something that has been burning for a long, long time. In other places, the clouds are strands of cotton twisted against the dark sky.

In the silent dark, it feels to Maggie as though the car is driving itself, that it is pulling her where it wants to go, past the high school and its playing fields, the chain hardware store that put the smaller hardware stores out of business, the mini-mall with the supermarket and the McDonald's.

They live in a split-level, set far back enough that the flood lights do not sense the motion of the car's tires as Maggie parks. Nor do the dogs sleeping in their kennels behind the chain link fence. She hesitates for only a second, taking in the utter blandness of the house's façade; the white siding, the well-trimmed shrubs bound in netting as though they had either just arrived or are about to be shipped off. A man could play Bach on his lunch break and go back to work at Auschwitz in the afternoon. This tidy little house sheltered the boy who revered Hitler, the boy who tried to kill her son. This house now shelters the man who would finish the job if he could.

A flock of yard signs, dense as feeding geese, stand clustered on the crown of the lawn. Maggie grabs the closest one and tugs hard. Stifling a yelp, she drops the sign. Blood beads at the tips of her middle and index fingers. An open staple. She shakes her hand against the pain; surely the dogs have heard her; surely, Sean Sr. will soon be flying across the lawn, his .22 aimed at her head. *Die, bitch.*

The driveway stays dark; the lawn still lit by the over-bright moon. She needs to work quickly; she needs to pay attention to where she grabs. The soil is moist; the metal stakes slide out easily. Clutching the signs, she drags them to her car and tosses them in the back.

Up and down the road she goes, stuffing her car with signs until even with the seats down, she can't fit any more. At the dump at the edge of town, she works her boots through the mud, then tramples the signs as best she can before heaving them into the gaping pit.

Back in their bedroom, Bruce is a large mound underneath the blanket. His snoring sounds raw as though he is in pain. Maggie slides in beside him and curls on her side so that their lowest vertebrae touch. Ordinarily, when he is snoring this loudly, she gives him a swift, selfish elbow, not caring if it hurts. Tonight, she keeps her elbows tight; she does not move a muscle, though she would like to howl in triumph. She enters the sound of his snores and tells herself to stay there. It is like trying to balance in the hull of a storm-tossed ship or in the belly of a whale. But she does not dare to wake him; she does not want to tell him where she has been, or what she has done. It is her mad, wonderful secret.

NINETEEN

Lying on his bed, looking at his laptop, Gunther hears his mother calling his name and decides to ignore her. It's Sunday morning, and just as he predicted, on their website, the Padrushkys are calling his mom an alcoholic scumbag who drives to Connorsville to get her "fix." Beside him on the bed, his cell phone is blowing up. All of his friends and hundreds of strangers, texting, tweeting that they've got his back. He's grateful, but he's scared.

Last night he dreamed he was running, not hurdling. He was racing across a red desert when he hit a dead end, a rock face that seemed to reach to the sky. He remembers looking up at it, searching frantically for a ledge to grab, but there was nothing, not a single rock or root to hang onto. Behind him, the earth was shaking; a herd of buffalo were stampeding. In the nick of time, he woke, jolting upright, in a sweat, still hearing the pounding of hooves.

There's a knock on his door, then his mom is standing there, dressed like she's going to work.

"Excuse me. Are you planning to get up today?"

He shoots her what he hopes is his most bleary-eyed look, pupils drifting, lids half-open. "It's Sunday."

"Exactly. And do you remember that Minister Gilbert is coming here in an hour?"

"Wha-a-at?" He puts down his phone. "You never told me that."

"Of course, I did."

Did she? Probably. He wasn't paying much attention. "What's she doing here?"

"I think the UU wants to offer their support."

Support. Like they're some kind of rickety old building or something. A falling down porch roof held up with a notched board like some of the roofs in Ms. Bev's old neighborhood.

"So, you need to eat something and get dressed, and I could use some help around the place, getting the downstairs to look decent."

He props himself on his pillows, still scanning texts. His mom doesn't move.

"I mean it, Gun. Get ready. You're not going anywhere until after the minister's visit."

"Chil-*lax*. I didn't say I was going anywhere. I'm going to help you." Is he though? Most likely, not.

"Thank you. I appreciate that."

He expects her to close the door, leave him alone, but she is still standing there, one hand on the knob. Then her chin drops; her shoulders start rising and falling in little jerks.

Oh shit. "Mom? You okay?"

She doesn't answer.

"Mom?" He throws back the covers, swings his long legs over the edge of the bed. The floorboards are cool under his bare feet. "Do you want me to call Dad?" On Sunday mornings, his dad is always at the Club.

His mom lifts her chin, her eyes runny and grateful-looking like he's handed her a bouquet of Mother's Day flowers. "No. I just need your help."

"You sure, Mom?" He's thinking of how crazy she was last night, yelling at him and his dad even though she was the one who screwed up. "I think you might need to talk to him."

"Dad'll be home soon—before Minister Gilbert gets here. In the meantime, let's just get our act together."

Our? But that's his mom. In front of his eyes, she snaps herself whole like a tent frame. You'd never know that a minute ago, she was in pieces.

◈

From the top of the stairs, Gunther can hear his mom and dad greeting the minister in the front hall. His mom is talking too much and too fast, the way she does when she's nervous; his dad is the opposite. The more nervous he gets, the quieter he is, until it is almost like being in the same room with a giant rock. He's a little bit more like his mom. Bad vibes make him nervous, make him want to crack jokes, do stupid stuff to make people laugh. At least that's the way he was before the incident.

As soon as his mother sees him on the landing, she smiles at him in a super-happy way that shows again how nervous she is, and the minister waves and smiles in a super-friendly way, too, that makes *him* nervous. He remembers his first grade Sunday School teacher, someone's mom, telling his mom, "I never notice a person's color when they walk into a room." Even by that age, he knew that was stupid. He always noticed, and people, white people, always noticed him. They more than noticed. They stared. Like Minister Gilbert is staring at him now, like she is remembering all of a sudden what he looks like, that he is black.

"Hi," he says and joins his parents. He doesn't know Minister Gilbert. She's new since he graduated from Sunday school. He never goes to the Unitarian church anymore. Only his mom goes from time to time, and that's because someone started a group to raise money for the victims of police brutality.

"Gunther."

The Minister's hand is small and firm. She shakes hard like a man.

"Why don't we sit in here?" his mother says. She herds the minister into the living room while his dad cuts past them into the kitchen. He wishes he could follow his dad, but he knows he'll be in trouble if he does.

Instead, he drops onto the sofa, the end farthest from where the minister is seated in the leather chair that is usually his father's. The minister's hair is cut as short as a boy's, and she is wearing a white sleeveless shirt and khaki pants the same shade as his own. The big brown chair makes her look tiny, like he felt in Dr. Bowman's chair. Her feet barely touch the floor.

"You have a beautiful house," the minister says, scooting forward.

Gunther follows her gaze. He doesn't think of his house that way, it's just his house. But for the minister's visit, his mom cleaned up the whole downstairs before he even got out of his shower. She stuffed all the newspapers (she's keeping a scrapbook of the stuff written about him), the file cases, the books that are usually piled on the dining room table into the hall closet and closed the doors of the TV hutch. It looks like a different house this way. Like a library almost; tons of books on the shelves; his mom's piano in the corner. They look like different people; his mom in clean jeans, pink polo, low-heeled sandals; he, in his preppy outfit, the shirt with the thin blue stripes his mother likes and the perfectly-cuffed slacks. Only his dad in his grass-stained jeans and t-shirt looks normal because he's stopping home from work.

"Coffee?" his mother is asking Minister Gilbert. "Tea?" She bumps him with her hip to make room on the sofa even though there is plenty. Is it some kind of signal?

"I'm fine. All coffeed up. Anymore and I'd start to shake."

"Bruce," his mother calls to his father. "No coffee needed."

They listen to his father clattering in the kitchen for a moment before his mother says, "Tell your father no coffee. We need him here."

"I hear you, Maggie." His father comes back, empty-handed, into the living room and pauses, surveying them, before settling into the sloping seat of the pine rocker.

Minister Gilbert brings her palms together at her chest like she's going to pray. "So, you're wondering why I'm here."

His mother is nodding, tilting like a long jumper getting ready to launch. His father clears his throat, his knees splaying.

"First, let me say, this visit is long overdue. I know I should have checked in on you all sooner, and I apologize."

Gunther hears his mother suck in her breath. He hopes she isn't going to tell the minister off.

"That's all right," his mother says. "You're here now. We appreciate that. Especially since the new turn of events."

"How are *you* doing, Gunther? Are you okay?"

The minister's eyes are dark brown, almost black. Folded into the curve of one nostril is a mole the color of dried blood. Gunther swallows and looks away, his voice caught somewhere in his chest. So many people ask him this question, he should be used to it. But sometimes, like this time, when it seems like the person really means it, it catches him off guard.

His father tilts forward in the rocker. "We're doing better since Padrushky was put in a real jail. You probably saw that in the paper."

"I read about it, yes, and that's one of the reasons I wanted to meet with you." The minister clasps her hands; her mouth flattens. "You know the UU supports your family. In fact, recently, we formed a committee to look into the role that bias in our education system may account for the rise in hate crimes. We all recognize the seriousness of the hate crime allegation, and we want to be there for Gunther—"

"Remind me," his mother says, cutting a look at his father, "we've got to get our dues in."

Minister Gilbert shakes her head. "That's not what I'm here for. That's not the issue. No. I had a visit yesterday from a group of UU members who feel that it's important that the other boy be supported as well as Gunther; they feel strongly that the other boy—"

His mother tenses instantly. "Are you talking about Shawnee Padrushky?"

"Yes. The group is worried that this young man will not get the services he needs in jail; they feel this young man needs *psychological* help. He's only seventeen—"

"We know how old he is," his father says.

The minister flushes. "Can you understand? These members want the UU to adopt a more *inclusive* view; one could argue, a more *compassionate* view—"

"And you're listening to these kooks?" His mother sounds like she'd slap the minister if she could.

"'Kooks'?"

"That's right."

"Wait a minute, Maggie," the minister says. "These are people who, though they support Gunther, believe in the possibility of *rehabilitation*—"

"For an addiction to hate?" his mother snaps. "Bruce? What do you think?"

His father doesn't answer. He's looking up at the ceiling, at the ugly punchbowl of a light that his mom always says needs cleaning.

"Bruce?"

His father is usually the calm one, the one who can get people talking normal again, the one who can settle parents at meets, reminding them that "it's supposed to be fun." His dad doesn't look like he's having fun. He is massaging the knuckles of his right fist, kneading and pinching, like he's trying to work a ball of stiff clay.

"You're going to let these people brainwash the congregation?"

The minister blinks. "I'm sorry. This wasn't meant—"

His father tips forward in the rocker so violently that it looks like he might fall into the minister's lap. "Have you read the signs, the Padrushky's website? Have you heard what they're saying about our family?"

"It's terrible, I agree."

His father's face is a deep pink and his cheeks are sucked in like someone who's about to spew. "Goddamn right, it's terrible. These people are out of control. They're hate mongers, and you want to give them a platform?"

"That's not quite the idea."

"What's the idea then?"

"A couple, Lily and Mark Manlius, perhaps you know them, would like to address the congregation next Sunday."

What the fuck?

"If these people are talking in church, so are we."

Minister Gilbert nods. "That's what I was going to offer, Bruce. That's what I believe is fair. Equal time for both points-of-view."

The minister turns to Gunther. He knows that he's supposed to say something; he doesn't know what. His stomach is kinked; his chest aches. He cuts his eyes away to the floor, wishing he could disappear.

"Would you want to speak to the congregation next Sunday, Gunther? Your voice would be more than welcome."

"Me?" He glances up for a second. The minister is looking at him like a teacher who's caught him daydreaming. He looks down at the carpet, at the bits of lint his mother's vacuum didn't find. "No."

"Gunther?" His mother's voice is sharp as a jackknife. "Do you get how important this is?"

"Yes." *What's important is getting back to his room, diving under the covers, hiding for the rest of his life.*

"You mean you get it, and you don't want to stand up to these people?"

"Maggie." He knows what his father is trying to do; tamp down the fire before it starts blazing. Only he doesn't realize how mad *he* sounds.

"I'm talking to my son. You can say something when I'm finished."

He wishes he could quiet his brain, go numb. He knows what his mom wants; his dad, too, even if he's not saying it. It's what everybody wants. Including Ms. Bev. They want him to be a hero. They want him to be like Martin Luther King, Jr. or somebody. He isn't. He wants to be. But he isn't. He read somewhere that real heroes are scared, or they wouldn't be heroes. Well, that's crap. He's figured out that he's just scared. Where his guts should be is jelly.

"Gunther?" His mother and father are looking at him in that way that people look at him these days, wondering what's inside. As if he fucking knew.

"You guys can talk. I'm not going to. Why do I have to defend myself? Why doesn't *he*? Why do I have to prove that that kid tried to kill me? That he belongs in jail? If those asshole Unitarians don't get that, it's *their* problem." He can feel his eyeballs warming, going liquid, a blob of mucus rises in his throat. His mother's arm comes up around his shoulder. He shakes it off.

"I'm sorry, Gunther. This is a very difficult subject, I know," says the minister.

You don't.

"I simply want our community to feel that they can express their compassion for all sentient beings and consider all of the angles."

"Is that your view?" his mother asks. "Is that where you stand on this? You want us to join hands with the Padrushkys and this couple and sing 'Kumbaya'? *We're* the ones who need the community's support. We need people to rally against the Padrushkys' lies. We need people to acknowledge that a hate crime was perpetrated against our son. We need to know that our community won't tolerate racism. Can you understand that?"

Minister Gilbert pulls herself to the front of her chair. "I came here to ask your family to speak to the congregation as well as the Manlius's. My hope is that this will be an occasion that promotes cooperation and understanding."

"Short notice," Bruce says.

"Very short, and I apologize for that. Still, I hope you will accept my invitation and that you will let me know as soon as possible."

"'As soon as possible'," his father says. "You mean today."

"Yes," Minister Gilbert says, planting her feet and standing. "Today would be nice."

Gunther feels his mother's elbow, nudging him to get up.

"Good-bye, Gunther." The minister aims her hand at him.

"Are the Padrushkys coming, too?" It makes him feel sick to ask, but he's got to.

"It didn't occur to me to invite them."

"Why not?"

"That's a good question. It's not meant to be a forum or a debate, simply a conversation." Minister Gilbert hesitates. "Do you want me to ask them, Gunther?"

"No way."

"But you asked."

"I asked because you're not going to catch me near that place if the Padrushkys are there."

TWENTY

In the mid-morning sun, he is just a man in his gym shorts and a gray muscle tee, the sweat searing a large triangle down his back, his sunburned shoulders burning an even deeper red as he rides his mower, headphones clapped over his ears, across his steep lawn. Squatting in the drainage ditch, Joanne raises her rifle, sights. Right now, she could plug Harter easy as a deer feasting on backyard corn, plug him right between the shoulder blades or through the heart. He wouldn't know what hit him. But that isn't what she wants. She wants this man to know that he is going to die. She wants him to confess his sins before she shoots him for committing them.

The sky is perfect; the clouds stuck up there like cotton to make the blue look bluer. Dragonflies cruise in the cattails above her head. Through the scope, Joanne watches Harter as he cuts to the end of his swath, then begins to double back in the other direction. He points the mower downhill to start the turn, his forearms straining as though trying to control a running horse.

She takes a deep breath, holds it, then fires. The front of the mower sinks on the exploded tire like an elephant dropping to one knee, before it rolls, flipping Harter head first down the slope. He lies on his side on the uncut grass, moaning, grabbing for his shin or his ankle, Joanne can't tell which and she doesn't much care. Still wearing his headphones and faced away, he is not aware of her approach until she sticks the end of her rifle to his neck, presses deeply so the red flesh turns white.

Harter turns his head to look up at her. His eyes are cartoon eyes, Joanne thinks. Black and white and popping like marbles. They only pretend to be scared.

She draws the trigger back. "Tell me exactly what you did to my son."

TWENTY-ONE

MONDAY MORNINGS. Hopper hates Monday mornings just like everybody else he knows. But this particular Monday morning is already up his butt and has put him in a really bad mood. First, fucking coffee filter folded so the coffee tasted like brown crayon swirled in hot water; next, his secretary, Martha, called in sick. The temp won't make it until noon. And just now, his cell phone has pinged, reminding him of his first meeting of the day—the Cannons.

Ever since his Saturday morning breakfast with the town honchos, he's been weighing the options. He likes to think of himself as a confident man; a smart guy, canny. Yes, it would be nice to have a headliner, the kind of high-profile case that might get noticed by the higher-ups in Albany. On the other hand, he's not stupid. In this state, the Judge is elected; the DA, too. The State versus Padrushky is a case that could make or absolutely destroy his career. Forty-eight hours ago, the odds looked good to win it; then along comes the alleged witness, and the odds aren't as good. He could win it; but not the way he wants to. The operation is successful, but the patient dies.

He likes this county; he likes his job even though sometimes it feels like the really dangerous criminals go in the front door and out the back before they have time to brush their teeth. Their junkie flunkies go to prison instead. So, much as it galls him, the truth is, after Saturday's breakfast meeting, he's ready to settle the case. Better that than blow it.

The Cannons are seated around Hopper's small round conference table; each with their glass of water (he didn't offer them the terrible coffee). Hopper drops heavily into his chair, clears his throat.

"Okay, folks, first of all, thank you for coming in on short notice. Believe me if it wasn't important, I wouldn't have bothered you. What's happening is a few new pieces of information have come up—"

"Like what?" It's Maggie, eyes narrowed, mouth set.

Hopper hauls in a deep breath, lets it out. "Look, guys, my intuition and experience say we win it. We have the evidence, the witnesses. I've reread the law on this case so many times I could recite it in my sleep and probably do. You'd have to check with the wife on that. However—" He works the pause but doesn't overdo it, because these folks are smart: They've got their eye on the ball. "I've had cases I thought were air tight go bust, and ones I was sure I'd lose, succeed. Twelve people in a room. You can never completely predict the outcome."

"We're not dropping the hate crime."

Hopper would like to whistle at Maggie's quickness, but he keeps quiet.

"Is that what you're saying?" Bruce asks.

"Preliminary now, just thinking." Slow down, Hopper tells himself. The idea is to lower the boom so gently they don't feel it.

"Explain." Maggie Cannon, court savvy, and from Downstate. The city. Not a shred of sympathy for this town.

"My fault. I'll take it slower. Right now, we're headed for trial. Three hundred possible jurors, county residents. We interview them, whittle them down. It's going to be a battle on every one, given the stakes. Then two or three weeks of trial time. Okay, we expect that. Expensive, but that's why we pay taxes—to see justice done. Say the trial starts early August. Then we're talking media circus through—"

"High tourist season," Bruce says.

Hopper nods. He'll play it like a revelation. "Good point. Which will only add to the feeding frenzy and Padrushky, Sr.'s incentive to cause havoc."

"It sounds like you've had a visit."

"Maggie—" Bruce puts a hand on his wife's shoulder.

"I don't follow you."

"I work for the Court, Hopper. I'm not stupid."

Definitely not. "A visit from whom?" He's not stupid, either, but he can fake it.

"You tell us. The Mayor? The Chamber? I don't know. The town fathers. The guys who run the show. The *money*."

Hopper hesitates for a moment. Go with the gut, he thinks. Spill it. "All right. The guys you mentioned. And a few others."

Bruce cuffs the edge of the table with the heel of his hand. "You could have said that right off."

"I should have."

"Who are the others?"

"Want to guess?"

Maggie Cannon locks his gaze; her eyes, he notices for the first time, are hazel. "Dick Romley, asshole extraordinaire."

Bruce Cannon flinches at his wife's expletive; Gunther stays rigid.

"Bingo. Who else?"

"Better not be Sean, Sr."

"Damn close." He's netted their attention all right. "Father Lambert."

Bruce Cannon squares his shoulders. "Why was *he* there?"

"Surprised me. Cajones."

"The Padrushkys' priest," Maggie says. "Not so surprising."

"Why *him*?" Gunther's voice is soft. "He doesn't know me at all."

Hopper gives Gunther a long look. His face is all angles and his skin looks ashy. He's lost ten pounds in less than a month. A kid who didn't have any weight to lose. In a dark navy suit and white shirt and those gold-rimmed glasses, he'd be very appealing on the stand. At least to the women on the jury—the white women, because Hopper knows the county's demographics. Out of three hundred in the jury pool, maybe ten African-Americans; and defense counsel will sure as hell find reasons to excuse every one of them for cause. Gunther, slim and studious-looking; Bruce Cannon, good guy, a local, salt-of-the-earth type. If he can swing it, he'd prefer to keep Maggie Cannon off the stand. They have the notebook, the hard drive, the witnesses. The case should be cut and dried; but still you've got Youthful Offender status denied and insanity ruled out. You're looking at twenty, twenty-five plus. Defense milks it. Sean Jr. makes parole in his thirties, hardened by years in prison. No education, no trade. So, the defense gets those same nice women feeling sorry for Shawnee Jr., wanting him to get psychiatric help, wanting redemption for such an innocent-looking, once-pious, young man, and they get the secretly racist men, plugging for the white boy. No matter how you slice it, a jury trial is always up for grabs.

Hopper clears his throat. "This is going to be hard, folks, so take a deep breath. Here's the latest. Father Lambert claims he has a parishioner willing to swear a deposition stating that this fall, she witnessed Sean Padrushky, Jr.'s being bullied—well, hazed, more like—by a gang of football players. The alleged witness says, according to Father Lambert, that she saw Gunther in the group of boys surrounding Padrushky, half-naked, outside the high school tunnel. Gunther's the only one she says she recognized for certain because—"

"We know 'because'," Bruce says.

Gunther buries his face in his hands.

"What bullshit," Maggie says. "If Padrushky was hazed, why didn't he come forward with it in the first place?"

"That's the aim of hazing—brotherhood of silence, Stockholm Syndrome, whatever." Hopper's speaking to Maggie, but he's watching Gunther; the way he's looking up now, his jaw set; his gaze idling in neutral. He's not going to reveal anything. He's not going to say a word. "Gunther, want to weigh in on this?"

Gunther shakes his head. "Not really."

"We can't afford to ignore this development, no matter how much we dislike it."

"*We*?" Maggie is glaring at him with lizard eyes. "Right."

Hopper takes a deep breath. So, this is where their paths will part, he thinks. The Cannons are going down their road, and he is going down his. This is where it will get ugly and hard. This is where their opinion of him will be sealed as Hopper, the prick, the traitor. He is sorry about this. He genuinely likes the Cannons; he genuinely feels for the boy. But here's the deal: It's the People of the State of New York versus Padrushky, not Cannon versus Padrushky. He represents the State, not Gunther. "Listen, I understand you're going to be disappointed, but here it is—I'm offering a plea to Padrushky's lawyer."

"What?" Bruce snaps. "You just said we'd win it."

Hopper narrows his eyes. "And you're not hearing my words, Bruce. I said I *thought* we'd win it, but now they've got a witness to an event that's going to put Gunther in a very uncomfortable position."

Bruce shifts to face Gunther. "Is this true, Gun? Were you there? Did you see this happen?"

Gunther stares down at the table as though it has opened into a bottomless cavern. Sweat beads along his hairline even in the chilled room. If the kid took part in the hazing, Hopper thinks, he's feeling relieved; if he didn't (witnesses almost always get it wrong), he's seething. "What really happened, Gunther?"

He doesn't answer. He picks up a pencil left behind from a previous meeting, twisting it in his fingers, tipping it side-to-side, and Hopper thinks *tightrope*.

"No one's going to lick my balls."

"Gunther?" Bruce Cannon's expression is startled, pained. "What're you saying?"

"They wanted to get me next. They said so."

Inside the conference room, the air conditioner kicks on with a loud rush. Maggie covers her mouth as though she might be sick. Bruce shakes his head.

Go slow, Hopper thinks. "So, it happened, but you didn't tell anyone? Not even your friends?" Gunther looks at him, and what Hopper sees is fear, pure fear percolating with indignation, pride.

"I don't snitch."

Hopper exhales a silent, hah. "Okay. I get it. I see it now." Gunther's not going to tell who stole the yard signs, either, he thinks.

"I don't." It's Maggie, looking grim. "What did you think was going to happen if you told us, Gun? What did you think we were going to do?"

Gunther stares ahead. A muscle jumps in his temple.

"Gun?" Bruce reaches for Gunther's shoulder, is shrugged away. "Can't you just talk to us? We're not mad at you, we want to understand. Mom and I, well, we don't understand when all this was happening. If we're mad at anyone, we're mad at ourselves. We could have helped, if we'd been paying attention."

"How would you help? Call the principal? Call the cops? Then everyone would know I told. I'd have been dead a long time ago."

"Dead? Is that what you were worried about?"

Gunther folds his arms on the table, burrows his face as deep as it will go.

"If the trial goes forward, would Gunther have to testify under oath about the hazing?" Maggie asks.

Sharp lady, Hopper thinks. "I wouldn't mention it, but I can't guarantee it wouldn't come up under cross-examination." He watches Bruce and Maggie hook glances; Gunther remains still.

"What's the offer you're considering?" Maggie asks.

"Padrushky admits on the record that he targeted Gunther because he was black, but we agree not to seek the hate-crime designation."

Gunther's head pops up. "That joker says what he says, and it's not a hate crime?"

"That's right," Hopper says.

Bruce shoves away from the table. "What kind of BS is that?"

"I'm telling you, folks. Trials are risky. In my book, half a loaf is better than none. I want to offer something that guarantees that Padrushky will be punished, that he's going to jail."

"If you go that route, what are our chances in civil court?" Maggie asks.

Hopper shakes his head. "You need to talk to a retainer attorney about that. It's outside my bailiwick. But I can tell you that Federal statute is broader than State. The scales of justice only have to tip a little bit—and you already established assault."

Maggie straightens. "To add to everything else, we had a visitor, too."

"Who was that?" Hopper has the feeling that Maggie is speaking in code. He doesn't know why.

"Sandra Gilbert, the Unitarian minister."

Bruce cuts in. "Some Unitarians are supporting the Padrushkys."

"You're kidding me."

"They're going to address the congregation a week from Sunday. I guess they've never heard of victim's rights."

Maggie's eyes are hawk-bright. "We're going to fight back."

Hopper shoots a thin stream of air through his front teeth. "Okay. What are you planning?"

"We're getting a campaign together that's going to jam that church with Gun's supporters. We're getting the NAACP out of Albany and Binghamton, the college, the unions. We're bringing them all to Connorsville. The coverage is going to be amazing. And we're going to speak."

"I see. Wow."

"What are you thinking?" Bruce drops his hand from Gunther's shoulders, faces Hopper.

What he's thinking is pre-trial publicity if Judge Adkins doesn't adopt the plea. What he's thinking is jury selection. What he's thinking is how the Padrushkys are going to make the hazing incident public. And Gunther's going to get accused of stealing those signs. What he's thinking is a media stampede that will dwarf the others. "May I say something I may not have the right to say? Cancel the rally."

Gunther looks up; Bruce and Maggie stare.

"Ridiculous," Maggie says.

"Why, Hopper?" Bruce asks sharply.

"You don't know where this can go—how it's going to play. You don't want to lose control of the public's perception."

"You mean *you* don't want to lose control of public perception—you and your friends in City Hall. That's why we're organizing," Maggie says. "We're not going to let the Padrushky's racist agenda brainwash this entire community."

"Gunther? Where are you on this?" Hopper watches the boy staring at his hands as if hoping to find an answer in his milky nails.

"I don't want to testify about the hazing. But I don't want Padrushky to get off being charged with a hate crime, either. I want everything to disappear. I want to disappear. I wish I'd never been born."

TWENTY-TWO

THE MOMENT MAGGIE ENTERS her basement office, she is filled with relief. It is a rectangle with only one small window close to the ceiling, a generous cell, but when Maggie closes the door behind her, she feels as though she has entered a cave of safety, a zone of privacy, in which she can think her thoughts.

After the meeting with Hopper, she is trying to wrap her mind around Gunther's confession. She is trying to understand how she and Bruce could have been so blind to Gunther's pain. She remembers Gunther asking them for permission to play football, how he hung around one morning, scowling, while they read the paper in the kitchen. He was giving them what she called "the vulture look," glaring at them through slitted eyes as though he despised them, anticipating that they were going to say no. He was right. Bruce and she did not want him to play football. They worried about concussions, they told him. They thought he was happy with track. "It's just for the fall," Gunther said. "To keep in shape." They were surprised, but they relented. Maybe he needed a different crowd. Maybe it was important that he try something new.

Now Maggie realizes that they fell for the trap. Gunther wanted them to say, 'no.' He wanted them to protect him from Coach Harter. What else had he needed their protection for? What else had he wanted them to see?

TWENTY-THREE

THE DOGS SAVED HIM, Joanne tells Lyle. If she shot Harter, who would take care of the dogs? She couldn't leave them without a mother.

Lyle sits, shaking his head. It is Monday afternoon, and the café Joanne has chosen in Connorsville does not have air-conditioning. "Oh god," he says, "I'm so glad you didn't shoot him."

Joanne looks at her brother. He is, without a doubt, a Boston terrier with his overshot lower jaw and his pitiable, well-spaced eyes. Not her favorite breed. "I got this from him, though." She pushes the paper across the Formica table top. "A signed confession, the shit."

"You held a gun on him, and he's not pressing charges?" Lyle draws the paper toward him, slips on his reading glasses, but not before glancing at the heavily-iced cinnamon bun that has just been delivered by the waitress.

Their table is in the back beneath a framed print of man wearing a fez. There is no one around them. On such a warm afternoon, the rest of the café's customers are sitting at the tables out front.

Joanne watches Lyle's lips pucker as he reads what she typed, what Harter swore to. Her nerves—tiny, grabbing hands—pinch at her stomach. "You know how fast he'd die if people knew what was going on in that locker room?"

Lyle puts up a hand to show her that he is still reading, but she can't stop. "Do you get it? Do you get what these kids did to Shawnee? Did you get that Gunther Cannon was on that team? We've got proof now that Shawnee was hazed and hazed bad. Can anyone blame him for what he done?" Joanne hears her voice getting louder, higher. She doesn't care.

"I got to explain something to you, sister." Lyle pats his forehead with his napkin, then crumples it and sticks it in his empty coffee cup. "I explained it to Shawnee, who unlike you and your husband, understood. If we were to prove that Shawnee was mentally ill—that he snapped, and that's an *if*—then he's going to a mental hospital. Lock the gates and kiss the key good-bye. If Shawnee is committed to a mental hospital, there is no guarantee that he gets out—ever.

"If we accept a plea, no trial. No possibility of losing the trial. Shawnee's out of the can in ten, maybe even eight, years for good behavior. Guaranteed. But if we lose, sister, he's in for twenty-five."

Lyle takes off his glasses and pushes his face closer to hers. His breath up close smells oversweet, like creamer.

"Here's some more bad news. It's Shawnee's decision, not yours, not Sean, Sr.'s, and the young man has already told his lawyer, me, that he would accept an offer. And one more thing, Joanne—" her brother folds the confession in half and slides it across the table to her. "Do not show this piece of paper to your husband; I am not representing him for murder."

Sitting there, Joanne has an urge to leap at him, grab his throat. Instead, she tells herself, *stay*. "I don't understand. Why didn't Shawnee tell us he was hazed? Why didn't he tell you? Or the police? Why doesn't he want to save himself?"

Lyle sweeps up the cinnamon bun in both hands and holds it to his open mouth. "He's nuts, Joanne. You know that." He closes his eyes and sinks his teeth into the bun until his lip disappears in the icing.

Joanne pushes her chair back and stares. She has been wrong about her brother, she thinks, he isn't a Boston terrier: He's a jackal.

TWENTY-FOUR

AFTER A DRY WEEK, THE SPRINKLERS ARE ON, flinging rainbows across the close-cropped greens. The sickly maples wave their tar-spotted leaves, the black sarcomas signaling their doom. The spray treatment did not work. Padrushky was hazed; Gun was next. Gun was in danger, terrified. How could he have missed all of that? Bruce wonders as he steers his golf cart up and down the asphalt lanes. Why didn't his son confide in him? Why didn't he trust him? Bruce stops the cart, hops off to tamp down some divots that lazy golfers have left in their wake. The questions scruff his heart; they hurt. Was it lack of trust or something else? What did he keep from his own father? Oh. He remembers. Nightmares for weeks; each time he woke, screaming. Everybody in camp got hung, the big boys said. You couldn't escape. That was the worst part. He knew it was coming. It came for everyone; he hoped it would happen quick and be over quick and then he'd never have to worry about it again.

Then one night after Campfire, after roasting hotdogs, after stuffing fistfuls of marshmallows into his mouth, making his cheeks huge, it was happening; a crowd of boys, his bunkmates and others, were on him. He remembers the shouts and the tugging; a kid's hangnail scraping his cheek like a cat's claw. He struggled as hard as he could against his attackers; he was strong, but not strong enough. He can still remember his dread as the fire in his biceps gave way and he was theirs.

In the strobe of flashlight beams and screeching boys, he hardly knew what was happening, but then there he was, hanging from a post, from the elastic band of his underpants hooked on a nail. His weight ripped the hole at the waistband wide and wider, but the elastic held, and he tilted forward from the post like a cherub, his belly hanging, his arms reaching toward the ground. Then the flashlights went out; the boys snuck away.

In the warm night, fireflies glowed their sympathy, and crickets mocked his pain. In the dark, he shouted, punching at nothing. What you didn't do was cry; he knew that; everybody knew that. You didn't tell, either. Like Gunther said.

No, he didn't tell his father anything about his hazing, or his rage at being betrayed by his professor, denied his PhD. Nothing about Maggie's miscarriages and how they learned that they were at the end of the line. Nothing about his worries about adopting a black child, either. The way his father raised him, silence was not cowardice; silence meant you were a man.

Clearly, he had raised Gunther this way, though he had not meant to. He had meant to change this. So, when did it happen? He couldn't say. It was like a spell cast over them; Gunther hadn't wanted to talk, and he had respected that choice. But now, looking back, Bruce thinks, it wasn't really Gunther's choice, after all; it was his.

TWENTY-FIVE

Ms. Bev's email address is written on the inside of the back cover of his school notebook in tiny print like it's some kind of secret. It is. It's his secret. He thinks of it sometimes as a life preserver or a trap door or a parachute. Sometimes he looks at it and thinks, if I need to get out of here, I will write her, and she will send me a ticket to London, and I will escape. It's hard to allow himself to even think that thought. The minute he does, he feels bad like he's betraying his mom, because isn't that what she's most afraid of? His dad, he thinks, would understand, but his mom would die. His mom tried to show that she wasn't hung up about Ms. Bev, but she was. She wasn't good at acting, even though she thought she was. After he'd spent an afternoon at Ms. Bev's, she tried not to snoop or act jealous, but she was always in a bad mood, and was always ordering him around and slamming things. Then she'd cut out altogether, saying she needed to get some exercise, and so even though she complained that she didn't see him enough, as soon as he got home, she would disappear.

He tried to talk to his dad about it once, but he wasn't interested. "Don't worry about your mother," he said. "She's a big girl."

So, he didn't worry for a while, but then his mom and Ms. Bev had the big fight and Ms. Bev left, and he didn't know what to do really.

Now, sitting at his desk, he stares at his notebook. His mom and dad are downstairs making dinner. He's supposed to be doing homework. But he can't focus. The thought of next Sunday, of having to talk in front of the Unitarians; the meeting this morning with Hopper. He should feel better that his parents know about the tunnel, that they're not blaming him for not telling, and he does, but there's the other shit. Hopper's shoving the hate crime to the side—Padrushky's attack will go down as bad blood. It's not fair.

He flips open the notebook to a bunch of diagrams of molecules that look like the toys he played with in kindergarten. There's a quiz tomorrow, and he's got to copy them, name them. Strangely, he doesn't mind. He's starting to like Chemistry. In Chemistry you break things down so small that human beings don't seem to matter. Life at this level, he thinks, is more bearable than walking around in his skin.

Then, like his hand's not connected to his brain, he pinches a hunk of pages, turns them over. He's looking at the lower left-hand corner of the inside cover, at the tiny formula that equals Ms. Bev.

Without thinking, he is typing. What the fuck does he have to lose?

Hi Ms. Bev,

Gun here. Remember me? How's it going? Kind of sucks here, but I guess you know. Thanks for the books you sent. I haven't had time to read them, but I plan to. Maybe after I graduate.

So be well,
Gun.

When Gunther gets downstairs, the kitchen table has been set. Even the water has been poured. His mom and dad look up at him, smiling. His antenna's up. Usually they'd be all over him, wanting him to do something, get something. His mom's made his favorite string beans with the bread crumbs and the garlic. His dad has made his roast potatoes. Now it's definite. There's something up, and he wishes he could turn around and go back upstairs, though his stomach is growling at the thought of food.

"Did you get your work done?" his dad asks, popping the cap off his beer.

"Kind of."

His mom raises her eyebrows, but keeps her mouth shut as she spoons string beans onto his plate.

"It's Chem."

"Ouch." His dad hands him the platter of potatoes. "Hey, Maggie, want to check the chicken?"

"Not really." But she gets up anyway, rattling the oven door and pulling out the rack. "Done, I'd say. Perfect."

Chicken, string beans, potatoes. His favorite.

"All right, then," his dad says. "Let's eat while it's hot."

There are always two messages in his family, *Eat while it's hot* and *Wait until everyone's served*. He's never figured out which rule trumps the other, but usually it's his dad who calls the shots.

For a while, everyone is chewing and swallowing and making the humming sound people make when the food tastes good. His dad finishes one beer, goes for another. He opens the refrigerator and asks over his shoulder, "All right if I offer Gun a beer?"

His mom shrugs. "If he's finished his homework."

He shakes his head. "I don't need it."

His dad shuts the refrigerator. "Good choice," he says.

"So," his mom starts. "Today's meeting was pretty intense."

He nods, puts down his fork. So that's what's going down. He should have known.

His mom and dad exchange looks, while his mom reaches across the table for his dad's beer. "I could use a slug of that."

"I can get you your own."

"No." His mom takes a long pull, wiping the bottle lip on her sleeve before handing it back to his dad. "Gun, dad and I have talked, and we know this may be uncomfortable, but it's time, we think, to have some conversation with you."

No, he thinks. Please, no. The last "conversation" he remembers was "The Talk" with his dad. It was right after the Halloween when he wore the Lil Wayne costume, and it was super embarrassing. His dad really didn't seem to know that what he had to tell him was old news. "So, what's up?"

"Well," his dad says, "first, we want to apologize. I mean, mom and I feel terrible. We let you down when you needed us. You don't have to forgive us, because we can't forgive ourselves. But we both think it's important that we talk honestly, that we hear from you. That you tell us how you think we can support you better than we have."

He stares down at his plate. His string beans are cooling, and the potatoes are losing their sheen. Why did they have to bring up this shit at dinner, when all he wants to do is eat? "Don't worry about it, okay? You guys did all right. I'm okay. It's not your fault this town is so fucked up."

His mom is looking at him, just looking, like he's a person made of glass she's afraid will break.

"Gun, I need to tell you that I love you. You can't imagine how much."

"Love you, too, Mom, Dad." He means it, he thinks. Only it isn't enough.

TWENTY-SIX

SHAWNEE'S FATHER IS SHOUTING on the telephone. His father is always shouting. He can see his father now. When he shouts, he turns the purplish red of a throbbing cock, purple and shining, his arms pumping, his fists flying.

"Dad?" he asks. "Are you saying something?"

The rant pauses. He can hear his father straining to breathe through vines of mucus. "What did they offer you? What the fuck did the DA put you up to? You aren't in your right mind. You can't make your own decisions. You can't trust no one. Not that son of a bitch uncle, not that son of a bitch DA. What the fuck's Hopper getting out of this, did you think of that? How many times, son, how many times do I have to tell you—it's me and you against this fucking world?"

He stays on the telephone for another minute, the bottom of the receiver pressed hard against his jaw. His father's voice grows hoarser and hoarser. He sounds like an auctioneer or a politician. Like the Führer himself. Slowly, he lowers the receiver, letting it dangle on its metal cord like a strung cat, and steps away.

How funny it is to think of his father shouting himself to a whisper, busting a gut to speak when no one is actually listening.

◈

The shrink is a bald man with dark eyebrows that look like they are propped up by something, stuck in permanent surprise. He's wearing a suit, no tie, no belt either. Maybe it's a safety thing. The shrink reaches across the table to shake his hand; he's got a few questions he'd like to ask if that's okay. A few? No, a *slew.* He's pretty sure the man's a *Jew.* Ask away, he's not going to answer them.

Ever hurt animals on purpose? How do you think a criminal record will affect your life? Anyone close to you whose death would upset you? How long would it take to get over this death (in days)? Do you bully others often? Are you satisfied with the way your life is turning out? Where were you born? What was your childhood like? What are your earliest childhood memories?

He used to think his father's chair, a La-Z-Boy covered in blue sateen might be magic; that when his father sat in that chair, he got strong and his brain charged up like it was plugged in a socket. When his father got in that chair and shoved back, it held him like a giant hand and his eyes closed, and watching him, he knew his father was hatching all the plots and ideas and schemes that fueled him through the day. Ideas like the end of the world was coming a lot sooner than anyone expected; ideas like the coloreds and the Mexicans were going to be taking over the country in the next five to ten years before white people could make enough babies to catch up. Ideas like aliens were already in cahoots with the terrorists—no other explanation for how the Towers came down. His father had a lot of ideas about the water and the air, too, and the way the government was controlling the people, controlling him, even though he was on to them and knew more than most.

One afternoon when he was eight or nine, he climbed into his father's chair. He wanted those ideas, and he wanted to taste his father's power. The chair felt as big as a boat; as electrifying as a space capsule. He tried to tip back, but he wasn't heavy enough, so he sat up, and that was disappointing like sitting in a barber's chair or a dentist's, so he closed his eyes and a man's face appeared against the dark billboard on the wall inside his forehead, a space created just for visions it seemed, because once he'd seen Jesus there, looking so sad, his eyes downcast and his long, hippie-hair (his father could never quite forgive that) falling over his shoulders; he looked like he'd lost something, his best friend or his dog.

This man wasn't Jesus. He had a small head and black, swept-back hair, small, tight pupils and a tight mustache. He opened his eyes. The man frightened him. He didn't look sad like Jesus; he looked angry in the same way his father looked angry, his face purpling, engorged, when he talked from his chair, this chair, of the evil in the world.

The slap across his cheek woke him so fast he leapt, no flew, out of the chair like he had acquired a super power, or the chair itself had flung him onto the floor and finding himself on the carpet in the middle of the living room floor, he knew he wasn't safe.

His father stood above him, his fist raised, the toes of his boots already in motion. "Who do you think you are, little shit? No one sits in my chair."

How many friendships have you had? How many sexual relationships? How did you feel about those relationships? How important were they? Have you had any verbal or physical fights with friends? How did they end? How did you feel? What's the difference between a friend and an acquaintance?

His friends are Brothers. They would die for him, and he for them. His Brothers saved his life over and over every night with their support for his plight, for their support in the fight. He has no friends, no acquaintances. He has Brothers. Unlike any others.

Do you ever feel depressed or sad? What's the most depressed you've ever been? Have you lost anyone you felt close to? What do you mean by close? How did it affect you? How would you feel if you lost someone close to you? Are you a loner? Have you ever been in love?

He launches himself across the table so fast the shrink hardly has time to back up his chair. Then the guard is on him; slipping him into a Full Nelson; banging his forehead against the wall.

◈

He sees himself as a boy sitting next to Father Rand at the organ. The church is empty, the pipes run up to God. His fingers on the keys are slender, the nails well-shaped and clean. Father Rand says you must always wash your hands before you play the organ. You must treat your instrument with respect. He does. When he sits at the organ's keyboard, his lungs are tight with awe. One touch sends the sound spinning, arcing into the heavens. He is playing top hand; Father Rand, bottom, when the priest's fingers suddenly cover his, when the priest's lightly-haired knuckles tent his naked ones. His heart stops; his fingers freeze. Gently, ever so gently, Father Rand embraces him with strong arms, the cotton of his long sleeves brushes his arms like silk. Father Rand holds him close, holds him with such tenderness, with such love. Like a mother, he thinks. He hoped that he would never let him go.

TWENTY-SEVEN

"DO PEOPLE CHANGE, YOU THINK?" Gunther draws a deep drag off the joint that Woody has passed to him, feeling his lungs expanding like those plastic bags he liked to pop with a knuckle-punch at recess in middle school to make the girls scream.

It is Saturday again, apparently. The day before the big deal at the UU church. Ever since he and his parents met with Hopper, the days of the week have been disappearing, reappearing, like drifting mosquitos you grabbed or missed. Only school keeps him on track.

"Heavy," Woody says, mockingly, closing his fingers on the joint that is coming back to him. He and Gunther have gone up into the hills past the trailer park, to their old spot under a shelf of rock they call the Bat Cave. "You mean, like, change their personality?"

"Yeah." But that isn't what he means. He is thinking of Shawnee Padrushky. He is wondering what happened to that kid? Did Shawnee hate him because he mocked him that afternoon in the locker room? Did he hate him because he left him in the tunnel and ran? Or was it really only because he was black?

Woody reaches into his pocket, takes out a pack of gum. "I thought for a while that you were changing on me, man."

"Me?" He tries to make his voice sound surprised. What has Woody seen?

"Yeah, when you got all into football, I was scared you'd gone to the other side. But you came back."

Gunther sits up and tosses the pebble in his hand as far as he can into the trees. "Those guys were assholes."

Woody pops the gum in his mouth, then offers a piece to Gunther.

Gunther shakes his head. "I gotta tell you something."

"Okay."

"About why I quit the team." His gut is twisting now; his desire to confess, a rushing river. "Those dudes were sick. They tackled Padrushky in the tunnel; they were messing with him real bad. Nasty shit. And they were going for me next. I was booking, man. I thought—" *I would die.*

Woody stops chewing, his gaze fixed on the far hills, purplish in this light.

Gunther nods. He can't stop his toe from tapping; his thigh from jiggling.

Woody pulls himself to sitting, his fingers touching the pimples on his cheek, reading them like braille. "Wow."

"Are you pissed?"

Woody shrugs. "Nah. But I could've planned some booby traps."

"Like what?"

"Trip wire in the shower. Bucket of piss lands on their heads?"

"Good one. We'd both die."

"Smiling."

All around them cicadas chirp with an intensity that makes Gunther think of tiny, revving chainsaws. There is something else he wants to tell Woody. “I’ve been thinking about my father.”

“Your father’s cool.”

“My *other* father. So, this is fucked, but somewhere there’s a man who’s my biological father and even though all this stuff has happened, like I was almost killed, he doesn’t even know. I mean do you think he ever wonders what happened to his kid? Do think he’s ever sorry?”

Woody pulls in his knees and hugs them. The rims of his nostrils have turned a rashy red and his acne has flushed to a deep purple.

Shit, Gunther thinks. Woody’s father. He didn’t think about that. Woody’s father hasn’t been around in years.

“Hey—,” Gunther starts to apologize, but Woody cuts him off.

“I got to take a leak, man.”

“I’ll wait.”

Woody stands, brushing off the seat of his jeans. “Can you believe this shit?” he says. “The best fucking weed I’ve ever had.”

“Yeah,” Gunther says. “Great shit.” He can take a hint. When Woody returns, Gunther stands. Without saying a word, they head back down the trail.

TWENTY-EIGHT

JOANNE POURS A CUP OF COFFEE for herself and rests a hip against the kitchen counter. She's finished her dog chores and now what? She knows what, but she's been pushing it away. She's got to fix Shawnee's doorknob. The police might have stuck in a little flathead, tripped the lock, but no, they had to rip out the entire mechanism, leaving a ragged hole, stained dark around the edges, like a bruised eye socket. Every time she passes Shawnee's door, she thinks of him, wishes that a miracle happened and that she will find him in there at his desk, or on his bed. She wouldn't even mind if he growled at her, as he always did, to keep out.

The new knobs are yellow-gold. The metal is cool and slippery as jelly. The directions are simple. You only have to be sure you face the lock shaft in right direction, or you could lock yourself in. Joanne lines up the knob assemblies on both sides of the door. She inserts the inside screws, twists them with her fingers. Soon Stubby and Sallie appear. Nothing goes on in the house without their inspection. They sniff around the edge of door, nose the packaging.

"Leave it," Joanne says sternly. Stubby and Sally cast looks of apology her way, then turn around and pad away.

The hush of Shawnee's room is like an empty church. Deep shadows engulf the pristine carpet, the tightly-made bed. The computer desk is bare; so is the top of the bureau and the cork board and the walls. The black curtains form a neat pile on the side table. Who folded them? Did she? Is it possible she came into this room after the raid and folded the curtains and made the bed? Her actions then seem long ago, impossible to remember in any detail.

She pulls out Shawnee's desk chair, a chair he was happy to find at a flea-market outside of town. Maroon cracked leather and brushed aluminum arms. He told her he liked its *Teutonic* lines. Something that made no sense to her. Its what? *The way the arms flowed from the back, the way the curves of the octopus-like base echoed the arms.* She shook her head. Talk about lines in chairs was crazy talk as far as she was concerned, though she pretended to get it, because for once her son had shared something.

Seated in the chair, she rests her arms on its arms, swivels the chair lightly right and left, then leans her elbows on his desk, her face in her hands.

Only a week ago, there was hope. Father Lambert told them that some members of the Unitarian church were taking up Shawnee's cause. They, too, wanted Shawnee to get help, not jail time. The donations to 'Save Shawnee' came flooding in. "We're raising thousands of dollars," Sean, Sr. crowed on the website. For a few hours, he seemed to put aside how mad he was that the signs had been stolen off their lawn and up and down the road. For a few hours, he let off his mutterings about letter bombs and *shooting the Cannons a message.* She didn't dare tell him that today a whole bunch of those donation checks bounced.

Then this morning, Sean Sr. tells her that Shawnee has accepted Hopper's plea deal. The hate crime designation will be removed, but Shawnee has to swear in writing that his motive for shooting Gunther Cannon was hate. It's his choice, Sean Sr. says: He won't listen to his father. Would he listen to her? She doubts it.

Even when her son was little, he didn't trust her. She could feel it. He was scared of her dogs; he hated their barking. Pinching her jeans, he would try to keep her from leaving him to check on them. Once he followed her into the kennels during feeding time. As soon as the door opened, the dogs began to bark and to hurl themselves against the chain link. They were hungry, but harmless. Even above their loud barking, she could hear Shawnee's screams.

She found him curled in his closet. With the door closed, you could still hear the dogs.

"Go away," he said. "I hate your angry room."

TWENTY-NINE

"Hi honey." His mom looks up from the pages she is marking with a blue pen; his dad, too. "Grab something to eat and come back out here on the porch. We want to go over the speech with you."

His speech. Shit. He wishes he was back with Woody, back up in the hills, far away. Somehow with all the other stuff going on he managed to slide the reality of the speech to a different compartment.

In the kitchen, he slaps together a cheese sandwich on the healthy bread his mother insists on buying, pours himself an iced tea from the pitcher in the refrigerator. His high is wearing off and he's starving. In the cabinet under the island, he finds a bag of potato chips and tears it open. It's four-thirty in the afternoon, according to the clock above the sink. Why does time have to move so fucking slow?

Stepping carefully, he brings his plate and his glass out to the porch. He's got to seem normal, he tells himself. He's pretty sure he can pull it off. He's been straight arrow so long his parents never suspect a thing.

"Take a look." His father offers him a typed page, but Gunther shakes his head, his mouth full of sandwich.

"All right, finish. Then you can look. It's our latest draft."

His mom is wearing one of his old track t-shirts, "The Lake Village Fliers." It's loose over her narrow shoulders, and maybe because he is still a bit buzzed, he thinks she looks older and tinier than he remembers.

"We want you to read the draft out loud and then we'll edit it, so it sounds more like you. It's a bit formal right now, but we think it gets the points across."

The points. Which points? Once he was a person, now he's a cause. And the cause is supporting *him*, whoever *he* is. Last week, after Hopper's deal went public, a video went viral, a ten-second clip that a kid in the park shot on her phone and posted on social media. It's him streaking across Main Street—Shawnee after him, pointing his gun, shouting what he shouted. The banner she pinned to it runs across the bottom, white letters on a blue background: *They say it's not a hate crime...if not, what is? Turn out for Gunther Cannon...Let's show a bro some love...*then there's the date and place and time to protest at the UU.

Heidi Light is the girl who posted. She's a sophomore he barely knows. He should be grateful that some people have his back, and he is, but he wasn't a *bro* to Heidi Light until last week.

His father sighs, rubbing his face so that his reading glasses push up on his forehead. "It's still rough, but we'll get there. Meanwhile, about a thousand things need to be done—"

"Did we tell you about the buses? And there's a group making signs tonight in the high school gym. I'm sure you know that. We should probably go. Kathie Schechter's working on t-shirts. She's donating the whole shebang, and the book club—"

Gunther takes a gulp of iced tea. Suddenly, he is choking.

His father slaps him on the back between his shoulder blades, but the coughs keep coming. His stomach hurts.

"Down the wrong hatch," his mother says sympathetically. "Raise your arms. Walk around."

He gets up and stumbles down the porch steps. He feels like a doofus holding up his arms like a cheerleader. The cough is slowing, but his eyes are watery, and his knees feel weak. He drops his arms. Along the edge of the mowed lawn, daffodils have opened and purple clover and a plant with springy red flowers that make him think of Dr. Seuss. Slowly he turns back to the porch where both of his parents are looking at him with concern.

"Maybe now's not the time to do this," his father says.

His mom frowns. "We don't have a lot more opportunities. I thought it's why you came home early, Bruce."

"*We* can still work on it. Gunther seems to need a break."

"I don't feel good. I got a headache." A headache almost always works as an excuse. His mom freaks about headaches.

"A headache? Why didn't you say so? Go upstairs, lie down. Be sure the shades are pulled."

"Take an ibuprofen, Gun," his father adds, squeezing his forearm as he goes into the house.

"Take two," his mom says.

"Okay." Just like that he is released. He has to tell himself not to smile.

PART IV

GATHERING

ONE

At ten thirty a.m. on Sunday, the hall of the Unitarian Universalist Society of Connorsville is growing warm, even with the windows partly opened and the ceiling fans spinning. Every pew and folding chair is occupied and has been for at least an hour, except for those in the front marked "reserved" with sheets of paper taped to their seats. On either side of the hall, cameramen jostle for position, ignoring the elderly ushers' attempts to move them up to the balcony. Some in the audience sneak glances at the cameras; others point them out boldly to their neighbors.

Earlier this morning, a line of chartered buses lumbered bumper-to-bumper down Main street like parade elephants. They emptied out into the public parking lot across from the Society. The riders organized quickly behind a large banner: GUN'S LIFE MATTERS. On the other side of the lot, another demonstration was forming. This group held signs, white block letters on a tomato-red background: SAVE SHAWNEE. Six police officers astride bicycles blew on their whistles as they pedaled backwards and forwards, funneling the crowd toward the church.

◈

Charlotte, seated in the middle of the front pew, is feeling odd, dizzy as though she skipped breakfast, which is not true. She ate a large breakfast at May's—toast, eggs, and bacon—and even so, she is filled with the swirly, nervous feeling that Marilyn calls getting "emotionful." Ever since she called Joanne Padrushky, she's been feeling this way, expecting every morning when she picks up the newspaper from her front porch to read a headline: Mother of Shooter Murders Coach. Still, it's been a week since she made her anonymous call, and no one has murdered anyone. Charlotte is divided between relief and disappointment that Harter is not dead.

◈

This morning has been hell. A screaming match between him and Maggie and Gunther, provoked solely by their nerves, over where his socks and Gunther's have disappeared. Because they had. Swiped by a malevolent hand. Shepherdess of socks, Maggie lost track of her flock, fell asleep on the job.

Then, she found them, right where they were supposed to be, rolled and tucked in their respective drawers. The world was not as cruel and insane as he made it to out to be, Maggie snapped, but he could not bring himself to apologize. Gun, either. Though he could be excused. The kid is a wreck.

Now as they speed down the road to Connorsville, Bruce reminds himself that they are not off schedule. Woody showed up on time, hair trimmed, face scrubbed. His manner easy. Maggie, wearing a simple black dress, is managing the texts, and assuring his mother that her ride has been arranged.

In the back seat, Gunther and Woody are sharing a pair of earbuds, their heads bobbing to an invisible beat. Every once in a while, something in the music tickles them both, and they look at each other, grinning.

Bruce squeezes the wheel hard. He swallows.

"Are you all right?" Maggie asks.

"I wish I knew what we're facing."

"Me, too."

From the back seat comes the sound of the boys, singing off-pitch. Where they don't know the words, they fake it. Bruce inhales deeply. Maybe it won't be so bad, maybe Gunther's more okay than they are.

Sean Sr. is circling the block in his truck, circling and circling. Each time he comes to the police barrier, the cop lets him through, though it is clear they are getting pissed. He hasn't decided yet if he's going in. Father Lambert is saving him a seat; he is saving one for Joanne too, but Joanne said no way, she's not going to that circus, she has better things to do. Like what? he asked. She didn't answer.

In Connorsville, people line the street all the way to the church, pumping their signs hard and shouting Gunther's name.

"This is marvelous," Gunther's mom says, rolling down her window. "Look at these people."

Woody elbows Gunther and points. Bunched on the curb, the Lake Village High School cheerleaders in their blue and yellow costumes spot Gunther and begin to cheer.

"The school must have bused them," Gunther's mom says. "Isn't that great?"

Gunther nods. He was doing okay until now when suddenly his hands are so cold he has to tuck them under his thighs, and he's got to let out gas. Lowering the car window, he scans the faces of the crowd—so many he knows and so many he doesn't.

In the hall, the audience is chattering in the self-conscious way of guests at a wedding. Pews to the left of the entrance belong to Gunther's supporters; pews to the right, Padrushky's.

Maggie, entering the hall from a door behind the stage, is startled at the size of the crowd. They are packing the pews and the choir balcony; they are lined up in the aisles, and back through the church vestibule and onto the street. "Can you believe this?" she says aloud. "All this support." "It's not all for us," Bruce says grimly. But she ignores him. *We're not alone,* she thinks. It's a revelation.

In the front pew of their packed section, she spots Charlotte, broad-faced and smiling, and her book group, no Bunny, sitting a few pews back. There are people from the office, and dozens of teachers from the high school, the track team parents seated shoulder-to-shoulder as though watching a meet. And so many other familiar faces. People she knows from the library, the doctor's office, Zumba, the café. And so many people whom she doesn't even know. These amazing people who on faith boarded a bus to stand up for justice. She squeezes Gunther's arm. Her heart soars, and she wants to shout, *Thank you.*

Sitting between his mother and his father, Gunther looks down at the program, at the order of speakers: Minister Gilbert; Lily Manlius; Gunther Cannon. His heart is beating in rapid thumps and his ears are making a whomp whomp as though someone stuck a synthesizer in his head. It says his name on the program, but his mom and dad promised that if he got too nervous to get up in front of all of these people, like he was going to throw up in public, they would take his place. Right now, he isn't sure what he's going to do.

In the car, his phone was blowing up and he and Woody were

listening to beats. It almost seemed like he could get into it. Now with the sound of the crowd, the camera people crouched in the aisles, the people holding signs, some for him, some against, he's scared. What's to stop a shooter, Padrushky's dad even, from running in here and gunning him down?

◈

Bruce fidgets with his program. The temptation to survey the Padrushkys' section to his right across the aisle is acute, but he's keeping the blinders on. For the past month, he's been living with the weird sense of being the focus of a skewed popularity contest. Seeing the crowd lined up to get into the church as he and Maggie and Gunther were ushered past them, he kept his gaze low. Shit, he probably knew half of the people on that line, at least. And some were carrying signs for Padrushky, and some for Gunther. Half-waves and sheepish smiles; turned shoulders and ducked chins. Gunther's friends, thank God, cheered as they passed. He patted Gunther on the shoulder, who allowed the weight of his father's hand for an instant before shrugging it away.

He's not like Maggie, who is waving and smiling to people in their section as though she's the Queen. What if Amy, his secretary, is in the Padrushkys' section? Or any of his Club members or grounds people or caddies? How will he ever talk to them again? Work with them? He can't pretend that it's okay to have a different opinion on this. He can't; he'd rather quit.

◈

Minister Gilbert, wearing a purple robe over a purple tunic and pants, positions herself behind the podium as the audience rumbles its greeting. Under the camera crews' high intensity lights, her hair gleams and the lenses of her glasses sparkle as though she has just emerged from a perfect dive.

"Good morning. Many thanks to all of you from near and far who have brought your willingness to dialogue and to listen in the name of better understanding for our community and, I hope, our world.

"Today our service brings together two differing views on an issue that has caused our community great pain; I will, therefore, ask you to open your minds and hearts and to conduct yourselves with civility, mindful that we are all human." Through the open windows of the church, something unintelligible blares from a loudspeaker as a car drives by. Both sides of the audience, unnerved, twist toward the sound.

Minister Gilbert taps the microphone. "Your attention, please," she says, frowning the audience back to silence.

"Two weeks ago, Lily Manlius and her husband, Mark, members of our congregation, approached me with a deep injustice burdening their hearts. They had learned of the unfortunate incident that took place in Lake Village earlier this spring and were deeply moved by the sad irony that a hate crime had in fact engendered hate in our midst, and so they asked to address the congregation with an unusual, though compassionate, view of the situation.

"I felt, of course, that the victim, the apparent victim, of the incident, should also be offered a chance to speak. I am grateful, therefore, to the Cannon family, to *Gunther*."

As though on cue, the high school students whistle and stomp. "Gun-ther, Gun-ther."

"*Please*." Minister Gilbert coughs heavily into the microphone, withering the cheers. "In order for this program to continue, I ask that everyone refrain from *partisan* acknowledgement." She shoots a look at the Cannons' section. "I want to again thank the Cannons, the Manlius's, our congregation and all of you who are visiting us today for supporting this dialogue and for helping us to create peace on earth and good will towards humanity.

"And now, a *polite* welcome for our first speaker, Lily Manlius."

◈

Charlotte, clapping lightly, feels a sneeze coming on. Someone has placed a cut-glass vase of peonies on the stage in front of the podium and their heavy perfume mixed with the smell of mildew rising from the humidity-dampened carpet is causing her nose to tickle and her throat to close. Tucking her nose into the crook of her elbow, she sneezes and sneezes again, apologizing aloud each time she comes up for air, but neither the bearded man to her right, nor the slender black woman on her left, seems even slightly interested in her or her allergies.

◈

Sean Sr. stands stock still inside the doors to the hall, looking at the woman at the microphone. Just like he told Joanne, Lily Manlius, his son's so-called savior, is a rich hippie chick come upstate to play farmer. Everybody knows her type—skinny, flat-chested woman of a certain age—struts down Main street in her high-end muck boots and brand-new Carharts, preaching organic this, organic that, like God is a giant eggplant in the sky. Of course, she farms organic; she can afford to. Her vintage Ford pick-up might as well have plates: TRUST FUND BABY.

"Why're you being so pissy?" Joanne asked him this morning before he set out for Connorsville.

"I'll tell you why," he said. "Rich Bitch doesn't know jack shit about our son. She's never even met him, but out of the blue, Shawnee is *her* cause, *she's* talking to the public. Don't bother to ask if *we* have something to say."

Then Joanne was quiet, because everything he said was true.

But he shouldn't be putting the woman down. He ought to listen to her. Maybe she and her husband have money enough to do something for Shawnee. Maybe they know somebody; Downstaters are always bragging about how they *know somebody*, like they have the power of God to make things happen.

◈

Coming into the kitchen, Joanne glances at the wall clock clapped to the wainscoting above the kitchen sink. Ten forty-five. The event at the church is starting. Perhaps she should have gone with Sean Sr. to keep a leash on him. But Father Lambert can do that. And who knows, after what she done to Harter, she might be the one getting hauled into the paddy wagon by the end of the day.

◈

"Thank you, Minister Gilbert," Lily Manlius says. "Thank you for allowing me to speak to these beautiful people." Her voice is breathy, but sure. "Thank you, everyone, for your compassionate attention." Lily folds her hands and bows, revealing a neat pink part from which her white hair springs in long waves. Some in the audience, though seated, bow back.

"My husband and I want you to know that we are here today as healers, not haters We are coming to you after an experience that happened to us as a result of a full week of silence and prayer during which Mark and I came to see an injustice manifesting in our community, a cruel injustice of the judicial system that has denied a young man, a minor of seventeen, the psychiatric care he desperately needs, remanding him instead to incarceration with adult criminals. Sean Padrushky, Jr. was a spiritual young man by all accounts, a superb musician with absolutely no history of violence, and one day, he suffers a breakdown. He—"

"Save Shawnee! Save Shawnee!" a husky man starts from a back pew; soon he's joined by another and another, until the whole section swells in jubilant chorus.

◈

Sean Sr. moves down the aisle, shaking off the elderly usher's attempt to stop him. "Them's my people," he says.

Bruce nudges Maggie with the nudge you give your seatmate on an airplane or bus just before you lose the contents of your stomach, a warning jab, so that the one beside you might find a way to take cover. Even as his elbow connects with her elbow, he is willing himself not to allow the spasm to complete itself. Not here, not now. Besides, the nausea is not caused by something he ate, clearly not. It's the circumstance. He has never been this angry in his life. It is beyond what he has ever known. He is sick with anger. Literally. It isn't the heat; it isn't the smell of something rotted, stinking, like the stench of a dirty terrarium, or the rank odor of an animal's cage; it is sitting in this church, hearing dozens and dozens of people, supposedly reasonable and educated people, cheering for the kid who shot his son.

Turning in his seat to look over at the chanting mob, Bruce spots Padrushky, Sr. coming down the aisle, striding swiftly as though he is planning to take the stage. In a flash, Bruce is on his feet. He wants to stop Padrushky in his tracks, push him right back out those doors and into the street where he'll take care of him once and for all.

On stage, Minister Gilbert is attempting to quiet the crowd, shouting into the microphone for quiet and frantically pushing her palms against the noise of the chants erupting from both sides of the aisle.

"Padrushky," Bruce says. "Coming down the aisle."

"Sit down," Maggie says. "You're scaring Gunther."

"He's right there."

"Should I call the police?"

"Dad?" It's Gunther. "He might have a gun."

◈

Lily Manlius comes to the edge of the stage, bending to speak to the man in the black leather coat. "Excuse me? Would you mind stepping back?"

"How about you step back? I'm Shawnee's dad. I want to talk."

The cameras zoom in on Sean Sr. leaping on stage with the spring of a panther. When he reaches for Minister Gilbert's mic, the fringe on his leather jacket swings. As he brings the mic up to his mouth, he looks like a country singer about to croon a song, Charlotte thinks. But the audience isn't certain about what he's up to. All around her, she hears the rumble of confused voices threaded with soprano pitches of surprise. If she were steno-ing this, she thinks, it would type up as a cluster fuck of nothing.

"I can't talk if you all don't shut up," Sean Sr. says.

Wipe the smirk off, Charlotte thinks. *You'll be in trouble.*

"Shame on you!" a woman calls from the back of the church. "Did you crouch in a corner waiting to die?"

"Be quiet!" a man answers from somewhere in the Padrushky section.

"I will not."

"Tell it, Sister." To Charlotte's surprise, it's her seat neighbor, a woman a quarter of her size, dressed like she anchors the TV news. *Tell it, tell it,* others join in shouting, waving their 'Gun Lives' signs. Not having one, Charlotte shoots her fist in the air.

"Come on," his dad says. "Let's go."

"I'm with you." His mother reaches for her purse under the pew. Gunther smooths his palms on his thighs. The chill has moved from his hands through his body. His teeth click uncontrollably. From the moment Sean Sr. took the stage and the heckling broke out, he felt as though the building was tumbling down on him, the shouts were bricks breaking over his head. He agrees with his dad. He wants to get out of here.

Minister Gilbert gavels her fist on the podium, her face flushing a hard red. *"For the love of God, people. Sit down and shut up."*

The unexpected rudeness has an effect. The audience quiets like smoked bees. They take their seats again, relieved, it seems, that someone is back in charge.

Sean Sr. is still on stage, his feet planted, his arms crossed. "Mrs. Manlius said I could talk."

Minister Gilbert glares at him, then cuts a look at Lily who nods. "Keep it short."

Sean Sr. tips his hat back, moves downstage. "My son, Sean Jr., is a victim of a conspiracy to get a judge re-elected. He's good boy, but he's nuts. He needs help, not jail."

"Sit down, clown," a man calls out.

Sean Sr. pauses, squinting. "Who's the son of a bitch?"

"I am."

The audience swivels, and Sean Sr. jumps off the stage, his fists cocked. "Bring it on, asshole," he says.

Father Lambert, clutching his robes and scuttling quickly across his pew, is the first to reach Sean Sr. Behind him, a police officer, gun drawn.

"Stand down," Father Lambert orders sharply. "He's not armed."

"He's under arrest for disturbing the peace."

"No," Father Lambert says. "I'll take care of him. He's in my charge." He reaches for Sean Sr.'s fists, squeezing them gently as he lowers them. "Let's go home, son. For Shawnee's sake, for the sake of God, our Lord and Savior." Then he puts his arm across Sean Sr.'s back and walks him slowly out of the church.

◈

Only Lyle has read the journal, but when Joanne asked about it, he told her to leave it alone. She didn't need to go there, he said. She agreed.

After that, they didn't talk about it. The journal was still being held in evidence; but Lyle gave a copy to Sean, Sr. to lock away in the safe. For once, Sean Sr. had obeyed.

The safe sits on the plywood table in the spare room. Steel and brass. Not a cheapie. Joanne presses in the combination, not hard to remember, Shawnee's birth date. A September morning; early; Sean Sr., calm as a pin. That night he placed everything by the side of the bed, his boots, his jeans, his shirt. He would have made a good vet.

The digits connect; the latch on the handle compresses. Jumbled inside the safe are a heap of medals from Sean, Sr.'s collection, a box of gold coins that Sean swears are worth thousands. On the top shelf is a large manila envelope stamped, CONFIDENTIAL. Joanne grabs it. Her whole body is trembling, and she has what her mother used to call the sick spins, the feeling that she is being turned and turned in the dark, like a child blindfolded for a party game. Clutching the envelope against her chest, Joanne sinks to the floor, her back against the wall.

"Wait," Minister Gilbert says, "you're leaving us, too?"

Bruce stops, Gunther and Maggie behind him. "We wish we hadn't come."

"Well," Minister Gilbert says, her voice straining, "I'm sorry about that. Really, really sorry. Gunther?"

Gunther stares down at what strikes him now as his pathetically shiny shoes. Why the fuck did his father have to say anything? "It's okay," he mutters. "It's chill."

"I know you wanted to speak."

Gunther shakes his head. "Nope."

"I know everyone here still wants to hear from you. Your voice is very important." Answering her, it seems, his section bursts into a chorus of yesses.

"Hear that? Would you consider it? Can you take a minute to think?"

Gunther stands stiffly. A minute? How about his whole life? He looks out at the audience. Everyone is turned his way. Their eyes on him like he's the star, like he's Usain. *He* would get it. *He* would understand how you see them, and they don't see you, even though they're looking.

His mother is frozen halfway to the exit, and his dad is already at the door.

"Wait up. Where the heck do you think you're going?" It's the woman who first called out Sean Sr. He remembers her voice.

"Home," his father says.

"No, you're not. You're not robbing these people. We got up five o'clock this morning to get on a bus to stand up for this young man. We want to hear Gunther. We came to hear what *he* has to say." The woman turns to him. She's tall, with high cheekbones and tawny skin. Her eyes are on fire.

His mom cuts the woman a fierce look. "No one's going to force my son to do anything."

"We can wait."

We. Gunther glances over his shoulder. Behind him, a blur of faces, some black, some white, stretching their necks toward him and nodding like their heads are going to fall off.

"But I hope you're not going to let that man get the last word."

The top page of the photocopy is the front cover of a composition notebook, the kind with stiff covers peppered with black and white confetti. In the blank white oval on the front, is a darkly-inked swastika. Joanne blinks and takes a deep breath. Her mind is filled with opposing thoughts: She can't read this; she has to.

It is in the note, the suicide note: *I loved someone; I thought he loved me*. The words tumble in her mind like veined pebbles she cannot crack. Who is *he*? Dewey Harter? Father Rand? Sean, Sr.? In her mind's eye, she sees Shawnee's face. His eyes are her father's eyes. Pale blue, and bright, the result of recessive genes on both sides of the family. Whenever her father came after her, she closed her eyes, let her body float away. Did someone come after Shawnee, too?

One other time she saw those eyes, on a blue pit. A rescue. She worked with that dog all morning wearing bite gloves and a catcher's mask. No good. By afternoon, she had to put him down.

◈

Standing behind the podium, Gunther tugs the hem of his suit jacket, tips the microphone closer to his mouth. The audience seems to be holding its breath, watching his every move, the way the audience watches a jumper line up a free throw. Only this seems to take longer, he thinks, so many seconds longer. Still he remembers his parents' coaching, *Take your time. Talk like molasses. It's theater,* they said. *Slow it down so every word counts.* And so even his actions he tries now to slow, moving through space as though it is water, resisting the urge to hurry up and get it over.

Inside the box of his mind, he can hear nothing except the enormous reverberation of his heart. All week long, his dad and mom had worked on the speech. Every word. Every period and comma and question mark. Every pause. His mother and father had argued, was it too this, too that? Were they really Gunther's words? Would it sound like they'd written it for him? Which they had. He didn't mind. He was too scared to write it himself.

Looking out at the audience, he catches the eye of the woman who challenged him. She is sitting again with her group of friends, and the fire in her eyes has changed to love. It's beaming at him, it's shining in her eyes and in her smile. Dipping his chin, he rests his palms on the edge of the podium, straightens his elbows. His dad, pressed tight against his mom, looks so worried you'd think he was watching him walk a tightrope over Niagara Falls. His mother looks nervous, too. But suddenly, he isn't.

"This isn't the speech my parents wrote," he says, touching his breast pocket. "This is real. My own words. The way I see it." His voice in the microphone sounds weird to him. Like it is coming from a metal box. "And by the way, I don't like microphones, so I'm going to turn this off"

A few groans of protest rise from the audience, but Gunther ignores them, switching off the mic. Now his voice sounds okay to him not like he's a politician or a valedictorian. Now he can speak like a human being.

"When I was a little kid, I remember I came home from school one day and ran up to the bathroom and started brushing my teeth. Not my teeth, actually. My gums. I had my face pushed up to the mirror and my lips pulled back, and I was scrubbing my gums so hard they started to bleed.

"Some of you sitting here know. Most of you don't. Like my mom. No offense." His mom nods. "She was confused. Like 'watcha doing?' 'They're all brown,' I said. 'Everyone else's got pink.'" He scans the audience for a second, waits for them to get it. "Yeah, I was trying to brush color away, so I could be like everybody else in my class—everybody white." He cuts his eyes to the Padrushky section then focuses again on his people.

"It's lonely. It's lonely to be different. It's lonely to see other kids' parents look at you and think, *danger.* It's lonely to study slavery in school, and everyone in the class looks at you, all ignorant, like you, personally, were a slave.

"I never knew how lonely until what happened in the park. I guess I had fooled myself. And maybe my friends. Damn, I didn't know until then it was *dangerous* to be me."

Glancing up at the balcony, he sees that those who have been fanning themselves have stopped fanning and are bending toward him as though he is a magnetic force.

"You." He turns to face Lily and her husband, who have returned to their seats. "You want Shawnee declared insane. Well, *hello.* What do you think I want?" Murmurs ripple through the audience, and he sees his mother's eyes fly open. "If Shawnee's insane, I get to go on with my life; maybe someday let go of this. I get to say only a lunatic would hunt me down, shoot me in plain sight, for no reason except I'm black."

Lily is nodding at him; her eyes bright. He feels sorry for her.

"But here's what's bothering me. If Shawnee's insane, if I let it go down like that, I'm spitting on the ghosts of all of the people, all of the innocent people, black people, gay people, Jewish people, Muslim people, you name it, who were murdered because they were different from you, like being different means you're dangerous, you're bad."

Maggie clenches her fist to her mouth; shoulders lightly heaving, and Gunther wishes his father would put his arm around her, but he does not. "I'm a member of the club now. It's not black only. It's not the club you want to belong to, believe me. No matter how much you care about me, you can't join. My mom and dad can't. They just can't. And it hurts them real bad. But those people in my mom's family who were killed in the Holocaust? They belong. The black kid killed for wearing a hoodie or carrying a cellphone, belongs; the gay kid lynched on an empty road, belongs." His father's head jerks up. *Is he crying?* "Once you've looked into the eyes of someone who wants to kill you for no reason except you're different from them, you belong.

"Now I'm going to tell you something about me, something I've been scared to tell. Padrushky was bullied and attacked, but not by me; I was next; they were going to haze me, too. So, I ran for my life. That's how it felt. I didn't stop for anybody.

"*I'm* the danger? Me, with the brown skin and the chip on my shoulder? You really believe that? Because sitting here in this room, filled with *you* people, when Mr. Padrushky was here, I was so scared I could've peed myself. See, that man and his son hate me for *being*. And the kids that attacked Shawnee, they hated him, too. That's right. You heard me. That's my only crime. Maybe it's his, too. The crime of being. How do you beat that?"

EPILOGUE

ONE

In the days and weeks after Gunther left for school, the house still feels too empty; the rooms, too quiet. A colleague of Maggie's, an older woman with two grown daughters told Maggie it was "empty nest" symptom. Before long, she will love it. The others in the office whose nests were also empty chimed their encouragement: "Yes, yes. It's great. You can think your thoughts again; you have freedom; you have *privacy*." Maggie took this in, pretended to find comfort in their predictions, but she envied the parents who still had their kids at home, whose lives were still ordered by sports meets, fund-raisers, and packing lunches.

The week after Sean Padrushky, Jr. was sentenced to eleven years in a federal prison, Gunther sat his parents down at the kitchen table and announced that he had something to tell them. *Ohmigod*, she thought, bracing herself. *It's Bev. He's going to live with her.* Thank god she kept her mouth shut.

"Of course," Bruce said. "What's up?"

Then, pushing away the dinner dishes, Gunther placed his laptop on the table and began to type. "I want to show you guys something." He turned the laptop to face them.

The screen filled with an autumn scene of sunlit maples ringing a campus of ivy-covered brick. Next, a trio of students, black, white, Asian, gaping over a microscope; then, a line of student hikers against snow-topped mountains. Finally, white letters on a black background: *Brookvale: An Inclusive Community for Students from Around the World.*

"A prep school?" Maggie asked.

"It's incredible, mom. They got a program where you can volunteer in an orphanage in Africa over Winter Break. The teachers write about the students, instead of grades. It's thirty percent students of color. I want to go there." Gunther kept his eyes on the screen, clicking through menu tabs.

"Leave us?" Bruce frowned.

"I'd be home on vacations."

Bruce drew the laptop closer, peering at the screen. "I'm not saying, 'no,' Gunther, but the money."

"They've got a lot of scholarships, and even though it's past the deadline, they said—" Gunther grabbed back the laptop, slamming the cover. "I knew you wouldn't listen." He shoved back in his seat. His eyes were puffy and dark. Even with the Padrushky ordeal settled, Gunther wasn't sleeping well.

"Come on, Gun, give us a break," Bruce said. "This comes out of the blue."

"Show us again," Maggie said.

Gunther sat glaring at the closed laptop. The kitchen still smelled of the gristle and char of the leftover steak on the platter in the center of the table. The oven clock buzzed.

"Okay," he said, "but don't make any cracks. Don't say anything negative until you've read it all."

Gunther found the site again quickly and spun the laptop to face them. Dutifully, they read through the school's mission statement, the academics, the admissions, the alumni accolades. They examined the photographs of happy, beautiful students of many colors peering into microscopes, scaling a rock face, taking part in a drum circle. When she and Bruce finished with the website, they found each other's gaze. Seventeen years ago, they'd signed the adoption papers, pledging to their son to sacrifice and to love. Here was the test.

Bruce cleared his throat. "We get it, Gun. This is the place. We'll see what we can do."

"Yes!" Gunther pumped his fist, then looked them both straight in the eye. "Thank you, Dad. Thank you, Mom. You're the best parents in the world."

TWO

"YOU'RE THE BEST PARENTS in the world," Gunther said; Maggie knows this isn't true. Still, after he left for boarding school, Maggie holds onto those words like smooth, reassuring pebbles you fondle in your pocket. They are words, after all, that she was never able to say to her own parents. Perhaps she and Bruce were the best parents in the world at that moment when they had, for once, seen exactly what Gunther needed and had given it to him. She is grateful for this.

But she has been a selfish parent, as well. She thinks of this often, and she is ashamed.

◈

From the moment Bev spotted them in line at Price Chopper, she had been their savior, or at least, their teacher, for the first thing she said was, "What are you doing with his hair?"

At lunch the next day at the house, Maggie watched happily as Gunther lost his shyness almost immediately, introducing Bev to all of his action figures as though she were a long-lost friend. Bev and she were both from Queens, they discovered; their high schools were rivals, and both longed to move back to the city. Bev was a full professor of English at the state college in Connorsville. Though tenure, she said, was a double-edged sword.

Soon she and Bev and Gunther were hanging out on weekends when Bruce was working at the Club. Yes, it hurt a little when, outside of Lake Village, strangers would tag Bev and Gunther with smiles, assume that they were mother and son. Neuroscience, Maggie told herself. Human brains crave symmetry. She and Bev were quick to correct the misidentification; Bev laughing afterward that "Gunther had two moms."

Two moms. Bev anointing *herself* as co-mom. She was gratified. She treasured Bev's acknowledgement like a medal she'd earned for being a good white person. Then, she was confused. Gunther had two moms, true—his birth mother and Maggie. Who was Bev cutting out?

The older Gunther got, the more time he wanted to spend with Bev; the more he seemed to need *her,* not Maggie, not Bruce. Maggie told herself that it was a good thing; it was what she'd planned all along. *It takes a village,* she was fond of saying; ironic now. But sometimes a self-sabotaging revision of Billy Creighton's simple logic ran through her mind, *how can you be his mom? You don't match.*

It had been a good week, Maggie remembers. A co-worker found Judge Adkins' toupee in the men's room, and the resulting memes were a hoot. Even better, the school secretary had called to give Bruce and her the heads-up that Gunther had made Honor Roll; *Honor,* not *High Honor,* but she found herself feeling ridiculously proud. She hung up with the secretary, called Bev. Bev before Bruce.

Bev whooped when she heard the news. "That's my boy," she said.

Her remark rattled Maggie. *My* boy? "Can we share?"

They met for lunch that afternoon at a table for two in Lake Village's one Chinese restaurant. The table was *their* table, hers and

Bev's, snugged in the corner, semi-private in the near empty room.

Maggie watches Bev flip the pages of the menu, humming a little hum of appreciation at all of the choices. She knows what Bev is going to order because she always orders the same thing, the Tso's chicken with its golden glaze and the pork fried rice. An egg roll comes with it, a cup of soup, too. Bev will order wonton, and she will order chicken noodle. The waitress, a large girl with shiny black hair and gold hoops, waits with her pad. She smiles at Bev. "I know what you want."

"I'm easy," says Bev.

The waitress turns to Maggie. "And you?"

"Tofu and vegetables; plain rice. No egg roll."

Bev frowns. "I'll take it."

"You will?"

"I'm not wasting a good egg roll."

"It's yours."

Out the window, they watch the Garden Club ladies on Main street hover around the brick planters, poking at the moist dirt with the tips of their trowels, ripping out old roots. Each team has made a neat pile on a tarp beside the planter. An older couple, she in quilted vest and he in tweed jacket, are pulled gently past by a small white dog. Mid-April, the town revives itself for the tourist season, sprucing up the window boxes, hanging new flags. The Chamber of Commerce has been cooking up marketing ideas: an Easter Egg Hunt on the grounds of the historical society; a May triathlon. The bridge season stretches from March until Memorial Day weekend, when the snowbirds come back to Lake Village to launch their sailboats and re-inhabit their lakeside homes.

"Crazy, isn't it," Bev says, dragging the bowl of fried noodles towards her. "We live in this place."

Maggie nods. She'd like to eat those noodles, but she's been trained from girlhood to resist. *Wasted calories*, she can hear her mother say.

Though calories have never been an issue.

"I know why I'm here, but remind me again why you and Bruce are?" Bev dips her noodle into the small bowl of apricot-colored duck sauce. "You were living in the City, right? You were living where there's a life, you know? Where there's *people*."

Maggie sips her water. She knows Bev means *black* people. They've been down this road before. Bev knows their whole story, how she and Bruce decided that Gunther would be safer growing up in Lake Village, in a place where everyone would know him, than in the city. His birth mother even requested it. It's a story that Bev's accepted, though in all the years of their friendship, she's never said that she approved. That's not Bev.

"You must have had a shitty week," Maggie says. "The Dean again?"

Bev grabs another noodle. "The Dean, the Chair, my so-called *colleagues*, who care more about shingling their houses than revising curriculum. There's so much bullshit I can take before I—" She pauses, crunching. "I'm sick of wasting my time."

"Quit."

"Right. Jobs in English. You tell me where to find one. And if there are any, they're in Podunk, Nowheresville. Kansas, Nebraska. No thank you. It's bad enough being a token here."

The atmosphere in China 15 was what it always was. The aquarium by the front door, filled with goldfish wending their way through the murk; the smiling kitty figurine on the counter with the endlessly waving paw; the slightly tawdry, yet cheerful garlands of paper lanterns, entwined with dusty tinsel. Everything—smells, décor, people, the same.

But Maggie that afternoon is poised to strike. She knows precisely where to place her chisel's tip, and with what force to bring down the hammer that will sever their friendship with one neat crack. *My boy*, Bev said, as though Gunther were her son.

"But I'm thinking, Bev," Maggie says, "if you really want to go somewhere else, you should. I know it's hard to get tenured jobs, but let's face it, you're a woman, you're experienced, and you're black."

Bev, beautiful in the rays of afternoon light that pick up the shine of her many cascading braids and the gleam of her lips, opens her eyes wide, her left eyebrow arcing like a dolphin in mid-leap. "I don't believe your words," she says. "I don't believe what I'm hearing, and I hope to God you don't mean what you say."

◈

What was wrong with her that afternoon? She was jealous as all fuck, that's what was wrong. She and Bruce raised Gunther to judge others by how they acted, not by how they looked. They raised him not to see himself as "other." What they'd done, Maggie thinks now, is pretend. To Gunther and to themselves. They pretended that color didn't matter when, in this world, it did.

She owes Bev an apology. She owes Gunther an apology as well. But how can she ever explain how it was that afternoon in the hospital, when for the first time she held Gunther, when his tiny fingers gripped hard to her forefinger, and he clung. Oh, how he clung to her and she to him; and oh my god, the joy that filled her to know that he was her son.

THREE

IN THE LATE AFTERNOONS, when Bruce gets home from work, he has gotten in the habit of grabbing himself a bottle of beer from the refrigerator, then heading upstairs to heave himself onto Gunther's mattress. He lies there feeling the narrowness of it; the relative weakness of the springs. Beneath him, the camouflage print of the comforter spreads like a forest floor, and he breathes in his son's sweat and the deodorant he used to mask it. The ache he feels is horrible, a grabbing and twisting, dead center of his chest. It won't let go. He misses Gunther.

This week he visited his mother. The day was unexpectedly warm, so they walked outside on the grounds, enjoying the smell of moist earth and leaves. "Do you miss him?" he asked his mother.

"Him? Which 'him' do you mean?"

He had put this clumsily, he realized, in hopes that she might allow him to talk about Gunther.

His mother stopped. She was dressed as always with great care: a boiled-wool jacket; matching slacks; a woven shawl. "Don't you dare include Gunther. Your son is alive."

Bruce takes a last sip of his beer, sets the bottle on the floor. Then he relaxes, sinking into the hollows that Gunther's body has carved, into the many layers of smells, into his once-occupied cocoon. Yes, Gunther is alive. He and Maggie speak to Gunther often. He loves his classes and has already made friends. He is happy at Brookvale, he tells them.

When they visited over Parents' Weekend, they could see the change in him. He was relaxed, confident. Several of his friends were girls eager to make their acquaintance.

There were changes in Gunther that he and Maggie didn't like, as well. He'd picked up some of the preppy lingo; the cadence of his speech was different, every sentence seemed to rock up at the end like a question. One night when they were all on speaker phone, Gunther told them in a mocking tone that at Brookvale, he was just one more "Oreo" in the cookie jar.

Bruce decided to play it cool. "It makes my teeth hurt to hear about all that sugar," he'd said. Maggie, appalled, was silent. "He's an 'Oreo'?" she said after they hung up with Gunther. "Even at 'all-inclusive' Brookvale, kids label themselves?"

"That's not the point, Maggie." He was remembering the most recent photograph that Gunther had shared with them, a line of his friends, linked arm in arm, each swinging a leg high in a chorus-line kick. They were smiling, laughing, mugging to the camera, and in the center was Gunther, open-faced and happy, so happy he seemed ready to lift off the ground. "Gun's happy there, because he belongs."

FOUR

THE FIRST THING HE DONE RIGHT, Sean thinks, was to fire Lyle. Family or not, if you want something done right, you got to pay for it. But Lyle had more than just fucked up, he'd brainwashed Shawnee into accepting a plea. Now that they were rid of Lyle, the new lawyer was filing an appeal; the new lawyer had friends in the legislature who were looking to change the statute that minors were treated as adults when it came to hate crimes. The new lawyer had neuroscientists and psychiatrists lined up talking about "hot cognition" and "plasticity" and "frontal lobe development" and other ways to prove the obvious that teenagers are dumb in oh, so many ways.

He's got a full-time job now between managing the website; the donations to the Save Shawnee fund; the meetings with politicians and their aides and the aides to their aides. There are hundreds of folks out there who are helping, and even Joanne lends a hand. It's something they agree on as it turns out, that the law should be changed; that Shawnee should be free sooner than the court mandated.

Sometimes Shawnee calls. He don't talk about much, still it's good to hear his voice. He sounds different; he has to speak fast because there's only one phone and a bunch of other people want to use it. No doubt he's grown a pair. Solid brass. In the middle of the conversation, Shawnee breaks off to curse someone out; he can hear Shawnee shouting at some asshole to shut up and wait his F-ing turn, and sometimes the call is cut off for no reason and you can't call back. Then, it's like being pushed off a cliff in the dark; it feels like a drop into nothingness, and he's not sure if it's him who got pushed or Shawnee.

FIVE

Lake Village hasn't changed much since Gunther left for school; May's is still here; the post office, the library, the police station, the park. He doesn't have to go to these places, Gunther tells himself. He doesn't have to mail a letter or grab a coffee or return a book. He doesn't have to go downtown at all, his mom and dad remind him. But something is grabbing him, daring him to walk down Main Street this afternoon, to see if he can handle it without losing his shit.

It is spring again. The sky is pool-bottom blue; the air filled with the smell of lilacs and mock orange. It's not Friday. It's Sunday. The first time he's been back since he left for school.

No one at Brookvale knows much about him. No one knows, except the headmaster and the school shrink, about the incident. No one knows he's the-kid-who-was-shot-because-he-was-black. At Brookvale, he's like a superhero changed back to his human identity. He gets to be normal. Or at least pretend.

He still has flashbacks. He still has nightmares and wants to pancake when he sees someone who looks even a little like Shawnee Padrushky. But not as bad as before. Dr. Alfred explained that trauma is like any deep wound to the body; it will take years for Gunther to recover. He nodded when the doctor said this, but to himself he was thinking, *I'm better than that.*

He walks down the sidewalk, keeping his head down, trying not to look at himself in the long block of glass storefronts, mirrors that travel with him. He's prepped out these days in duck boots and jeans; his hair twisted in beaded dreads. At school, he has friends who look like him, and friends who don't. Once, in the fall, Woody showed up at his dorm. He'd hitchhiked to Vermont, walked the five miles from town. It was cool to see him, and awkward as hell. His Brookvale friends were like was-sup? Woody was his best friend from his old school, he told them. He didn't explain more than that; Gunther knew they wouldn't understand.

One day in their session, Dr. Alfred told him that it helps the families of murder victims to see the place where their loved one was killed. The survivors need to see to believe, he said. Perhaps, some day, you could visit the scene of the crime.

In a second, Gunther was out of his chair. "I wasn't murdered," he shouted.

In the park this afternoon, there are families with small children, everybody in their Sunday best and a few boys, no one he knows, hiking a football and fumbling it. Walking through the wrought iron gates, across the lawn and around the asphalt loop, Gunther counts his breaths, slowing them. With each step, he expects people to pop-up out of nowhere, blocking his path like hostile characters in a video game—Ryan shouting; Shawnee, pointing his gun. No. No one appears. But he walks another loop just to be sure, before crossing the street.

ALICE LICHTENSTEIN received an MFA from Boston University, where she was named the Boston University Fellow in Creative Writing. She has received a New York Foundation of the Arts Grant in Fiction and the Barbara Deming Award in Fiction. She has twice been a Fellow at the MacDowell Colony. Alice is the author of three novels: *The Genius of the World* (Zoland Books, 2000); *Lost*, (Scribner, 2010); and the *The Crime of Being*. *Lost* was a long-list finalist for the Dublin IMPAC International Award in Fiction.

Lichtenstein's stories have appeared in several literary journals, including: *Narrative Magazine*; *Post Road*; *Short Story*; and *Digital Americana*. Her award-winning story, "Revision," was nominated for a 2020 Pushcart Prize

Lichtenstein teaches fiction-writing at Hartwick College in Oneonta, NY. She has also taught fiction-writing at Boston University, Wheaton College, Lesley College, and the Harvard University Summer School.

ACKNOWLEDGMENTS

So many wonderful people have helped and supported me in the writing of this book. First and foremost, I thank my incredible husband, Jim Bercovitz, a constant source of love and encouragement. Next, I thank my dear friends, Sue Helwig and Sara Hanlon, who read and critiqued draft after draft with loving candor. An enormous thank you to Michelle Miller for generously sharing her insight and experience. Thank you, too, to Lee Fisher and to Regina Betts, president and vice president, respectively, of the Oneonta Chapter of the NAACP. Their leadership in the Oneonta community is nothing short of heroic.

Thank you to the Bercovitz family, Yvette, Richard, and the late George Edward Bercovitz. Thank you to my parents, Immanuel and Nancy Lichtenstein, and thank you to my sister and brother-in-law, Elizabeth and Thomas Torak, two remarkable artists.

To Jacki Hunt, Jeannie Kell, and Joy Webb—thank you for assuring me countless times that I would finish (and publish) the book. Thank you to the Huntingtons, my driveway family extraordinaire. Thank you to Dr. Alex Frank and Stacey Mandelbaum for their love and support. Thank you to my dearest Anne Pollack whose work in bringing the arts to survivors of human trafficking is a constant inspiration.

I would also like to offer thanks to Miriam Altshuler, the agent who is always there even when she isn't. Thank you, Steve Feuer, for sharing an important boyhood memory, thank you to Jim Helwig, for sharing your firearm expertise, and thank you to Laura Miller, for expert advice.

I would like to thank the remarkable team at Upper Hand Press: Stewart Williams, for his lovely design both interior and exterior, and Ann Starr, the editor and publisher one dreams of meeting. Ann's courage, pen, and insight are unsurpassed.